# Whitetail Shooting Gallery

ALSO BY ANNETTE LAPOINTE

*Stolen*

# Whitetail Shooting Gallery

A NOVEL BY

*Annette Lapointe*

aNVIL
PRESS

VANCOUVER • 2012

Anvil Press Publishers Inc.
P.O. Box 3008, Main Post Office
Vancouver, B.C. V6B 3X5  Canada
www.anvilpress.com

LIBRARY AND ARCHIVES CANADA CATALOGUING IN PUBLICATION

Lapointe, Annette, 1978-
    Whitetail shooting gallery / Annette Lapointe.


ISBN 978-1-897535-98-1

    I. Title.

PS8623.A728W45 2012        C813'.6        C2012-905488-7


Cover design: Carelton Wilson
Interior design: Heimat House
Author photo: John Galaugher

Represented in Canada by the Literary Press Group.

Distributed in Canada by the University of Toronto Press and in the U.S. by Small Press Distribution (SPD).

The publisher gratefully acknowledges the financial assistance of the Canada Council for the Arts, the Canada Book Fund, and the Province of British Columbia through the B.C. Arts Council and the Book Publishing Tax Credit.

Printed and bound in Canada.

for
*Lena Jill*

*Of course this land is dangerous*
*All of the animals*
*Are capably murderous.*
<br>— Jane's Addiction, "Of Course"

# « CHAPTER I »

LATER, SHE REMEMBERS THE GUN'S FIRE. The smell of it, sharp through her face like she'd breathed in a chemical accident. Mixed household cleaners and explosive sound.

She remembers being deaf.

Her whole life, she's been told things will make her deaf: walkman headphones, tractors, thunder, her sister screaming in her ear, Jason screaming in her ear, the attempt she made that one time in the shower to scream in her own ear. Ginger told her about concerts so loud they make your ears bleed.

Gunfire makes Jennifer's ears bleed.

Makes her whole face bleed. There's holes in her, suddenly. Holes in her face and her shoulder. Holes in her breasts. Holes in her leg.

Holes in her *horse*, and she didn't know a horse could scream, 'til right this moment.

Jason stands there staring at her. His face is white, and he turns and throws up, and then her horse bolts and she doesn't see him again for more than an hour. Her parents come, and separate her from Djinn, who's panting and bloody and needs buckshot dug out of her neck. They check her over and try very hard not to scream, and carry her — both of them, like firemen in the face of an explosion — to the car, and drive like fire for Saskatoon. Daughter on the back seat with holes in her face, bleeding and deaf.

They aren't all the way to the city before her hearing comes back, and she starts screaming, too.

They left her sister behind in the yard. She needs to tell them about this, how Tori is little, and Jason is still there, sick in the woods.

They left Tori alone with him.

She doesn't know how to explain they shouldn't have done that. It's only then she understands that they didn't see it happen, and they don't know that Jason shot her.


THEY CURL UP SEPARATELY, Jenn and her cousin Jason, on opposite sides of the treehouse.

The tree's been dead for years, raw willow starved out in the last drought before they were born and cut down to its component trunks. It was part of the shelter-belt of trees breaking the wind's thrust on the original farm. In the still-living tangle of willow behind them, there are foundation fragments. Outlines of a window. Pieces of machinery and bone.

The view through the Bear Hills goes on for miles. Blue semi-arctic night.

He didn't invite her here, but Jenn hiked out anyway, backpack full of pajamas and granola bars. The dark is a long, slow adjustment. It's never as black as she expects, but still dense with insects and shadow. The sandflies hum in clouds. They're attracted to the horses, and shift their collective intelligence occasionally towards the nearest dozing equine body, looking for sweat or shit to feed on.

It's cold. Ozone-smell all through the trees.

Last year, if he was going tree-camping, Jason would have come by to collect her. Waited while she gathered up her wrap-around-skirt cloak and film canisters full of dried plants, and otherwise put on her wizard skin. He'd have walked out after her. Paused sometimes until she was almost out of range and then hurled things at her head.

Low velocity.

One of the handful of scars on her hairline is from the week he carried rocks. Mostly, though, he threw desiccated horse shit or bits of wood. They dissolved on impact.

This time, he left her behind. He's thirteen, now, and she's twelve. He locked her out. She had to climb the tree because he pulled the rope up after him. When he saw her, he rolled onto his other side, like she was a shadow. She thinks about smothering him in his sleep, now. Not quite to death.

He shouldn't have left her.

His cape is gone. Jason's warrior outfit is lost, and he burned his princess hat. His comics are present, protected by the weight of a flashlight, but they're more *X-Men* than *Sandman*, and she isn't interested.

Jenn's claimed her own corner, and she brought her own flashlight. Her bag yields up a handful of Forgotten Realms novels harvested from her bedroom. Story about cracks in the earth that let out the spider-worshipping matriarchal dark-elves. Priestesses who tie up every miserable boy who locks them out, and have him flogged while they watch.

Almost/not quite pornography. It gives her ideas.

Next year or the year after.

She has no idea why Jason doesn't want her presence. He said he never wanted her, but he's carried her since she was born. He's older, fourteen months, prickly these days personally and along his jawline, and sometime last winter he walked away from her. There's something *wrong* with her, something partly based in her awkwardness and partly in her being a girl. Something that makes him watch her.

Bright eyes.

She thinks, *Turn around, bright eyes.*

*(Every now and then I fall apart.)*

"Don't sing, okay?"

Didn't realize she'd said it out loud. But she woke him fully, and he's irritated. Something *wrong* with her. But he pushes one of his comics (alt-world *Superman*, the story of the mysterious older brother re-enacting *Nineteen Eighty-Four*) and takes a Ravenloft novel from the bottom of her book pile. He makes a point of offering her a mildewed couch-upholstered throw-pillow for her head. Like chivalry. Not quite stripped out of his prince clothes.

She thinks, *Princess*. There was that year he spent wearing the skirt. It was adorable. A long time ago. Four years ago. Five.

Jason crawls into Jenn's sleeping bag long minutes after she lies down. He's cold and she's bed-warm. The space between them narrows until he's wrapped around her back and it's one in the morning (glowing faint green of her plastic watch stuffed against her chest, she's so *cold*). The two of them constitute almost one real adult, buried in this tangle of sleeping bag and knit clothes. Jenn listens to the horses shuffle in the grass below. None of them are asleep.

Dozes like that.

And then he leaves her. Gets up all in one move and climbs down the rope, leaving night air rolling over Jenn's body. The curled-up part of her brain whimpers. Rolls her half-over to see where he's disappeared.

He's not gone. Half-moon light's enough to see him, back to her at the trees, pajama pants around his hips. Aiming into the dark.

She's never been able to do that, and now she has to pee too.

Jenn's pants are around her ankles when Jason tackles her. Rolls her over, bare-skin ass into the bush, and she screams. Genetic memory of something being hunted. He's laughing before he's up again, and she's left with the urge to get on top of him and *piss* on him. See how he likes it.

He's fast, though. Up before she can snatch him, and she has to drag up her cold-maybe-wet pants to follow. Across the field with her bare feet stuffed in unlaced runners, shrieking for his blood. He's going to pay for this. She's going to throw him down beat him purplegreenyellow, bite his ears off, bite his tongue out, *eat* him for this. She's still bigger than him — just *watch* her.

He retreats, finally, behind the rain-soaked couch her father dumped by the treehouse in the spring, that Jenn's been reading on all summer. It's given her sunburn on her shoulders, belly, knees and a low-grade rash on the back of her legs. It's her territory.

He trips. Goes face-first into the grass and wild-rose brush. She can tell it hurts. So she sits on him, holds him down while he fights, and her insides twist from ribcage to hipbone, something completely new.

IF JENN WERE A BOY, she'd have claimed the family basement for her cave. It would be her birthright. She'd have crawled underground and lined her cement cave with clothes and animal hair, and she'd plot how to capture her chosen other-person, how to drag them down into the dark and chew on them.

Cave-person. Cave-girl. Cave-man, if she were a boy. Cave-woman doesn't have the same ring.

Jason lives in a cave. When he left Jenn's house and moved back in with his dad, he claimed the basement as his own territory. Only the furnace room, where the washing machine is, belongs to the house. Jason's basement is entirely defensive and all his. Jenn helped him carry a few things in, but he hasn't admitted her in two years. He had this expression like he was going to say her breasts kept her out, but that wasn't quite right. She could hear him not-say it. Other breasts might be allowed at some point, but not hers.

Not his mother's, either.

When she talks to her parents about Jason, they tell her he's angry at his mother. Because of the car accident, and the things before that, and the time his dad spent in jail. They were very upfront about it, at the time. Asked Jenn to stay at the dining table after dinner, while her sister fled to her room and her Barbies. For a second, she was terrified it was going to be her sex talk, and not just another "very special episode" her parents had decided to structure.

*Listen, Jennifer. There's been an accident, and we need to talk about it.*

*Your Uncle Garry and Auntie Sarah crashed their car. It was over the weekend. They were having a fight. You know how they fight?*

Loudly. Sometimes outside. She'd seen them, watched them from her blind in the pasture grass with a kind of ecstatic terror that mixed with the first elements of sex in her brain. This sound outside the edges of human existence.

*They do that in the car?*

*I don't know if they do it all the time, honey. But I think they did this time. They're both hurt. Jason's hurt too, but not so much. We're going to go pick him up in Saskatoon tonight, and he's going to stay with us.*

*How long?*

Her mother hesitated. *I think until his mom gets out of the hospital.*

*Is Uncle Garry dead?*

*No.*

*Why can't Uncle Garry take care of him?*

Parental conclave: *I don't want to talk about this right now. / You don't think we should tell her what's going on, all of it? / I think she'll be upset and we don't know it all yet. / I think she's upset already. / You don't have to be sarcastic. / Sorry. / I want to keep it out of the house. / Not an option. / I know.*

They didn't stop talking to each other, or looking at each other. Jenn left the table. Later, her mother stood in her doorway with an armful of blankets, like she was going to suggest Jenn surrender part of her room, but she didn't say anything. She made up a bed for Jason in the basement rec room. Carried Jenn's toys and books back upstairs with her and dropped them on the floor of her room. She said, "Clean up, would you please?"

They migrated Jason upstairs after a week, consolidating both girls into one room and consoling them with bunk beds. Jenn claimed the upper bunk and watched her sister stagger from point to point across the floor. Watched Jason shuffle into the bedroom that had been hers.

He came in, that night, and asked her to go to the treehouse with him, and she guessed if he was mad, it wasn't at her. His knees were covered in gauze and a white elastic fish net. Underneath, he showed her, there were lines of sharp black stitches. He lived with them for two years, leaving when he was ten to occupy their grandparents' old farmhouse with his dad. His mom didn't come back.

His mom isn't allowed in Jason's cave, even now, when she visits. He sits with her in the yard, or goes off with her in the car, and comes back and throws things into the trees. Jenn isn't allowed in, and Jenn's mother isn't. Her sister dives through the blanket-door with a kind of hurricane determination onto the couch cushions piled there to prevent brain injuries in small, determined children.

Jenn wants her own cave. If she could figure out a way to steal the basement, she could have one.

She studies what her friends have done. She has friends. She has her own little girl-wolf pack who understand her animal problem. Some of them are barely human. They've been digging down into the ground for years.

Ginger's basement is insulated from the rest of the world with wallboard and something soft and grey that eats sound. Ginger has only a thin sheen of girl over her pre-girl self, and she has boy instincts. It helps that she's huge. She crawled down into the basement all on her own, with her blankets and her clothes and that lizard she likes. It was a kind of declaration. She celebrated by taking her baby-pink clothes and her stuffed animals out into the backyard, and she phoned Jenn and said, "Get your dad to drive you over here."

"Why?"

"Just come. Do you have matches?"

Stuffed-animal bonfire. Jenn's dad came around the edge of the house to check on the smoke, walked back to his truck for the fire extinguisher, and put the whole blaze out without comment. (To Ginger, he didn't comment. Jenn was the subject of his careful, studied approaches on the subject of arson for months after that. He collected up the scented candles from her room. He put the matches for the wood stove out of reach. Watched her.)

Ginger's underground space doesn't have any remaining plush toys in it, only writing on the walls, a certain number of liquor bottles, and a pool table in the third stage of decay. The felt isn't gone yet, but there are holes nibbled into it. Ginger went through a phase of keeping mice and rats. Chinchillas, one winter. Lizards after that. The pit-bull she rescued from the neighbour who was planning to drown it. She rescues anything that isn't pretty or human. She finds homes for some of them, but there are creatures no one else would take in.

Snakes and bats. Really big spiders.

She has plans to deal with the cute, pretty human things. The people. She keeps pages carved out of yearbooks laid out on a cork board with sewing pins stuck through them. They're marked up with sharpie and some kind of deep-red liquid ink. Pretty girls, what they'd look like with their skins off. Male bodies: what she'll do with them. The inventories (lists on foolscap stolen from their classroom) are written in ballpoint pen, in script like tiny insect feet. Observations of chests and rib cages made when the boys peel their T-shirts off in the gym or chase each other around the rim of the town.

*Bite him lick him chew the space between his hipbones squeeze his wrists cup his balls hold him down and fuck him fuck him fuck him bite his head off nibble on his massive feet.*

The cork board isn't public. It isn't even in a part of Ginger's cave that her parents might see. Jenn ducked into Ginger's dog-den of a bedroom, looking for a cassette tape, one she'd borrowed before: Air Supply and David Bowie and Kansas mixed onto magnetic spools. Lizards watched her out of their red-washed terrarium. The bed-nest was in the corner. Jenn saw a flash of dick and turned. Saw the plans.

There were pictures, taken with a cheap disposable camera riddled with beach sand so the film scratched. Ugly, but clear.

It was Jason's body, taken at school and cut out, then laid on an inked-in medical table for examination and sex.

Jenn seriously thought about taking the picture. It was a good idea. But if she had a cave, she could have plans of her own. She would show hers to her friends.

Her weird, damaged friends. There are only six of them, girls with the wrong social shape. They've formed their own tribe. They're teaching Jenn to play pool. Tell her, *Just try not to tear the felt worse than it already is.*

Donna, perched up on a pile of boxes, mutters about vectors and perfect math. Lines and angles. Jenn can feel her watching. She shoots.

Strike balls. Scratch felt. Donna is sketching something on the unpainted wallboard with a stinking black marker. She's discovered something the rest of them haven't twigged to yet, or she's gone insane. Unlikely, though. Donna loves this kind of locked-in, crazy-person performance, like it makes her more real than the rest of them. More real than the people in her family. But she's also obsessive and visual. These beautiful, repeating patterns she sketches over everything she can touch. Like she's been drinking coffee since before dawn. Since before birth.

Donna whispers, "Fractals."

"The muppets that live under the repair shop?"

"Those are Fraggles." She keeps sketching. Ginger snorts.

Donna's not allowed to draw things like this at home. Last winter, her father found her sketchbook and burned it in the front yard. It's not that he doesn't love her or that he thinks she shouldn't draw. It's what she draws he has a problem with. She likes *symbols*. She likes Greek letters. She can talk Planck to her father until she's grey-blue from oxygen deprivation, because he's not going to acknowledge the difference between pagan arcana and particle physics or pure math. It's all deviance to him. He has to make her understand.

He's trying.

Donna has notebooks cached in all her friends' rooms. When she accepted Jenn, Jenn could tell right away, because there was a notebook stuffed into her closet when Donna left for the night. Only Ginger's parents, who are screaming rednecks but for some reason not religious ones, have actually invited her to *decorate*. They like Donna. They don't seem bothered, hosting a pack of deviant girls without a full set of social skills among them. *All you girls, you wanna draw on the walls, you go ahead.*

Jenn doesn't have Donna's flare or Ginger's aggressive handwriting, but she's pencilled on one corner of the wall, *antiquis temporibus, nati tibi similes in rupibus ventosissimis exponebantur ad necem*. She found it in a box of her mother's university textbooks, written in the margins, and stole that page.

*In the good old days, children like you were left to perish on windswept crags.*

She's not sure whether it's aimed at Jason or her, or some other kid she's never met, but she likes it.

Ginger says, "You're contaminating my space with geek germs."

"Your room is full of lizards. You don't get to complain," Jenn tells her.

"Their names are Bowie and Jagger, and I love them. If you talk smack about my lizards, you can stay at school over lunch and see who kicks your ass."

GINGER IS OBVIOUSLY the progeny of the people raising her — she looks just like them, blonde and towering — but they must wonder where she came from. Her parents have piles of rock and country tapes, and a love for CCR, and Ginger likes *Tin Machine*. Jenn looked into David Bowie a bit, holed up on the second floor of the Saskatoon Public Library, and now she has a copy of *The Man Who Sold the World* (on vinyl, Bowie-in-drag cover) to give Ginger for her birthday. Her mother went shopping with her for it, in and out of all the used-vinyl stores in Saskatoon until they turned up the right record. She needs to get it right.

Jenn thinks her mother'd like to know Jenn has a safe place to hide, but she's not about to tell her. Down in Ginger's cave, the Alice in Wonderland effect is in full swing. *We're all mad, here!* But when the lunch hour is up, they have to go back to school. Return to the big, sprawling, single-storey brick complex full of old linoleum and plastic chairs and an atmospheric soup of personal enmity.

*I hate you and I hate her and she hates me and she hates him and he hates him and he hates her and she hates me and we all hate each other.*

*All you need is love thy neighbour. Very hard. Very far away from you.*

It's like this every day. They spend six hours in the brick school-cage. An hour and a half or two hours on the bus. Then homework. Go to bed at ten. Get up at six-thirty.

Every day, she feels like a sick animal being poked with sticks. *Let's teach her abstract mathematics at 9:15 a.m.! That'll learn her!*

Jenn learns, but only as much as she'd have learned anyway. She's like her mother, down deep under her skin, smart the way few people ever will be in a town that brews fetal alcohol syndrome like gestational moonshine. Her teachers are grateful she's paying attention; it means they don't have to worry about her. She isn't going to attack them when their backs are turned. Instead, they can lock down the horror show of the other kids, who're all waiting to turn on each other the instant adult supervision wavers.

They fucking *bite*, the assholes she goes to school with. Jenn grew out of that years ago. Privately, she suspects that compared to them, she's normal. She's even stopped carrying live animals around inside her shirt.

She keeps small bones in her pencil box, but they're quiet. They don't scream during class at all.

Ginger isn't so trustworthy. She throws things at smaller kids. Donna chews on her own arms. Jenn slouches further down in her chair, and the teacher currently pacing stops to scratch Jenn's head. Fingers in her hair like she's the only calm animal in the room.

Boy two rows down reaches forward and gouges his pencil into the neck of the guy in front of him.

Scream.

Books, papers, pencils, sandwiches, spit-snot-blood fly and the desk gets kicked over and that's *it*. Fighting in the dirty linoleum aisle until the teacher comes and kicks them apart. He snarls over them while they spit at each other, then drags them off to the vice-principal's office by their hair.

Biologicals smeared all over the floor.

It's like this every day. She wants her mother to know *that*. Wants her father to know. Because they thought growing up in the country, on the family farm, in an extended family setting, engaged with agriculture, would be good for her. They send her to school here every day. And they won't even let her live underground, where she might be happy.

DONNA'S BEDROOM HAS none of her artwork on its walls. There's just a framed picture of herself, age four, and a small hole where the nail used to stick to hang the picture of Jesus. Jenn was visiting, actually, when Donna had that showdown with her father. She'd taken the picture down and shoved it under her bed. Her fathered walked in without knocking, reached under the bed, and put the picture back up.

Donna went after it, then, with a very fine brush and some India ink. She wasn't artistic about it. She just removed Jesus's face. Not even an edge of a halo left.

Her father walked in half an hour later, looked at the picture, and took it away. Brought her another one.

She found the stinking marker from her backpack and wrote *NO* across the glossy image.

Her father said, "You know your rejection of Him hurts me."

Donna explained to him, very calmly, that every pink-and-blue picture of Jesus she saw made her want to drive around the country establishing roadside shrines just so she could throw things at them.

He nodded, took the picture away. Later, when Tori and Donna were walking through the living room, he caught Donna and hugged her against him. Buried his face in the top of her head.

She still sings for him when he preaches. Every Sunday, in black dress pants and a nice blouse with her hair all braided back. She has this voice. Not always pitch-perfect, but there are octaves and decibels of it that you don't expect. Between hymns, she sits at the back of the pink stucco Church of the Family in Christ and reads.

She can parrot back the whole detailed sermon on loving your children even when they make you crazy. Spits sometimes when she does it, like she doesn't believe him. He watches her like she's a terrorist he won't negotiate with, and doesn't respond.

He negotiates with other people, though. He makes deals with everyone else in town. *I'll do X for you if you'll come to church this Sunday.* For most people, it's physical help: fencing or roof repairs or a ride into Saskatoon. He's been known to act as go-between for romantic conversations and business deals. And in return he gets an extra body in the pews in front of him the next Sunday, one more human project. Like he really, really believes that he can persuade them, if he can just make them sit still and listen long enough.

Jenn's sitting on Donna's floor, reading her social studies textbook, when her father finally makes his offer.

Donna can have sleepovers on the weekends if she'll make a real, sincere effort to convince her friends to come to church on Sunday morning. Just to hear her sing.

Donna turns her head to Jenn. Says, "You could sing with me, if you want."

Jenn's more tempted than the pastor realizes. Or he realizes and he's just not letting it show. Girls who aren't good at basketball, who have thick waists and have no depth perception and their jeans fit awkwardly and their shoes are always dirty and their hair resists arrangement and their skin breaks out and they know too many answers and aren't good in a fight. Those girls sing. To themselves, in little groups. In drama club and the short-lived school choir.

He abjures the drama club for complicated reasons, but he's seen the girls clump up and practice carols for Christmas performance. Twos and threes and Donna solo singing *O Holy Night*.

It's a good trick if you can do it.

There are weekends when Jenn doesn't want to be home. She doesn't like the way Jason's looking at her, or she's restless and loud and her parents want her out. She gets a ride into Bear Hills and sleeps in Donna's room and sits beside her at the back of the church for an hour on Sunday. Stays with her afterwards, all day.

Donna's parents can't deal with her all the time. There are negotiations, and she's surrendered to Jenn's parents' custody. Two weeks. Jenn can remember when she didn't want to share her bedroom.

They nest in extra blankets. They have sleeping bags and air mattresses and bed-pillows and couch-pillows and potato chips and root beer and makeup and *YM* and *Cosmo* from the Bear Hills Co-op gas station. From 8$^{th}$ Street Books & Comics, all the way in Saskatoon, they have *Hellblazer*.

It's not quite a blanket fort, but when they were young enough for blanket forts, they were too young to get their hands on occult-horror comics. John Constantine's lover is gone and he's down among the dead men. Vampires and dead ancestors. His memory of the horrors of Margaret Thatcher eats at his physical body.

In a shoebox under the bed: *Interview with the Vampire*, *Queen of the Damned*, and *Flowers in the Attic*. Blood-red lipstick. Episodes of *Forever Knight* taped off TV.

The vampire material's addictive, and Anne Rice is vivid adolescent porn. Jenn finds the battered paperbacks when her mother turns her loose in the tangled used book store on Saskatoon's edge. *The Mummy, or, Ramses the Damned. Cry to Heaven.*

More and more of what they read is boys kissing/hugging/licking/biting/bedding boys. Pretty, pretty immortal blond Aryan psychotic boys. It has to be boys on boys because all the girls are crazy and screaming half-naked in the woods.

It's an interesting idea.

As long as it's summer, and Jenn's parents want them out of the house, they might as well try it. Jenn's mother works late and her father does field work, and the house is echoing-empty. Jason's lurking, across the home quarter in the old house, but he doesn't want to come out and play.

Tori, baby Tori who's somehow growing up skinnier and quieter than the rest of the family, is Jenn's responsibility, but if she won't come out of her room, that's not Jenn's fault. She can keep her slightly bruised little self in there forever if she wants. All the Barbie dolls can stay in there too.

Tori talks to them — the dolls — like they really talk back. You have to wonder what, exactly, Barbie has to say.

Possibly some interesting things. Tori learned to sew just so she could make Barbie jeans and baggy striped T-shirts. Two or three dolls have deliberately close-cut hair. Sometimes, when Tori's been carried away by their parents, Jenn and Donna invade her room and stare at the dolls. Donna says she thinks Tori's Barbies might have fangs.

They have this other conversation, then, along the lines of, *If you think my sister's so interesting, why don't you go play with **her**?*

*Because **we** aren't **playing**. Wench.*

It's possible, too, that someday they'll take Victoria with them. Until then, Jenn and Donna go into the brush-filled pasture on their own.

Jenn's family — Jason's family too, she supposes — has two sections together forming the home farm. One square mile is open: hayfields. One's bush: pasture. There were at one time four family residences, though only two of them are left, kitty-corner and a quarter of a mile apart. Shared stables and outbuildings in the middle. Barbed wire around the two yards, and along the surveyed boundaries, and the rest is open. Christopher Robin had the Hundred Acre Wood. They have six hundred and forty acres, and no plush animals lurking, waiting to be told stories.

There are animals. They're tiny and desperate and they all bite. Cattle move through at a distance. Coyotes and foxes eat the mice. Half-dressed girls prey on anything they can catch.

Theoretically, because they haven't caught and killed anything, yet. Still, stripped down to tank tops, jeans and work boots, gloves and knives and lipstick battle-marks, they could start eating raw meat any time. Insects ring around them, and the branches cut Jenn's arms everywhere they hit. She and Donna come in every night looking like meat that isn't quite dead. They crawl out in the morning with comics and vampire books and basic food and carve their own spaces out of the fallen trees.

She wonders if this is what her parents meant when they told her to go outside and play.

Almost-sixteen is possibly too old for girls to build tree forts and stage imaginary battles.

They did this when they were younger, too, but then it was *Star Trek* instead of *Dungeons & Dragons* and vampires, and they didn't feel quite so savage doing it. They weren't big, hulking girls then.

They take the horses out sometimes, when they're dressed for it. Horses add to the whole medieval ethos. Jenn's father likes the look; he brings them horsehair ropes from farm auctions and helps the girls shape them into neo-Elvish gear. He tries to talk to them, sometimes, about Tolkien, and Jenn has to express to him that they're not interested, really. She isn't a fucking *hobbit*.

All they really need now are capes, like the cape she had when she was twelve. But capes would scare the horses. Catch on the trees.

Maybe it looks like fun. Enough that Jason crawls out of his cave and starts watching them. Jenn spots him in the almost-dissolved treehouse. She sees flickers that make her wonder if he's building hunting blinds. What the hell he wants.

It gets Donna's attention. She watches him back. Hunts him.

It's a serious business. She smears herself with mud. When the sun keeps catching on her pink T-shirt, she takes it off.

She jumps on him all at once, out of a bush. Rolls him down and sits on his chest. Knees him in the face and sort of drools on him, like a psychotic zoo animal.

When Jason was nine and came to live with them, he played with Jenn in the pasture. When he was ten and eleven and she was almost friends with him, they co-claimed the tree house, and they shared it peaceably. He walked away from her. At some point between then and now, he lost the will to go into the chokecherry naked.

How she thinks of it.

She's almost sure Donna won't eat him.

Donna bites him, but just that once, on the shoulder. And eventually she lets him up. Rocks all hundred and ninety eight pounds of herself back on her boot heels and glares.

Jenn doesn't remember Donna hitting him, but Jason's one eye is swollen almost shut and his nose is bleeding. He's shaking.

What he says is, *Cunt. I'll kill you.* Then he runs. Not at her. Away.

Donna steps in behind Jenn and bites her softly on the neck.


THEIR PARENTS HAVE some kind of bilateral trade agreement in place. When Donna goes home, Jenn goes with her.

The only horses in Bear Hills are the imagined ones they shape around the hemp-rope swings in the manse's backyard. Summer ate itself, and there are bags of school supplies in the front hall. It's half-cold out. Jenn's layered into a sweater and jacket, all her clothes on like a respectable young lady. Rope fragments sliver into their palms.

Inside, there are small children in the living room, all ranged around the coffee table doing Sunday school homework. Only Donna has a desk and a room of her own. She's the oldest of five. The sixth one was a miscarriage. "It's buried under the swing set."

Jenn stills her swing. "Really?"

"Just behind."

"Boy or girl?"

"They didn't tell me."

"This is when you were little?"

"It was last year."

Jenn looks for soft places in the ground, watches Donna when she can't find the spot.

Donna says, "Run."

She gets up without looking at Jenn, scrambles over the fence like there isn't a functional gate, and takes off. The dried-out climbing vines shred where her runners hit them.

She's fast for a fat girl. Faster than Jenn realized when they were in the pasture and the ground was soft. Bear Hills at the end of August is idyllic. It's rimmed by Manchurian elm trees, interrupted by caragana and lilac hedgerows. There's Manitoba maple in the empty spaces. Still, there are gaps and shadows, spaces you can lose a girl in. And then you come to the end of a street and shift from unmeasurably old pavement to gravel, and then suddenly there's just grass in all directions and no windbreak. No lights. No paved roads branching off in sharp directions. No houses for a couple of miles.

There's a feedlot in the distance. Silos in the further distance. Jenn can't see any of them in the dark.

Air and grass moving. There's a disorienting number of stars.

Donna's in the middle of the field beyond the closed-up hospital when Jenn catches her. Bloody air (the first sign of a lifetime of intermittent asthma) runs into her lungs and comes up so coppersalty she keeps trying to spit her own breath back onto the ground. The white nylon of Donna's bra glows like it's under black light. Bare pale skin. Donna's sweater is pooled at her feet.

Under her sweatshirt, Donna wears a tangle of hemp and leather and silver jewelry that Jenn vaguely remembers her buying at the provincial exhibition. She's been drawing on herself in ballpoint pen. Medium-blue ink looks black in the dark, disappearing under her four-hook bra and crawling up under her hair.

Random patterns and numbers and Planck. It runs down her sides. Catches where the waist of her jeans cuts into her belly.

This is nothing like a gothic landscape, and Jenn is starting to get that she was wrong. She's not a hobbit, but vampires are entirely the wrong symbol-metaphor-fantasy mode for her universe, and this is not a body that elves would recognize.

She thinks about werewolves, and coyotes.

They were in the pasture, and Donna bit Jason. Donna bit *her*.

Jenn pulls off her own top. Underneath, she's wearing medium-beige rubber and nylon. Different breasts, different shape, still heavier and less sexual than she wants to be. She says, "Have you got a pen?"

"I *always* have a pen."

"Not a permanent one."

"Yes."

"Do me like yours."

"Take off your bra, then."

It's cold. Jenn didn't run as hard as Donna, and she's cooling faster. Bare flesh in the wind, and it's maybe eight degrees above freezing. No humidity. No insects, because it froze and snowed and melted last week, and they're in the desert season now before winter. The pen's ballpoint roller has something tiny and sharp caught in it that hurts her once every couple of centimetres or a distance Jenn thinks is probably an inch.

Whatever Donna's drawing isn't vines or symbols. There's no continuity in her movements at all.

"I'm cold," Jenn says.

"I know. Hold still or I won't be able to see."

All the way down her back. Jenn feels gaps form on her skin where there isn't enough light to draw. She doesn't know how long this will last, or how long it's been since Donna took a shower.

"I washed my hair bending over the tub when it got too greasy."

"Aren't you kind of . . ."

"Sticky. Yeah. I wipe down every so often. Ten days so far."

They don't have to take gym anymore. Not since last year. Jenn thought that would be the end of other girls staring so closely at her naked torso. She doesn't miss the locker-room predators with their pretty-girl eyes. Assessment of your underwear and the fat bunched at your waist. Zits on your back. Worn-out elastic on your panties. The last time you shaved your legs. Your posture when you have no pants on and everyone is staring at you.

In the dark, in the field, she can at least have pants. Up close, Donna smells worse than Jenn does. She's now allowed to judge.

She won't be able to see what's on her back. She can't imagine how Donna drew on herself. Even double-jointed girls are limited by physiology and fat. Her body doesn't infinitely bend.

Donna licks Jenn along the waistband of her jeans. Passes Jenn her sweater.

Thirty breaths between that and the moment that Donna's father calls, "Baby, is that you?"

"Yeah." Donna stands like she's never been half naked in the open air.

"I was looking for you all over."

"Well, where did you think we'd go? There's nothing out here but grass." It's true.


WHEN THEY WERE LITTLE, Jenn and Jason both lived with both their parents, and they played hide and seek all over the farm. There are more than a dozen buildings still standing, and a square mile of low brush. Open fields.

In early October, years after Jason's mother grabbed the steering wheel on the highway, years after Jason's father comes back and reclaims him, Jason mostly watches her from a distance. Jenn goes riding on her own. Traces of ballpoint ink itch in the folds of her knees. She's wrapped in lace-up boots and extra socks and a sweater, then a windbreaker and mini-gloves whose fingertips she cut off with sewing scissors. Hair up under her Pony Club helmet, resurrected since her last concussion. Animal-accident prone. She comes in with almost-numb fingers and toes. Djinn chases through the brush under Jenn with all the determination of a overgrown kid-pony, but she comes back steaming and exhausted. Jenn slides down and her own knees give. She staggers, trying to put her saddle away.

Jason lets her hang everything, nice and neat, before he pushes her down.

Big boy all over her back. He sits on her waist, pushing her face-down into the barn floor, and only letting her twist face-up when she whimpers. Says, "I've been looking for you for hours."

She can't think why he would. Not for hours. "Why?"

He laughs. Leans down (*knees on her, twists, grinding little bones against the concrete floor*) and kisses her. Wet mouth open tongue-less. Just like he does this all the time.

"I want to show you something. Come on."

He takes her to the machine shop. His builder tendencies kicked in early. Jenn remembers their first shared Christmas, he duct-taped all her toys together. When he was twelve, her father taught him to weld. Taught uncle Garry at the same time. So now, every so often, she hears Garry say, *Why don't we just weld those bits together and see what they look like?*, and then for hours the yard smells like hot metal and oxygen.

Eventually, they'll build a giant dinosaur robot out of the fragments of a century of farming. Their great-grandparents bought the farm from its original claimants most of a century ago. Jenn's father and Garry go to estate auctions and buy sixty-pound lots of scrap iron, all packed in collectible wooden crates. Other people, who've wandered out of Saskatoon to try this farm-living business, go to those same auctions and buy up metal fragments just because they've realized you can't have a barn empty of these things. But they get bemused by the metal parts and re-sell them.

Just keep the insurance company calendars from the 1950s, with the pictures of girls and horses, captioned *Three Little Fillies*, or *My Favourite Blondes*.

Jason's carved a section of the machine shop for himself, away from the welding zone. He has a spot-soldering gun and pieces of computers. It's technological wreckage. Jason bought an Apple II and a Commodore 64 through the *Western Producer*, convinced his dad to drive him out to wherever they were, just so he could peel away their layers in this dusty room that'll be too cold to work in without gloves in another week.

"No, it won't. Anyway, these run better when they're cold."

"They run?"

"They almost run. I'm working on it."

Behind him, on the trestle table, there's something built out of random circuits and tiny lightbulbs. A steroid-fuelled nightlight, she thinks. A space gun. He's working from a World War II manual for electricians. It was their grandfather's. He likes — liked — Jason best. Better than either of his sons. Better than Jenn, whose pockets full of mice annoyed him beyond language.

"This is what you wanted to show me?"

He pauses, shakes his head. "No."

Jason wanders past her, towards their grandparents' house. His house, since their grandmother moved to Victoria to age quietly in the absence of winter, and Garry took the place over. Jenn doesn't go in, as a rule. The house smells like engine oil and yesterday's pan-fried hamburgers, and it's monumentally empty of any sign of Jason's mother. Just, there's a towering hibiscus tree in the back porch's corner, and Jenn's almost sure that was hers — ex-aunt Sarah. She liked plants, and macrame. Jenn can see the tree's silhouette through the filthy glass, just enough that she suspects it isn't dead.

The tree might have a name. She isn't sure.

Jason changes direction in mid-step and moves back, diagonally, across the home quarter to her house. Inside, he takes his boots off and piles them in the corner. Hesitates by the basement stairs, then turns and goes in. Upstairs, past Tori's room to Jenn's.

Her room has his smell in it, and her bed is tangled like he slept there all afternoon. The radio Jason sort-of built and gave to her, in the last year they were friends, is in pieces on the floor. Its guts are everywhere. Around it on the floor, there are pages she gradually recognizes as parts of her vampire novels, excised with a utility knife and impaled on the softwood floor with thumb tacks.

Grins at her like maybe he jerked off in here earlier, in a place she won't find for a while. Like he's still a member of the family who can come into her room when he likes. Like he has any business contaminating her mother's grand architectural design with his filthy boy-body. He's reeking all over the natural wood and clear sunlight and artisan-woven rug in the corner. His smell's in the ancestral quilt on the bed.

"What did you *do*?"

He says, "I was going to fix your radio. Since you broke it."

"You aren't allowed in here." She stares. "You cut up my books."

"I read them first. And I have to ask: *manhood*? I mean," he ripped a mutilated page loose from its pin and lifted it into the light, *"The swelling of his manhood that would never again fulfill its intimate purpose, but showed itself still willing,* my god. How do you read this shit?"

Hot flash runs through Jenn's face and she grabs at the page. Grabs all of them that she can reach, and the shell of the book, and stuffs them into her underwear drawer. Dares him without actually saying anything to go digging through her less-than-sexy selection of panties. If Jason braves her array of floral cotton and over-stretched elastic, at least she'll be able to use that against him in the future.

She says, "You read it too."

"I've actually gone out and *bought* porn, girly. I can't *be* embarrassed anymore. This is just for fun. Sticky fingers in everything, you know?"

"Sticky...oh." Hot in her face, again. "Never mind. I hate you."

Pause. He looks...not satisfied. Like he was expecting something else.

Jenn says, "I actually do hate you. Get out."

She kicks him. Pushes him back out her door and onto the stained-oak mezzanine. It would be a good moment for him to take a Scarlett O'Hara-style plunge down her mother's slightly-too-impressive stairs. Add some real drama to the day.

Tori sticks her head out her bedroom door. Stares at them. She looks half-interested, ready to go into full Prissy mode and scream like a girl, a banshee, a shop-class accident when Jason finally cracks his skull. *Oh Gawd Miss Jennifuh, you done killed him!*

Jason, Jenn thinks absently, would look good in a swirling red velvet dress. Especially one made out of curtains.

"Jenny, *fuck!*"

Because he actually did fall. Caught himself on the railing and he isn't going to die, but he's angry. Scared.

"I was joking. Jesus Christ!"

"You're ugly," she says. "You get things dirty all the time. Never come in here again."

"You don't think you might be over-reacting, you know, *slightly?*"

"Get out."

She walks past him, past Tori, and slams her door. Her poor book's pages are half-loose in the top of her dresser. Jason's skin-and-cheap-cologne smell is deep in her bedspread. She lies down on it anyway.

THE PHONE BY HER BED rings at eight-something that night, and Jason says, "You're right. I'm sorry. And possibly I'm an asshole. Do you want to come out with me?"

THEY DON'T HAVE A VEHICLE anywhere in the family that doesn't smell like animals. Jenn's mother's car, at least, should be lawyer-clean, but the smell crawls in. Jenn isn't sure how her mother's hung onto her professional reputation, since livestock-reek must follow her into the office. Into the courtroom. Black robes and white collar and eau de border collie.

Maybe her clients are comforted by it. Most of the people she works with look like they lie down with dogs. Some of them come to the office still in their work clothes, coated in animal hair and faintly organic shit smell.

Garry's truck has a thin coat of fur on everything. It's a trace from the three dogs Garry keeps all the time, maybe even sleeping with them. He loves those dogs. Kisses their heads when he leans over them in the yard. The blanket stuffed behind the bench seat smells like doggy happiness.

Dog-slime.

It's all over her jeans. On her skin.

She should spit on Jason a little. Pass on the love.

Jenn leans against the window and looks at the dark. Nine o'clock and it's a month since the equinox. It's black outside. They need all the running lights for highway driving. An hour and a quarter into Saskatoon, and she sits there watching signs flare and deer flash across the road. Three weeks to hunting season.

SASKATOON HAS CORRIDORS — long streets that feed the rest of the city and that travel compass points from one urban edge to the other. In the middle of 8th Street, the east-side corridor, there's a bookstore that stays open most of the night. Which isn't, of itself, that thrilling. It's a cove in a strip mall full of bars and sewing-supply outlets. Glowing sign, tired guy behind the counter, towers of used sci-fi novels in the back.

Jason picked the store for what you might call its *periodicals*, she thinks. Comics in sealed plastic bags fill bins and drawers. Jenn read comics when she was a kid. *Archie*, mostly. Some basic superhero comics her mother brought home for her from the gas station. Those were battered bits of newsprint with mostly incomprehensible stories. It makes sense to her, now, that each comic is only a fragment of the whole. When she started reading *Hellblazer*, it was a thrill. Then *Sandman*, filled with the need to look like an Endless goth girl. She's stopped reading, though, mostly. She can't afford it. The comics are expensive, and she has to buy them in bunches on her trips to the city. It's less money for clothes, junk food, vampire novels, silver jewelry like Donna's.

A guy leaning across the store counter is in heavy negotiations for a bound copy of *Batman: A Lonely Place of Dying*. Greasy hair punctuated with glued-in extensions and a T-shirt with binary code on it. Jacket tied around his waist.

Jason's hands twitch toward the comics. His collection was always better than hers. It'd be worth going into his house, invading *his* room, to find out what he has that she hasn't read.

She realizes, after, that he didn't come for the comics. His focus is the magazine bins. You don't sell old copies of *Field and Stream* wrapped in plastic. If you have back issues of *The Western Horseman*, you trade those in at the saddlery shops. This is a geek-boy haven, and geek boys spend their money on very specific things. Vintage computer parts. Paperback novels. Games. Comics. Porn.

The racks are full of porn.

*Playboy. Penthouse. Hustler.*

*Barely Legal. Bra Busters. Big Boobs. Busty Beauties. Celebrity Skin. Cheri. Chic. Cherry Pie. Club. Fetish. Finally Legal. Genesis. Gent. Hawk. High Society. Hot Talk. Juggs. Just Legal. Leg Action. Naughty Neighbours. Oui. Perfect 10. Plumpers. Ripe. Swank. Taboo. Tailends. Tight. VIP. Velvet.*

All in plastic, like the comics. Different reason.

Without looking at her, Jason says, "Don't browse too much.
Pick something and I'll pay for it."

"You have ID for that?"

"You're a very boring child, you know that, Jenny?"

Makes her skin crawl when he says that. So she picks something. And, really, it's not like anyone as bored as the guy behind
the register is going to bother age-checking anybody who isn't
giggling like a twelve-year-old and jumping up and down. Jason
just earns a *hey man* and a half grin. Plastic bag and a receipt. He
has a smeared look for Jenn, though, that makes her hunch her
shoulders, going out the door.

She's not going to sit there, a small-town girl in a truck cab,
goggling at porn. A handful of bills and change buys them
McDonald's from the place across the street. French fry smell
soaks her while Jason drives them back across the river. Down the
arc of Spadina Crescent to the weir overlook. It's this river-wide
half-dam that makes a tiny waterfall. There are spotlights
focussed on it, at night, and a parking lot in the shadow of the
railway bridge. Two or three other cars hulk in the lot. Their windows are faintly silver with breath-fog.

Porn doesn't have the obvious thrill for Jenn that it does for
Jason. She has all the necessary parts; she's seen them in the
shower. In the mirror on those mornings when she's awake
enough to strip down and give herself the teenaged-girl self-
loathing once-over that every magazine she's ever read reminds
her to do. She knows her body doesn't look like the ones in *YM*
and *Cosmo*. Even if she dropped ten (thirty) pounds, she wouldn't
look like that. She's five foot five, big feet, ribs low to her hip
bones. Zit scars on her back and breasts.

She saw other mostly naked girls in the years of torturous phys
ed classes. Mostly, the class inspired her to never participate in
group activities, ever again. Possibly never move again if she
doesn't have to. Basketball shorts come off, bras change from

sports to underwire, and you get a pretty good idea of what your classmates look like, even if you're making a point of looking at the wall. Bony girls, slinky girls, lumpy girls, big girls. Girls with bone flaws that throw off their symmetry and girls who could hunt you down on a playing field and rip your heart out. Basketball players in Bear Hills only run about five feet seven. They aren't tall. The most you can look for in local girls is sleek hair, unmarked skin, clean body lines.

Women in magazines glow from the inside. They're tan the way you can only get in a salon. They have longer bones. Longer limbs. Long, breath-thin waists.

Porn, Jenn discovers, is another thing entirely. The women aren't just flawless. They're hairless. Shadeless. She's never seen the frightening not-pink colour of Barbie doll flesh on a human being before. They look like Tori's nightmares, when the dolls wake up angry.

They have bigger breasts than any girls' magazine ever showed. The pictures are more ass-focussed than Jenn's ever had reason to worry about before.

"Oh god," she says.

"What?"

"I don't —"

"Look anything like that. I know. That's not the *point*."

"Somebody looks like this." It's her mouth, talking without reference to her brain.

"Not you. Big deal. I'll get you gay porn next time, and you can make fun of my body."

Impossibly globular breasts. Tiny, pale-pink nipples poking up unnaturally near the tops of flesh balloons rising out of nearly-exposed ribcages.

"Why show me this?"

He sighs. "You don't think it's funny?"

She screws her eyes shut. On her retinas, there are burn-spots from the brightness of the photographed asses. "Why would I?"

"Think about it for a minute."

"I should have stayed home."

He's unsatisfied again. She gave him the wrong answer. Fuck him.

Beside her, staring at the river, Jason hisses. He says, "Does it ever just *ache*? Like you could really think about sliding a couple of fingers in and riding your hand until your whole body just kinda snaps back and you could come 'til it's all out of your system?"

She doesn't look at him.

"Think about it. Porn is permission to think about sex in a lot of detail." He reaches over. His fingers brush the base of her skull. "It's not *real*, though. It wouldn't be anywhere near as much fun if it was real.

"It just kick-starts you. It's really hard to *not* think about sex when you're staring down the . . . throat. I don't know. Cunt. Seriously, I don't have an end for that sentence. But tell me you're not thinking about it. Sex. Even if it's just sex with yourself."

The conversation turned sticky, faster than she expected, even. Jenn wonders how long it would take her to walk the hundred-odd kilometres home from here. How far she'd get before Jason caught her and stuffed her back in the truck cab. She says, "Why exactly is this about *me* and sex?"

"Because you were mad at me, earlier."

"So you drove me to Saskatoon and showed me porn and talked dirty?" It's possible her outrage would be a bit more pointed if she didn't still have fries in her mouth. Years from now, she'll spend hours with a therapist discussing the connection her brain formed between sexual repression and fast food. "You realize that girls don't like porn?"

"Everybody likes porn."

"Why would I like this?"

"Because it's about sex, and sex is basically a good thing."

Jenn's startled. She thinks he might mean it. "Because you've had it so much?"

Jason stares at the river. Chews on a McNugget. "Everybody likes some porn. Because those vampire books of yours? Definitely porn. It's possible you don't like *this* porn. It's not my fault; you picked it. But you should see the stuff in my dad's closet. He thinks I don't go upstairs. Jesus, you should see the stuff at my mom's place."

He starts the truck. They've fogged the windows, just sitting at opposite ends of the cab, talking. The heater kicks in and starts the defrost cycle.

"What do you like, then?" Jenn asks.

"I'll tell you sometime. But seriously. What would you go looking for if you were looking at the pictures instead of grabbing blind?"

"I. No. No pictures."

"Really?"

"It looks like sex with Barbie. You can talk to Tori about that."

"She's twelve. I'd have to give up sex forever." He rubs at the window. "Tell me you don't enjoy it."

"I hate this stuff."

"No, I mean you and Donna."

Jenn blinks. "Hang on. What?"

"You and Donna."

"Are both girls? Play pool together? Can kick your ass in the pasture if you don't leave us alone?"

"Are not doing anything to reduce the whole butch image," Jason says. "And yes, seriously. She *draws* on you. You can deny it, but I'm in your family and I know."

"I. We're not." She shakes her head. "Never."

That satisfied him. She doesn't know why. "Hmm. I'm starting to believe you. Jesus, couldn't you guys have a little imagination. You're so fucking boring."

He'll pick her up and kidnap her inside a block, but Jenn gets out of the truck anyway. Listens to the water roar for a second or two before she starts walking. There's a footpath along the river that goes down into the bush; he won't be able to reach her there, if he's following from the road. She's down into it, close to the water and surrounded by naked chokecherry before it occurs to her that she's in the city, not at home, and it's entirely possible that there are people in these woods as well as animals. There was that girl, a year ago (three years? five?) who disappeared on the footpaths on the river's other side.

Leaves crunch around her as she curls up. There isn't anybody out here, not really. There isn't a pervert desperate enough to lurk in old grass just because someday one person might wander through. You'd be more likely to get sprayed by a skunk. You can hunt girls on 20th Street, and there are boys for sale five blocks from here in Kinsmen Park. They're hard to miss. She's easy. She's off the trail and burrowed down in long grass. She has her mini-gloves in her pockets. It's cold, but not freezing; probably not even zero. She could sleep here until morning and then walk down to . . . somewhere. Call home for a ride.

This neighbourhood is all residential. She's half a mile from City Hospital and the Mendel Art Gallery and some impossible distance from everything else.

She could knock on a door, maybe. Look for a block parent sign — do they still use those? Ask to use the phone.

She hears, *Jennifer!*

*Jenny!*

*Fuck!*

Fuck *him*.

The shouted, *Jenn*, in the distance is very, very small.

IT'S GOING TO BE WINTER. She needs to put on new skins.

Fleece and thermal layers in the barn, or one of her father's old coats. Underneath her barn coat, Jenn wears layers and some-times long underwear. Extra socks. Ugly, heavy, warm boots.

It isn't that cold, yet. It snows in mid-October, and the snow lasts until the day after Halloween and then melts. Just occasional glassy ice-patches are left, and bare ground. Snow at ground level where the sunlight doesn't reach, in the bush.

–5°C most days. Colder at night.

The first Saturday in November, they register for ice sports. Senior figure-skating lessons for Jennifer, late-beginner lessons for Victoria. Junior-coaching-staff work pays for half the skating, and it leaves her money for books. Jason stands in the opposite line, for hockey sign-up, and ignores them. When he's written onto the list and paid for, he goes outside and pretends he isn't smoking. He walks around Jenn all the time like she might explode if he strikes the right spark, like he's not sure whether he wants to try that.


DONNA CHASES JENN to the rink and chases her around the bleachers in the half-hour between the end of school and the beginning of CanSkate practice. She sits up high on the plywood seats and eats popcorn. Jenn leads toddlers through the basics of safe falling and bunny-hop jumps and tries not to stare up into the rafters and grin.

After practice, Donna leads her to the girls (Visitors) change room. The toilet enclosure is marked with her stinking perma-nent marker. It says:

*JASON H. SUCKS DICKS*

"Thank you. My cousin's name is written on the bathroom wall."

"Does it make you feel better?"

"Not yet. Maybe."

DONNA HAS HER driver's licence. She drives Jenn home after fig-ure skating in the road-boat pastor's car. The tapes they find in the glove compartment are mostly Christian country and pop music.

Donna pulls off the road four miles from Jenn's home. Pulls Jenn out of the car and into the back seat. She flattens against the vinyl seat-back and pulls Jenn against her, in a spoon. Breathes against the top of her head.

JENN SKATES WITH her own-level class from six-thirty to eight-thirty on Saturday mornings. It's the only weekend ice time that doesn't belong to one of the hockey clubs. She's used to doing this cold, exhausted, and hungry. If she tries to eat at this hour, she'll throw up. When they can beg their exhausted, cold, university-stu-dent coach to let them off, Jenn walks out to the concession, skate guards scuffing the concrete, and buys hot chocolate. Sugar and caf-feine and pain in her teeth from the boiling water.

"Jenn, were you ever planning on coming back? Because you're totally welcome to take the ice time your parents paid for and spend it sitting in the lobby."

"Coming."

Girls still working doggedly through the national fitness figure skating program at sixteen are never going to be Olympic skaters. Unless you're five feet tall and weigh a hundred pounds, you won't ever be partnered. So instead they learn classic figure 8s, inside- and outside-edge lines, dance patterns. Skate with a walk-man on to learn music coordination and try not to fall down.

Jenn's mother gets up at six and drives Jenn into town. Sits half-asleep in the driver's seat. "Do you *enjoy* this, baby?"

"I don't understand."

Starving and cold-numb by the time she leaves the ice. Her skating bag smells like sweat and the baby powder that's supposed to absorb moisture and keep her feet from freezing. Her mother's never been able to convince her to skate in sweatpants or thermal layers instead of leggings. She curls up on the bench in the dressing room and shakes, waiting for her core temperature to come up to human normal.

So. Get dressed. Deodorant. Donna picks her up at nine. It takes them over an hour to drive into Saskatoon for fast-food breakfast. Egg and sausage and cheese on a bun, or the pancakes that dissolve when you pour syrup on them. Cheap coffee.

Heavy teenage girls surrounded by layers of winter clothing sit in the low-density commercial wasteland, eating.

They drive home listening to Christian mix tapes. Sleep until mid-afternoon.


SHE WAKES UP, and Jason's sitting on the foot of her bed, cross-legged. It's not that she didn't know he was there, exactly, she just kind of thought he was a cat.

"I've figured something out," he says.

"Okay."

"You're not a guy."

"No kidding."

"I forget, though. I think you're like me."

Jenn sits up in bed in a t-shirt that's been washed more times than the rest of her shirts (not combined, but there might be some obscure mathematical equivalence that Donna could explain to her) and shows nipple shadows as well as the shape of her breasts. She can smell girl-sweat and vague sex smell — her smell — on her skin and the bedding.

Her bedspread is pink. Her bra is lying on the floor.

Jenn says, "Donna's my sister."

"Tori's your sister."

"Donna's my sister that I *like*."

Blink. Winter light in the room. He says, "I bought you a new vampire book." Its cover has roses and vague, suggestive blood. She should switch to werewolves. It would confuse Jason, and she's beginning to think that sex is more about dogs than ivory teeth.

Donna's going to like the werewolves. She'll grow out the hair on her legs and start biting harder, just to prove her love for people.

THE ANIMALS ACCEPT Jenn's accidents. They still love her. She understands Garry, from a distance, sometimes: only animals are always going to love her. Dogs. And horses.

Little girls who wish for ponies don't incorporate winter into their fantasies. Ponies live in endless green fields where the sun is always warm, and nothing shits. Fantastic ponies don't get nervous from smells on the wind or strung out from air pressure changes, or go into heat, drip sex and blood down their hind legs. They don't roll in their own shit. They don't need food/water/exercise when it's cold enough to freeze the breath in your nose.

What Jenn rides is clearly not a pony.

She rides a Polish Arabian mare, thirteen years old, fourteen hands high, bay. Height of a pony, personality of a desert war horse. Emotional fragility of a valium addict going cold turkey.

Djinn hunts the dogs. Rocks back on her hind legs and stabs at Garry's border collies and snarls when Garry gets too close, because he's a dog on some level, and Djinn knows that.

Jenn loves her.

She went with her mother to a breeders' auction, years ago, and found this animal shivering in the back of a box stall. Most of the way to starving. In the Bear Hills, conditions were dry. In the Cypress Hills, ten hours south, it was desert; three years of no rain and no feed. People were giving up. The auction wasn't just a selection of young stock and a few show horses. They brought in brood mares and family pets. Kid ponies. All these gorgeous, emaciated horses selling for meat prices. They looked like they were already dead.

Djinn had no mane, then. Hollows behind every rib. Her hand-inked pedigree, written on parchment, covered a page and a half in the catalogue.

Jenn's mother was having a good time. She'd had two glasses of wine and a couple of painkillers for the sprained shoulder she'd earned separating calves. Jenn didn't register it so much, then, but the combination was a serious one. It gave her mother ideas like bidding up the prices, just a little, to give the horses some dignity. She bought Djinn for $375. Gave her to Jenn on the way home. "Because her name's like yours, so I think she must *be* yours."

Drunk logic.

Jenn's had five horses. A kid pony and a barrel horse and the strung-out racetrack reject she rode for Pony Club, and the horse that dislocated her finger when it flinched. And Djinn.

Djinn — Tori has to explain this to people, individually and very slowly — is breed-registered under the name *O Mi Desert's Dream of Jeannie*. It breaks down to *genie*, and then to the Arabic word *djinn*. One of the fire-creatures, her father said. Because Jenn's apparently incapable of naming her horses anything normal, like Sunfire or Princess.

The mare's low enough in the back that Jenn can mount without a saddle. There are women who can make this a graceful process — kick, twist, on — but years of gymnastics and that abortive attempt at ballet didn't leave Jenn flexible or skinny enough. So she has to jump and then scramble, clutching at mane and spine while Djinn sidles around and occasionally tries to bite her.

She can forgive a lot of a horse that once let Jenn dress her up in a knight's costume, complete with lycra horse-mask and flagstaff banner. Who plodded twice around a ring at the Bear Hills rodeo grounds without going insane or killing anybody. Jenn was particularly satisfied when one extremely well-trained show horse threw itself backwards through a fence when its owners tried to dress it in that god-damned treehouse costume just one last time. (It was a good concept — the kids were the Berenstein Bears, and the horse was a treehouse, but the horse wasn't having it.)

Screaming bloody murder and tearing down creosote-treated posts. Horses speak almost entirely in superlatives and histrionics. Djinn too, but not that time around, and not in public.

Scratch of winter hair against Jenn's leg. Leather and horsehair crawl into her nasal cavities. The world smells like encroaching winter.

This square mile of chokecherry and poplar's stood in for dozens of imagined landscapes. Jenn hunts monsters in here. Bodiless things — fantasy fragments and bits of memory and desire. Djinn's willing to jump the odd log and she isn't afraid of coyotes. The home pastures are all posted against hunting, but the deer still scramble through as though they're just waiting to be shot.

There are about three thousand deer, she read once, in the Saskatoon area. Even more, further out. There hasn't been a large predator in the Bear Hills since 1973. Only human labour keeps the hordes of edible animals under control.

It's that time again.

Gunfire in the far distance. There are trucks patrolling the roads. Guys in orange jumpsuits come through town for gas and jerky and junk food. Kids from hunting families go through gun safety classes when they're about eleven, years after they're issued guns. No one in Jenn's family hunts, but almost everyone else she knows does. Even Donna's father goes the odd time, to keep the men company. They give him brown paper packets of deer sausage. It's like an offering, burned in the manse kitchen.

The Bear Hills Comprehensive High School rules explicitly state that truancy must be justified by reasons of illness or family emergency. The student handbook notes that hunting does not constitute "a good reason."

Driving tractor during harvest can occasionally constitute a good reason. Grain can freeze before the weekend, but the deer aren't going anywhere. You want to hunt during school hours, you need to live further north than this.

She wonders how far north you'd have to go to reach some place that was actually empty.

Nothing around her is empty, when she looks close. There are always cars, old and decomposing in the windbreaks around people's yards. Degenerating farm equipment lurks between the barns and the pasture proper. It's not a redneck thing, exactly — not that her parents just like looking at it — but they're keeping the parts handy. Before the tree house, when Jenn was still toddling, she napped on the back seat of a decrepit Chevy Nova, while her father salvaged parts between the haystacks.

Donna liked them, when she first saw the cars. *They make it all post-what-d'you-call-it? Apocalyptic.*

Jenn hasn't been able to call up a fantasy to match Donna's iron-integrated landscape. She's never been able to picture anything more modern than an elven arrow coming at her out of the trees.

Something wrong with her reading of the world, maybe, but it hasn't disappointed her yet.

It means she's used to stillness. She doesn't listen for cars or the walking dead.

There's quiet, though, and this other thing, like going deaf. Jenn hears the sound-crack, and then a gap in time. It's enough of a hiatus from the real for her to be genuinely shocked when buckshot catches her in the face. Just before she falls, it occurs to her that this is what Donna was talking about. Exactly the kind of scene she'd like.

Djinn is screaming.

Jason stands at the edge of a chokecherry tangle, just out of her reach, holding a shotgun in both hands and staring at Jenn like she walked out of his earliest, most primitive nightmare.

# « CHAPTER 2 »

WHEN JASON WAS A KID, about the time he started going to school every day, and long before the night his mother grabbed the steering wheel, his parents gathered themselves and him up and moved from Saskatchewan to the Gulf Islands off the coast of British Columbia. He remembers the trip only because they stopped in Vancouver to take Jason to an allergy specialist. Nurses laid him belly down and shirtless on the table. They made a map of his back and systematically marked him with allergens, then noted down everywhere his skin broke open. He's still not sure that isn't the worst thing you can legally do to a kid. But it proved what his parents had already observed. Jason's allergic to things. Animals, mostly. Some dust, some pollen. Random, unexpected foods.

Living on the edge of the Pacific helped. Everything he'd been exposed to long enough to develop allergies was gone.

Their particular island contained a fragment of almost-rainforest, and an assortment of wildly blue native birds, and a colony he thinks his parents probably fantasized about for years before they joined. Artists and touch-the-earth hippies had built the place up gradually. They'd been doing it for twenty years before Jason's family got there, coming in to replace the people who ran away to join corporate America. People got to miss television and retirement funds and hormone-fuelled hamburgers.

Everything he remembers eating was organic. Food that came into the colony arrived in someone's car, packed up from the health food stores and farmers' markets on Vancouver Island proper. The colony's garden became Jason's father's. He said he'd grown up carving food out of sand, and he didn't see why he couldn't do at least as well somewhere that it rained occasionally.

The garden taught them about blackberry infestation. Jason's father had to cut back the bushes all the time and burn them on the beach so they wouldn't re-root and spread. He kicked them sometimes, like sheer fury might discourage them.

His mother was an artist. She *is* an artist. But while they were living on the island, it became the most important part of her personality. She built sea monsters out of driftwood and old nets in their garage and hung them with salt-damaged glass. She built a totem-man in their backyard. Then a totem-woman whose cunt was the most obvious, brightest thing about her.

People came in, from other islands and the lower mainland and elsewhere, to talk about assemblage and found-object sculpture. It's how they met Gordon Watson. He used to be more functional. He was teaching, then, in Vancouver. Between 1980 and 1987 he wrote four books of poetry and art theory. He took photos that were displayed in Seattle and London. And he was just this rangy, hairy guy from Saskatchewan. He slept at Jason's family's house the first night he visited, and in the morning Jason and his mom found Gordon and Jason's dad sitting on a pile of crates in their backyard, both vaguely drunk on chokecherry wine Gordon had carried in his backpack all the way from Saskatoon. There was a bottle of dandelion wine, too, waiting. There was a lot of very carefully cultivated weed waiting to be smoked.

Gordon stuck around. He lived in one of the guest cabins for a summer and worked and talked to Jason's parents at night. At the end of the summer, Jason's mother decided she'd exhausted her sea-monster phase and went back to ink drawing and watercolour.

There were still totem-women. Nudes tacked themselves up on the walls at night. He found them on the kitchen table when he came in to breakfast, sometimes.

Yoni and Cheerios.

And then his dad threatened to set every inch of blackberry foliage on the island on fire, using gasoline if he had to. And it occurred to Jason's parents that they were, just maybe, in the wrong environment. Or his father was. Jason wonders if that move back to the prairies was when his mother started to get angry. She retreated to the bathroom and laced the tub with salty-sharp crystals that effervesced into the entire house. Sometimes she drank while she was in the tub. He got used to the house-cleaning routine, including a stage where she boxed up her empties and returned them to the Bear Hills SARCAN station for the deposits. When she'd amassed enough change, she bought him a second-hand Atari system, the first serious tech piece either of his parents had ever allowed in the house.

THEY FOUGHT ABOUT the Atari the way they'd fought about the TV. Whether exposing Jason to the electromagnetic waves of technology was fundamentally damaging. How close they ought to live, really, to the electrical towers that edged the neighbourhood. They were living on the edge of Saskatoon at the time, in this retro-1950s enclave by the meat-packing plant. The air stank. His dad was doing by-the-day construction work to pay the rent, and his mother, Jason thinks, was imploding. She was so *angry*. Angry enough to plant blackberries in the backyard, but they died without taking over.

Weekends, they drove out to the Bear Hills and stayed with his grandparents. More than an hour in the car, Jason in his pajamas in the back seat, and the CBC filling the space between his parents. He remembers deer running across the road, and his mother shrieking intermittently about animals and mechanical death. Jason's dad said, if she was so worried about it, why didn't she make Jason wear his seatbelt. Jason tried to picture that, lying down on the Toyota's back bench seat, somehow also strapped in. This feeling like a nylon twist in his gut was the only thing he could imagine.

His grandmother was a serious gardener. He doesn't remember his grandfather much at all — just this big, diesel-smelling man whose office he wasn't supposed to invade. His dad woke Jason up early on Saturday mornings, carried him over to his aunt Brenda's house, and left him there.

He watched television with Jennifer. Her parents had set boundaries around the TV, but at least she was allowed to watch. Just, she had to sit at least six feet back. They watched in the basement, away from her parents. His uncle Steven had marked the boundary of electromagnetic safety with green painter's tape across the braided rug. *Sit here. Stay.*

They watched channel 8, loaded with static. *Superfriends. Pink Panther and Sons. Smurfs. Ewoks. The Mighty Hercules.*

Her mother came downstairs, eventually, and threw both of them outside. *Go play.*

Jenn was younger than him, but reasonably interesting. Good at finding small, crawling things in the corners of the livestock barn and creating new homes for those things on the pasture's edge. All of the animals were Jennifer's. Jason's skin broke out on contact, and digging in the grasses left eruptions on his arms like he'd been electrified briefly, and then left to suppurate in a dark swamp .

He walked back to his grandparents' house in the late afternoon, and his mother stared at him. His face was marked with allergenic hives. There was a cut near his hairline where Jennifer had maybe accidentally caught him with the stick she carried like a sword.

He felt amazing.

His mother forced him into a bathtub that still reeked from her soaking salts and scrubbed him down. Covered him with calamine lotion or solarcaine or whatever she found in the medicine cabinet. And then he was confined for the rest of the day, lying on the couch watching re-runs of *Coronation Street* or *The Prairie Farm Report*. Long stretches of time that he doesn't remember now at all, but there were moments. Three-minute features about guys who'd invented completely new mechanisms out of pieces they'd found in their yards. New prosthetics for farmers who'd lost two or more fingers in a grain auger.

If you just lost one, Jason supposed, you were out of luck.

Gordon Watson showed up, though Jason doesn't remember when. He hitch-hiked out and slept on Jason's grandparents' porch. His family's farm was only six or so miles away. He wasn't going back, though, he said, until his mother died, and he and his sister could carve the place up and never speak to each other again.

So Gordon was in the car, too, when they drove home. He shared Jason's back seat and stared at the night world, so Jason had to sit up and watch the world too. He remembers there were so, so many stars. He was never awake, usually, that late. In the city, he never saw the stars, and on the island, it was cloudy most of the time, and the horizon was close. So the explosion of light in the moonless sky startled him. Even at the speed they were moving, the stars didn't shift like landscape. He watched that, and not his parents.

He doesn't think his father was drunk. He doesn't *think* so. He's sure his mother was. Gordon might have been.

There were sudden, bright deer in the headlights.

His mother shrieked, like she always shrieked, but she'd never grabbed the wheel before. She pulled hard, towards herself, and the entire car moved. That, that right *there*, was the nylon-strapped gut twist Jason had always expected his seatbelt to deliver. This moment of personal immobility while the back end of the car overtook the front, and they went into the ditch, in the dark. The impact broke the rear axle, and Jason's mom's nose. Her shoulder left its socket. His father broke his front teeth.

They sat quietly for a second. The radio antenna had snapped, but the radio was still playing static and occasional fragments of late-night chamber music. Jason licked around his mouth. He was looking for broken teeth, or words, or blood. Gordon next to him stared. Then he got out, forcing the door open with his shoulder, and started to walk away down the side of the road. He left his backpack and notebooks behind, and both of the re-corked wine bottles from earlier. Then Jason's dad got out. He stepped back and stared at the car. Like he'd never seen one before and couldn't figure out what had happened.

His mom said, "Are you okay, baby?"

Jason couldn't talk. His gut hurt. And his knee. When he looked down, it was covered in blood. From what? The car was soft-upholstered. None of the metal was torn. He burned, though.

The broken wine bottle at his feet gradually began to make sense to him.

His mom stared at the bloody mess. "Fuck," she said. He hadn't heard her swear before. She made a point of not doing it in front of him.

Now, Jason thinks his mom went after his dad because Gordon was out of reach. When the ambulance guys found Gordon, he was three and a half miles away, still walking, concussed out of his mind. He was lucky; she might have killed him.

Instead, she went after his dad. She might have been con-cussed, too, or only drunk. Her arm hung loose and wrong beside her, but she ran at him, screaming. Cursing his friendship with Gordon, and his prairie existence, and his inability to *watch the fucking road*. She told him that Jason was dead.

*Fucking dead, because you can't watch for deer. Jesus Christ!*

Jason checked himself over. He didn't think he was dead. He hurt all over, and after Jennifer's accident with the baby mice, his parents had both told him that after you were dead, things didn't hurt anymore. That for animals, particularly animals, it could be mercy. That he should let them go and not worry. For boys, they said, it was different. But they wouldn't let him die, and he shouldn't worry about it.

He definitely wasn't dead. He was almost sure.

He could even walk, if he tried hard. His seatbelt gave, after a while, and he crawled out of the car on Gordon's side, leaving bloody knee-prints behind on the sand-coloured velour seats.

His dad was crying so *hard*. Like, he wailed. He'd just sat down where he was and he was crying like Jason cried when his world was ending. His mom stood over him, still swearing, and Jason needed to get closer. He walked through the dark and the radio static into the cracked-up beam of the single surviving headlight. He said, "Dad?"

His dad looked at him. Looked at Jason's mom. Then he got up and hit her, very hard, in the face, and she went down like she was dead.


HUNTING'S NOT OFFICIALLY part of the family ethos, but that doesn't mean none of them hunt. Just, mostly, they don't do it with guns. Jason's spent the majority of his life with his cousin hunting him. Little girl watching him like he was a god, the first couple of years. More complicated after that. He hunches down in the bush, in dry leaves and the constant, thin layer of snow mould, and watches for Jennifer.

When she was little, she wore a bright paisley wraparound skirt as a cape; it made her easy to spot. It wasn't quite a hunter-orange vest, but it belonged to the same species of blindingly obvious. It gave him a chance. And then she stopped wearing it, and came after him with Donna, and they turned into a joint, monstrous thing: two scruffy fat chicks against one permanently bruised boy.

He's still braced in case Jennifer's other friends decide to join them. It could be bad for him. Ginger's scary as fuck — six foot two and armed with lizards. If her ragged edges ever start to show, no one in town will survive. The dust will settle, the morning after her rampage, and there'll be this bloody, big girl perched on the water tower like a flying monkey, chewing on bits of human bone while she studies the wreckage.

Jason understands the impulse. But in the interests of his long-term survival, he keeps the *Wizard of Oz* references to himself. He can't afford to be the Wicked Witch of the West, or Dorothy. He needs to be something easier. A wolf, or a dog. One of many. Shaggy animals all around him. Every boy should be so lucky.

He waits all summer for hockey season to start, and then the first week is hell. Muscles he used all last winter atrophied while it was warm. In summer, all the exercise he gets is fleeing cannibal females. Muscle strain, back on the ice, is a purple-white agony in his legs. It runs right up into his ass and lower back, a little preview of how much he's going to hurt every day when he's forty. It gets easier. By late November, when he steps off the ice, he feels like he could skate for days. Practice ends and the zamboni rolls out to smooth the ice for church-organized family skating.

The children are coming. The little fuckers invade the place and scream all over just to feel their voices bounce off the sheet metal on high.

Midget-level boys' contact hockey is as close to professional as most of them will ever play. The Saskatchewan Junior Hockey League and the Western Hockey League have already culled the best players and sent them off to new cities to join teams. The rest of them will play in small town rinks and beat each other bloody until their joints give out. Then they'll reproduce, join the old-timer's league, and haul their tiny offspring to twice-weekly Canskate classes until they're old enough to start hockey in their own right.

Figure-skating toddlers who can hardly walk stagger onto the ice in dulled skates, pushing chairs while proto-breeder teenage girls in leggings and bomber jackets cheer them on. Crash helmets and layers of snowsuit padding ensure you can't tell the girls from the boys, unless some truly demented moo-mommy sticks her two-year-old out there in tights and a skirt.

The really pretty-princess girls never seem to make it to school age. They disappear. Jason isn't sure whether their families migrate to some undisclosed, cultish location, or whether the kids expire from cuteness and hypothermia. Or their proto-breeder coaches eat them up, in a secret girly fertility rite.

He has to get out of the rink before they catch him. All of them have to. The young men are loose!

Nobody really expects them to go home.

Jason can always spot a guy he's played hockey with, even if they're not from his home team. It's blood-memory. He knows those guys even when he runs into them in Regina or Saskatoon or Battleford. They all have this physical connection where they lean in slightly towards each other whenever they pass.

Maybe half the players can legally drive. They take the new meat — grade nine boys with bloody teeth, still jacked up on the endorphins of full-contact play — with them, piled into truck cabs driving hard for the edges of civilization. Jason's dad won't help with this, and he doesn't tell his mother, but in other families, the dads played hockey, and they remember. Tell their wives it's time for a romantic weekend, clear out of the farm, leave room for the guys to run wolf-pack style in the bush. There are guys — Jason sees them around — thirty-five, forty years old, who still ache for ice and blood. They're fucking their wives tonight in Travelodge beds so that the boys can play the way they want to.

You don't *supervise* this.

The year Jason was new meat, it was deep winter in November. Enough snow on the ground that they had to start the night indoors. He remembers being down on his knees in an oil stain on the concrete garage floor.

This year, there's no snow yet. Every year it gets just that much warmer. He's waiting for the year it never snows at all.

The bonfire they built out of scrap wood, last year's cut brush and gasoline makes it look like they're having a party. It'd have to be the kind of party where aliens abducted most of the revelers and left fifteen hockey players standing very still, a set of electric stock-clippers whining in Aaron Kroczynski's hand.

Aaron is seventeen, and last summer he broke his nose in a fist-fight. It's healed now, and Jason likes the look. In profile, he looks like . . . well . . . he looks like Batman.

Black nylon jacket and black jeans. Braces holding his front teeth together. Grinning like a motherfuck, which isn't Batman at all, but his profile's right. He has vigilante edges.

He has a confirmation cross on under his sweatshirt. Appendix scar low on his belly.

Dark hair between his clothes and his skin.

"Dustin!" Howled.

They drag him out and play-wrestle him down, just like Dustin hasn't creamed himself thinking about how much he wants this. He's fourteen. He's been fantasizing about how this moment would feel since the first time he cracked someone's ribs.

The clippers — old, electric, they smell like mineral oil and cattle — go to his head, and sweaty, muddy-brown boy hair hits the dirt.

They shear him with the same setting you use to strip hair away from infected livestock. Close but not careful. They strip off his eyebrows and most of his eyelashes.

Dustin looks like a marine who got too close to a fire.

Guys roar.

Three more meat bodies tonight. At the end, there's no hair left on their heads. No details to tell them apart. They're turned into baby-white faces only marked by red, panting, half-split lips.

Whoever came up with fire night got off on the ritual as much as Jason does.

They throw all four naked-faced rookies into the fire-glow and jump them. Really grind them down on the bottom of the dog pile and hold them there 'til they whine. Then pick them up and wipe their faces and pour Jim Beam down their throats.

Chase them through the woods all night.

It's icy cold beyond the reach of the fire. Good training for the meat bodies; they have to get used to this. If your lungs burn at 5°C, you'll die at –20°C. They're building stamina. You play out here for hours so that sixty minutes of ice-play goes by like jerking off in the shower. Like you could do it seven times a day.

The farm's house is deep in poplar trees, a quarter-mile off the road. There's bush all around them. The limits of their range tonight are electrified barbed wire. Not enough spark in there to kill a teenaged boy, but enough to discourage an eight-hundred-pound animal. But Jason wouldn't go that way. None of them would. It'd be like sticking to the outer rim of a Halloween maze: you *want* to go to the centre and face down the chainsaw-wielding maniac and piss yourself. It's fun.

He goes hunting. Hide-and-seek doesn't really begin to cover it. He climbs dead machines in the dark and breathes in the smell of rodent shit and dry mould and rust in their cabs. Drops like dead weight right in front of the next guy who snaps dry grass in the dark and waits for him to scream and then screams back with his face three inches away, rolls him down and straddles him and holds his hands out of the way and *laughs* at him. Grins when he spits and calls Jason *fucker*. They roll up and go different directions.

There are places other than machines for him to lurk. There's a '60s-style bungalow, a prefab garage, a Quonset hut. Stock pens that smell like years of animal shit. Swing set and climbing rope. Platform treehouse that feels like his own treehouse. There's the hay-bale stack.

Last year's bales smell like mould. Dust and pollen and loose seed mix in his nose with the edge of mouse shit. Jason's in the lee of it when the first body hits him from above. Descending knees catch him in the shoulder and fell him like electro-shocked beef. Thighs wrap around his hips —

*Hi*

— and Jason's neck curves against the tongue sliding over it, from the collar of his jacket up to his mouth. Never quite touches his lips.

He grinds up hard, once, before the body on his vanishes. Jason's left rubbing the heel of his first against his crotch. He needs a second to remember that neither of them screamed.


And.

Outside the house, guys are still lowing, like shaving their heads turns boys into . . . not wolves. Dogs. Coyotes, maybe, or hyenas. Dirty animals that like dead things.

Jason's vocal cords hurt.

He tracked the owner of that tongue for twenty minutes, in and out and around and down. Followed him half by smell. And then he went inside. The blue of the house's porch light shows Boyd. Who fucking *lives* here.

It makes a difference. Boyd potentially has issues and history with that bale-stack, but he still had no trouble molesting Jason next to it.

Normal boys and dogs just piss on things to mark their territory.

Boyd's making coffee in his stocking feet, still panting from his run in the dark, when Jason comes in after him. Without turning,

Boyd says, "I thought I'd leave it out for them. See how long they'll drag tonight out if we keep jacking them full of caffeine."

"You going to yell *soo-wee* when you put it outside?"

"I think the smell will attract them without my help."

He's making cowboy coffee, boiled in Pyrex. There are no lights in the kitchen except the burner coil's glow. The coffee-smell crawls up into Jason's skull when he leans in against Boyd and mouths at his neck. Taste of T-shirt and sweaty boy. The stove's only faintly warm; there's a body between it and Jason. Boyd's ass against Jason's crotch tenses, and Jason wants to scream, *you **licked** me*, right there in his ear, but.

But.

Boyd says, "Did you want to go back out?"

"No."

He pulls a thermos out from the dark back-edge of the counter. "Let me fill this and throw it out there for them. Then I'm yours."

JASON BRUISES BOTH hips running into furniture and walls, because Boyd won't turn the lights on. He was bruised already, from the night's collisions, playing hockey. Living in his skin. He doesn't need more. Boyd leads him through the dark house. Maybe everyone knows the way around his own house in the dark. Avoid the couch. Scuff the carpet. Watch that hutch in the hall: it bites.

Door.

This home-ec class they had to take, somewhere in grade eight/nine, the textbook said, *The design of the modern home creates private and public areas, with the living room and perhaps the dining room overlooking the street, and the family bedrooms at the back, away from urban noise and traffic flow.* ©1968.

What street? What traffic?

Where the fuck is that *sound* coming from?

The hyena-boys are not respecters of domestic space and its expectations of privacy. If they want to come in, they'll just fly through a window, spraying glass and blood onto the carpet.

Boyd isn't kissing Jason, quite. Sucking on Jason's throat is completely different. Hands hook in his sweatshirt, and Jason's sure he'll fall over something on the floor if he moves. Clothes, homework, hockey gear, old toys, boots, chair — *something.* This room is just like Jason's room, except not underground, but only Boyd knows the safe path through. Everyone else falls into the toxic areas and disappears. He had to stay where he is.

There's just enough bare carpet exposed for Jason to kneel. Drag his mouth along Boyd's waistline. He tastes navel, body hair, denim barrier, and flesh pushing at him underneath it.

He's wanted this for months.

Boyd's dick is short and a little wet. Jason's seen it before, though not hard. Not *totally* hard, anyway, but they play on this huge adrenaline rush and then six or eight guys pack into the half-hot shower room, and everyone gets excited. Even hard, though, Boyd's easy to take in and small enough that Jason can suck without his teeth getting in the way.

He knows girls who do this all the time, but they hate it. He doesn't.

It's power. Suck a guy, push your face into his pubes and hum a little. Suck-pull on his too-thin skin and he'll whimper like an animal. Dig his fingers into your hair and beg for it.

Boyd comes with his shoulders pressed back against the wall and his hips way out, dick pushing at the roof of Jason's mouth. Makes him gag for a minute before he can swallow.

Jason pulls off, kisses his belly and stands up. Kisses his mouth before Boyd's neurons start firing and he pulls away.

Asshole. Jason didn't *start* this.

Boyd whispers, "Did you want coffee?"

"No."

The bed's right there, maybe four feet away. Hard as Jason is, the things on the floor that might destroy him aren't much of a concern. He steps on what might be Lego, staggering backwards to the mattress. There's a male body on top of him as soon as he falls. Jason doesn't even feel the bruise on his sole until later, when he's putting himself back together and Boyd's left him alone.

GUYS JASON PLAYS hockey with come find him, some evenings. Boyd collects him, sometimes, eight or nine at night, and they drive a twenty-mile loop around the Bear Hills highlands, playing tapes through car speakers and not talking. Every dollar Boyd's made working for his parents the last two years went into the sub-woofer in the trunk and the speakers he installed himself all over the cab. Bone-low bass runs through Jason's legs with the vibra-tions of the car over gravel.

Weekends, they drive in to the city and bring back pizza. It cools slowly into slabs of meat and grease in the box, delicious and slip-pery whenever Jason reaches in for another piece. Since he shook free of his mother's vegetarianism, he hasn't lived within the boundaries of pizza delivery. The closest he's ever come to ran-dom fast food in the middle of the night is piling five guys into a Ford Escort and driving to Saskatoon to pick it up. Devour meat and salt while he's tangled in the press of adolescent male bodies crammed into a subcompact. Stars and the emptiness of the high-way at two in the morning. He makes a point of not looking out the windows at the sky.

White-tailed bodies cut across the highway in front of them. Like they're daring each other to see who can hit the car.

His dad didn't want Jason to play hockey, but it was Jason's con-dition for coming to live with him instead of following his mom to her next artists' colony. That wasn't the end of the conversation, though. His dad reminds him about once a week that hockey's expensive and violent, and he spent the first year Jason played muttering about instilling toxic ideas of competition. But his dad pays, because he gets that he owes Jason this. Some of his friends were learning to play that year, and he wanted to learn so *much*. He was already old for it, but he went anyway. Not entirely sure why. He didn't watch the game on TV. He'd only been to the rink a handful of times, all of them with his aunt and uncle to pick up the girls after figure skating.

He didn't learn to skate in town. He wasn't going to do that in public, where people could watch him fall. He went out at night, on the yard rink his uncle made, and learned by himself. Once he was steady, he skated with Jennifer. Sometimes even with Victoria.

All their tiny bodies shooting around and colliding.

Once Jason could skate, his dad signed him up. Got him outfitted, drove him to practices. Came to tournaments and bought him rink burgers — actual meat, topped with onions — and cocoa, and wrapped him in an old, unzipped sleeping bag to keep him warm between games.

They sat together on the plywood bleachers in sub-zero-temperature indoor rinks all over west-central Saskatchewan, and while they were waiting for the next rounds, his dad read to him. Bag of kids' books over his shoulder that his dad took on every trip. And it's not that Jason didn't enjoy it, but he wonders, sometimes, how genetics led from that guy to him. They don't understand each other. If they did, Jason wouldn't have to fight so hard to be invisible in this place. Most of the boy-activity showdowns they've had, Jason's lost. He wanted to take hunter safety when his friends did. Not taking the classes meant he was missing a huge, necessary piece of cultural knowledge. It was so ingrained, here. At games that his dad couldn't drive him to, Jason ate deer sausage out of massive tupperware tubs and studied the gun racks in family vans.

There were deer everywhere.

He stood there, in his grandparents' kitchen with no grandparents left in it and argued with his dad that hunting was, at worst, a necessary evil. The Bear Hills were named for a top predator, but the bears are gone. The cougars and the wolves are gone. The last large predator in the region was shot in 1973, and the coyotes can barely keep down the mice.

So there are deer, so many that the ecosystem won't sustain them and the beef herds, too. If they were going to stay farmers, the deer had to go.

When his dad said no, he tried his mom on her next visit. He pointed out that deer were a cheap, freely available protein source for the people. So it was socialist.

What his mom said wasn't that hunting was wrong. She said it was grotesque.

He went back home to his dad, who'd started his own sculpting practice since he was left unsupervised. He muttered something about people who hung up deer heads as a form of advanced decor and what it said about their aesthetic sense.

Jason lost that argument. So instead what happened was that everybody else took hunter safety, and when they all crashed at somebody's farm after hockey games, they passed whatever they'd learned on to Jason. They gave him photocopied guide pages. Showed him how to strip and clean a rifle.

They don't hunt each other with guns, but they all know how to use one. Nights coming back from the city, they'll come up to sloughs five miles out of Perdue, and pull over. Dig a shotgun out from the tiny hatchback trunk and amass a pile of feathers, close enough to shore for one of them to dive in and drag the birds out.

Boyd's mom cooks them duck meat for breakfast like it's the most normal thing in the world.

JASON WALKS OUT of St Paul's Hospital in Saskatoon, and the first guy he tries to bum change off for the phone invites him to play hockey on the school grounds across the street. He finds out later that they play every night. Trucks illuminate the playing field after dark, one at a time in sequence, their lights sucking battery power until they're in danger of never starting again. The players are big guys, years out of high school, who hate their jobs and live for this. The teams re-form every night out of the bodies available. When Jason wanders over, there are five sandwich artists, three gas jockeys, three janitors, and him — the trauma case who wandered away from the emergency room.

Jason can smell body-warm, sticky blood mixed in with his sweat. (He was walking in the pasture, and he saw something. An animal.)

It's dusty dark. The leaves came down a month ago, and the continuing world's entropy pulverized them. Leaf mould and dirt and gravel and dog shit all sift into the soft membranes of Jason's nose and mouth, and then down into his lungs. He can feel them tightening up. The other guys pause for long seconds to hack the mess out of their throats onto the ground. The ball they're chasing through this mess sparks like an expensive yo-yo when you hit it. Between strikes, Jason has to follow the ball intuitively. It's easy. He could do this with no eyes.

He'd love to bring his team in some night and square off against these guys.

He should go home. Shower. All along 20th Street, guys brawl and people shoot up and girls a lot younger than Jason fuck for money, and right now he's still the scariest-looking thing out here. There's blood on his sweater and coat and jeans. On his runners, too, but they're probably dirty enough that it doesn't show. There's an edge of burning-smell on his skin and in his hair.

He looks like the last survivor of Armageddon or a really good hockey game.

Ball strikes the chain-link fence, and a girl on the other side jumps like she wants to step out of her second-hand red hooker shoes and throw it back. Chase after the ball and fight all of them for control of the park.

HE CAUGHT DJINN. He was crouched in the brush, just breathing through the shock. He remembers Brenda and Steven bending over Jennifer, and Jennifer crying, and a truck engine. In the quiet after that, he heard the horse.

She made noises that he'd never heard something bigger than a dog make. Her bridle was caught on a poplar branch. Everything his dad had ever lectured to him about horse psychology arranged itself in Jason's head. They have prey responses. Flight-terror. At some point in a stressful day, horses go post-traumatic. People in that state go on killing sprees with garden tools; horses shut down. Their brains conclude that *thishorse* is going to be eaten *rightnow*, and their minds, such as they are, go away.

They're not always wrong to do that. His dad was clear about that. Horses are moderately stupid, plant-eating herd animals. Their function in the large scheme of things *is* to be eaten. The whole carrying-humans-around thing is relatively recent, and their horse brains still aren't wired for it.

Jason's never seen a horse get eaten, but he likes the idea that if a large predator, maybe a cougar, starts eating a living horse, at least the horse won't feel it. A little neural fail-safe for the moments before death. It's how he would have designed things, himself.

Wild-rose brush was tangled all around the half-dead poplar she'd collided with. The reins were broken. Blood covered her neck and saddle, and that was when Jason decided that Jennifer was dead. His pretty, fat girl cousin had disappeared entirely into early November, leaving nothing but her crying little horse behind. And his brain went horse-sideways for a while.

It hasn't come back yet. It's why he can be playing hockey in ghetto-ish west Saskatoon instead of curling up in the dark at home and crying.

He cut the bridle. He felt vaguely guilty, ruining Jennifer's things, but it got the horse loose. He tied the remaining pieces of harness around her neck and led her home. Up close, she was bloody like she'd lost her skin. It was Djinn's blood and Jennifer's. It got all over him when Djinn leaned into his body just like he was a person and she was a small, scared animal.

While he walked, he tried to imagine an animal that could eat a girl and leave the horse alive. Jennifer was only thin muscle under baby fat — a snack, but nothing compared to eight hundred and fifty pounds of bay Arabian horsemeat.

He didn't know how to clean her up. Just left her in the barnyard, finally, and walked away.

He didn't throw up, but stomach acid burned the back of his mouth. He spit and it tasted worse. He realized he was going to have to go back to the pasture to clean up.

He took a shovel. The ground was still soft enough to dig a hole.

It was a pretty day. Quiet, in the absence of his family. His dad had gone up north for a day or two, and he thought his aunt and uncle had probably forgotten about him. All alone with the cattle and horses and birds. Jason could hear his own breath and the dry grass moving. And this low hiss like somebody couldn't quite remember how to breathe.

He found Gordon Watson by sound. Right there in the middle of their pasture. He had a blown-up rifle next to him.

He didn't cry until Jason dragged him loose from the rose-bush tangle, and by the time Jason came back with his dad's truck, Gordon was quieter. He was still sick-moaning like an animal, nothing like the sounds a grown man should make. He was only bleeding a little, but he was burned all over his face and hands, and lymph seeped out of every opened patch of him. It was overkill; the blood would have been enough.

The scale of blood isn't something Jason is familiar with. He's cut his hands on barbed wire a couple of times, and he remembers blood from the night his mother grabbed the wheel. When he has to stay with his mother now, he carefully doesn't look at the traces of her menstrual blood in the bathroom. All the measurements he's ever heard of the blood in the human body are in imperial units, and they don't mean anything to him.

He could tell from the mess of her horse that Jennifer must be dead, but he had no way of judging whether Gordon was dying.

He convinced Gordon to stand, and from there Jason was able to shoulder him into the truck cab. They came out of the pasture through the wire gate. For a second, Jason was genuinely pissed that Gordon didn't offer to get out and help him prop the posts and wire back up before the livestock wandered through. Then he remembered. And through the open driver's side door, he could hear Gordon making thin echoes of the noise Jason's dad made, that night. It made him sick. Scared.

Sick. "Shut up. *Please.*"

He drove on gravel until he found the highway, then put his foot to the floor until he reached Saskatoon. Never turned on the radio. The trip was scored with engine noise and wet breathing. He couldn't unwrap his hands from the wheel to even roll down the window and drown that noise out with rushing air. At St. Paul's Emergency, they wouldn't believe Jason wasn't hurt. There was so much blood on him. He had to strip down to his underpants and runners and let an intern touch him all over.

After, when he'd put his clothes back on, he explained in this very calm voice that his neighbour, Gordon Watson, had had a hunting accident, and could they please take care of him? He was still in the truck.

BY THE TIME the hockey game collapses, it's freezing cold. Jason hurts every time he pauses for breath. It's a school night, and people who work normal hours should be home in bed, but the guys on the field with him work noon to eight, or midnight until morning. They've only slowed down now because their bodies are giving out. Knees, ankles, lower backs: that's where male bodies give it up. Between plays, they crouch and grind their teeth. All these thirty-something guys, going down like hurt animals.

Any animal with that many chronic injuries would be dog meat.

He tries not to think about Djinn, still wearing half her tack and standing in the barnyard.

The guys walk him back to Emergency, but they won't come inside. It's like they think someone will lock them up if they go in there, and then they'll be late for work. They might hurt all over, but that's not an emergency; it's just the state of them. You can treat that kind of damage, but mostly, unless you're a world-class athlete, people don't. They just walk around hurt.

In horses, you can sever the tactile nerve just below the knee and end their pain. The horse can still walk; run, even. It works good, until the horse fails to notice that it's caught its leg in wire, and you wind up with a dead animal tangled in a hundred feet of fencing.

Inside the hospital, it's not such a bad night. The late CBC news is on, and a couple of people are reading old magazines on the public side of the security doors. When Jason lies down to sleep, he has a whole vinyl couch to himself.

LATER, WHEN JENNIFER can walk again, after he's sure she's not dead, Jason takes her to parties. She never used to go to them on her own. Her friends aren't party-goers, and she's afraid of half the school, but he needs her to come out and play. Feel the pulse of the landscape as something other than a fantasy.

He has this problem where he's always going to be sorry. It makes him responsible for her.

Jason didn't used to like girls. They were marginal in his universe, less interesting because they couldn't fight and wouldn't play with him. Occasionally, he'd see one he liked. Like, he'd run into somebody's girlfriend at a hockey tournament, and she'd be this really tough girl. The kind that would street-fight. And then he'd follow her around, to see what she'd start. Sooner or later, some other girl would look at her boyfriend wrong, and this chick would just tear it up.

Like cats. Blood and fur and fake nails flying.

This lecture they all got, back around grade eight: *It isn't **nice** to see young ladies fighting. It's even more disturbing to suppose we're educating young ladies who would want to fight. For **fun**. There are fights at noon almost every week! You think we don't know because these girls go off school grounds to have their dust-ups, but we know. It isn't much we're asking, you know, to have our girls not tear each other up like animals. Not over some stupid slight and certainly not over some boy.*

*Young ladies . . .*

He said, *There aren't any young ladies here.*

*You know what I mean, Jason.*

He knows. There are still no young ladies here. It isn't exactly finishing school. Boys fight in small towns every night of the week. And then they got women's lib and raised a generation of girls who play hockey and ringette and drink hard and get in each other's faces and behold! They've raised guys with tits.

Not all of them, of course. There are still *girls* around. He's just not interested in them.

He keeps his ears open. He remembers lounging outside whatever classroom, sometime in the before-now, when one of the basketball girls slammed herself up to Jennifer and hissed, *You wanna fight me?*

*Nope. You could beat the crap out of me.*

It might have been true, but he thinks Jennifer sold herself short. She never acknowledged how many of Jason's bruises were her creations. And all those strange girls who run around with her, they're warriors. And Jennifer had stick-swords in her hands back when Jason occasionally ran around in a princess hat.

His Aunt Brenda read him fantasy novels when he was little and impressionable. It turned him—temporarily—into a deviant. With a princess hat.

These days, it doesn't show. People like him. He's been going to pit parties since he joined hockey for real. Weekends, every kid in the hills gathers in the gravel works outside town, builds up bonfires and trusts the rock piles to break the wind. Boyd and his sound-addicted friends run their car stereos at full volume so you can hear it from the road.

Jennifer dances with her hands in Jason's back pockets, and for a second he remembers her knocking him down. It's an easier scene to hold in his head than her bleeding in the pasture. He saw her there, all covered in blood and falling off her horse. He thought she saw him too, but she's never said, and maybe she doesn't remember.

He's making her life better. She's his girl. No one's going to shoot her, ever again.

Bear Hills school dances aren't anything like the high-school-fifties fantasy of dances that he sees on TV, but they're fun out of all proportion. Filled with all the teenagers for fifty miles who have thick enough skin to go out in public. Kids drive in from other schools and other school divisions. You wear the cleanest jeans you own. Best T-shirt. Maybe something slinky if you're a girl, or not. Jennifer wears tank tops with jean shirts thrown over them. Her outline's like a bag lady, but he can see her tits so clearly whenever the light hits her.

Up close, dancing with him, she smells like girl-deodorant and fruit-laced glycerine Body Shop soap. He asks her, once, what he's smelling, and she says, *Teen Spirit*, and he thinks it's a joke until the next time he's in her bedroom and sees the Teen Spirit deodorant stick next to her hairspray. When they go out, her hair's combed big and stiff, and her bangs are sharp enough to take out his eye if he tries to kiss her wrong.

Jennifer's friends start coming too, once they realize that Jason's going to take her away from them. Donna and Ginger and that Amber girl with the nail-biting problem whose fingers sometime spontaneously start to bleed. They take Jennifer away from him and dance with her in a circle.

Girls dance in groups. Guys don't dance together, but girls can. They just form packs, dance in a circle, egg each other on while they shift their weight around and occasionally bend backwards. Sometimes break into a few steps of the line dancing they all had to learn in phys ed. All his life he's going to have a thing for scary-looking chicks in too much eyeliner and foundation makeup that doesn't quite match their skin tones. Jennifer's skin is so uneven now, there's no concealer she can buy over the counter that's going to do a decent job.

She's learning that getting shot earns you some respect in this town. These aren't people who necessarily *like* Jennifer, but they don't want her to die. It'd be like losing a part of themselves. Maybe they don't feel as strongly about her as it looked like they did at the school's mandatory prayer meeting, but they care some.

Jennifer didn't initially believe them. For the longest time, in the hospital, she thought they were making fun of her. The *from everybody* card that Jason brought to her, she shoved in a drawer.

He remembers the line of her back whenever she peeled off her hospital gown to squint at the damage. Just in the mirror, and just for a few seconds at a time. She made a huge point of not looking at her actual body. He's kind of sorry she wouldn't. The toughest girls he stalked never generated that range of bruising and scabs. He wishes she was proud of the new mess she's become. It's probably not right, though, that he finds her black-and-blue look so sexy.

JASON'S OLDER THAN Jennifer (and older than Victoria, though that goes without saying), but he managed never to feel protective of anybody until Jennifer was shot. The squishy feeling other people have about little animals passed him by. The cattle always gave him hives, and the horses locked up his bronchial tubes, and it made it hard for him to feel sorry for them. He'll never be a vegetarian. If their positions were reversed, the cows would eat him without a second thought.

Jennifer covered in blood was different. When he and his dad went to see her at the hospital, he found out she was raw meat under all that blood. It was a good, hard look at every bowl of homemade hamburgers his dad ever mixed up, overlaid with bits of uncooked chicken skin and yellow living fat where her wounds hadn't closed yet. At this point in the recollection, usually he drinks or throws up. For the next couple of months, he could only eat meat if it'd been processed to the point that he can believe it was never alive at all. Chicken nuggets are his friends. Fish sticks. Cover them with sauce and eat them with french fries and you won't know the difference.

He visits Jennifer a lot. Eats some of the food she ignores off her hospital tray. None of it's very recognizable either.

She never says anything about seeing him. So he keeps coming. Brings her books, first. Then, when her face starts to knit, he walks right into her bedroom at home and brings all her makeup to her, stuffed in a plastic grocery bag and topped with stuffed animals so the nurses won't see and stop him.

Losing the first term of the school year is easy. He just doesn't show up. He goes into Saskatoon and guards Jennifer. Jennifer doesn't go to school either, but she has an excuse. Eventually, the nurses throw Jason out of Jenn's hospital room. He goes home for new clothes and a shower. Steps around his dad like he isn't there. Drives into Bear Hills and collects Jennifer's homework from her friend Donna. He takes it back with him, walks into the hospital like he's never been kicked out. He sits in the pediatrics-issued rocking chair in Jennifer's room and reads all the texts and novels to her and writes down her answers to the assigned questions when she can talk enough to give them. The rest of the time, he answers them himself and puts the lot away for her to find later. Not that he's anywhere near as smart as she is, but he's done all those questions before. And she checks things over, mostly, before she gives her mom anything to hand in.

All her pretty math numbers look ugly in his scrawl, but they're all right.

If her mom's not there, he takes it himself, and gives the homework back to Donna. He walks into her bedroom, this one time that Donna leaves her mother to answer the door, and finds her lying almost face-down on her bed, drawing on her arm. Some of what she's writing might be Jennifer's name in an alien language. Miserable dark-haired math-freak girl looks up at him.

"Want to go see her?" Jason asks.

"When?"

"Now."

Donna stares at him. "It's the middle of the night." It's ten. Time for all the good students to wrap themselves in their heathered-grey nighties and go to bed.

"She doesn't sleep, really. Not on a schedule. They've got her on some massive painkillers so she kind of drifts all the time, but she wakes up if you visit."

"It's not visiting hours, though." Complaints, complaints from a chick already shoving her boots on. She pulled on her jeans and tucked her nightie in without ever putting on a bra. Or, he thinks, panties. He didn't expect a genuinely fat girl to look this interesting.

He says, "Family's allowed any time. 'Cause it's pediatrics." Then he pulls her into the guest bathroom by the front door and kisses her — no tongue, the way he'd kiss Jennifer. "Congrats. You just became family." He takes her coat collar and drags her out the door. Cold air blasts around his vocal cords when he yells, *Stealing your daughter!* back towards the house.

It's so cold they're surrounded by ice fog, driving to the city. The tiny heater in his dad's truck barely works. He has no idea how his dad copes. Whether he just likes being cold like it's some sort of penance for fucking up their family. On 22nd Street, he buys Donna coffee at Robin's Donuts and waits for her to thaw. Then he drives her the rest of the way. Walks her through Royal University Hospital's '70s subway-tile floors with an escorting hand on her arm and up through the halls and elevators to the pediatric ICU.

"Another cousin. We should make a chart with pictures for you," is what he tells the night nurse.

Pediatrics is set up for family to be there all the time. When they were all tiny kids, his dad told him, the hospital rooms only had plastic bucket chairs, but someone finally worked out that miserable parents were crippling themselves, sleeping in those. Now there's a rocking chair and a futon-ish foamie next to every bed, so that the family member on watch can hold their baby, or sleep. Not really designed for kids over six, but they hold patients here 'til they're eighteen, in the Winnie-the-Pooh decorated wards with railings on the beds so the kids don't fall out.

Jason curls up on the foamie while Donna cards Jennifer's hair and talks to her. When she pushes him over, later, he just slides. Wakes up in the small hours lying sex-close to a girl who isn't even a little bit his cousin. He thinks he can hear Jennifer screaming.

Donna says, "You shouted." His spit's shining on her palm, and after a second he understands she gagged him until he woke up. "Are you okay?"

Jennifer is asleep. Not screaming. When he thinks about it, he realizes she didn't even scream at the time.

Sirens five floors away, pulling up to another wing, sound to him like screaming.

Donna says, "Your pupils are huge."

"It's dark."

"Whatever." Breath on his face. "Stay here."

Time fractures while he sleeps, and then Donna's father is kneeling over him. He asks Jason, "Can you get up?"

The man walks him by his shoulders into the family lounge, where any sane distressed relative would be sleeping. There are soft-ish couches, and recliner chairs and a TV. The — fundamentalist, frankly really batshit — minister stands backlit by flickering fluorescent rods. Jason has what's probably a typical teenaged-boy moment of absolute terror in the face of an outraged father, multiplied by the sheer religious force of the guy's expression.

*You laid hands on my daughter. They aren't ever going to find your body.*

Think. He has to think.

*Your daughter's a lesbian! I did nothing!*

*Stop yelling at me!*

*You know, if you were yelling.*

*Stop looking at me like you're my dad.*

"Jason."

"Yessir."

"Has anyone talked to you?"

Jason doesn't move.

"Donna said you were screaming in your sleep."

He doesn't breathe.

"Sit down, boy. Drink something with no caffeine in it. I'm going to find you a trauma counsellor."

"It's, like, four in the morning."

There's just this second where he sees the man's true face. And Jason's never been seriously Christian, but he still didn't expect there to be fangs on a minister. "Trust me. I'll find one. And later, you're going to come talk to me."

NOW JASON HAS a reason to cut school: he's officially suffering from post-traumatic stress. There are a lot of pills involved in treating this, and most of them fuck with his sleep cycle. Occasionally, there's even a warm body, totally unrelated to him biologically, to talk to. At first, he thinks Jennifer told them something, but he realizes finally that they're worried he might lose it because his sense of safety in the universe has been disrupted. Like he might kill his family and the hospital staff, and the police will storm the place to find just him and Jennifer surviving, naked and covered in blood.

This, apparently, is what it takes to get a shrink's attention in this town. He wouldn't have one at all, except that Donna's father put on his witchfinder-general face and bellowed to heaven and hell until one came.

Once they're convinced Jason's not going for the machete, though, he's down to just the pills. Counselling is only for the *dangerously* insane. Jennifer has counselling sessions, but she doesn't tell him anything about them, and he doesn't think he should ask. Presumably, if she decides to spill her guts, the cops will come for him. Otherwise, he's safe.

THEY SEW JENNIFER'S face back together and send her off to school. Jason makes sure that she hands in all her homework, and that he never hands in his. By now, it's not just distraction; it's a plan. He needs to be closer to her. Their being in different grades isn't acceptable.

Around about March, when he's solidly failing his second semester, someone sends him to the guidance counsellor. She's a thick woman staring through 1980s owl-glasses with red frames, pink lenses — it's probably supposed to be symbolic, but if they were really rose-coloured glasses, she'd be a nicer person.

"Is there something wrong, Jason?"

It's a stupid question. If there were nothing wrong, he wouldn't be in high school. He'd have a different family, and the sight of deer cutting across the highway wouldn't give him nightmares. He thinks about workable answers to her question.

*I have this recurring dream where we're all made out of bats. Do you think it means something?*

*I'm plotting to destroy the school. I know those guys tried it back a couple of years ago and it didn't help, but I have the optimism of youth.*

*Did you think when you were my age that you'd wind up a guidance counsellor?*

*I know who vandalized your Respect Others posters. It wasn't me, but I supported the action.*

*You look kind of like a white rabbit.*

*Feed your head!*

"Nope. I'm good."

"If you didn't look so normal, I'd think you were on drugs. It's the only cause I can think of for this kind of academic decline."

"I'm not high."

*Just very, very well medicated. One pill makes you larger . . .*

"Mmm."

*I'd love some refined sugar about now. It was my first, best drug. I got my first hit from a dealer kid on Salt Spring Island. I stripped off all my clothes and ran around the yard screaming. It was awesome.*

*I told the psychiatrist that. She totally couldn't decide whether to make my nakedness the issue.*

*Where's Jennifer right now. Is she okay?*

Vaguely, he's aware that he's twitching like an attention-deficit eight-year-old. Possibly time to ease off on the Prozac.

"I just didn't see the point of my social studies project, okay? I mean, *the social contract?* Even you have to admit that making bristol-board posters illustrating the constraints of civilization is savage and pointless."

Her nose twitches when she's irritated. Somewhere outside this tiny room plastered with teamwork slogans, she has a real life with kids and a minivan. Those kids probably belong to a lot of teams. She has harder cases than him, but at least she doesn't have to work to figure them out. It's just the usual whirl of sex, drugs, slow chemical poisoning from pesticides, incestuous nightmares, seasonal affective disorder–fuelled binge drinking, and fetal alcohol effects. This child goes into special education. That one goes to jail.

"If I told you not to worry," he asks, "would you believe me?"

"Are you planning to kill yourself?"

Oops. He was a bit too calm there. She's supposed to listen for flat affect. "What? No!"

"Tell me what's the matter, then."

And so on and so on.

TWO WEEKS AFTER THAT, he and Jennifer write their deferred winter exams. Just the two of them in the principal's office with enough pens and pencils to build some kind of interesting model. Maybe of a dinosaur fucking a spaceship.

Jason watches her write, all those hours in the half-dark after school. He fails his own exams spectacularly. Sometimes he smears ink all over what he's written, just to make sure they won't pass him out of reasonable doubt. He thinks about writing *fuck you* all over one or two of them, just to ensure they'll be pissed off enough to let him fail.

The principal's eyes follow him when he takes breaks to go to the can. The guy's not stupid. That's why he never comes out of his office, just lurks behind the potted silk plants and issues ultimatums regarding inappropriate footwear and littering in classrooms. If Jason were principal, he wouldn't go out there either. These kids are practically fucking cannibals.

Construe that last statement however you want.

*Shut up. The only blood in my teeth is mine.*

So it's probably not surprising that he's dragged out into a totally film-noir moment on the last exam's night. He hunches down in his ski jacket while the principal stands opposite, smoking in the dark on the edge of school property.

The guy's got dignity. Not once has Jason ever seen him bum a cigarette off a student.

Cranky middle-aged squint traps him. "How is failing a grade going to make her happy?"

"'S gonna make *me* happy." More stable. More anchored in the real world. "I have to wait for her."

"I'd send you off to a character-building boot camp if I didn't think you'd run away the first night. I bet you know where she is right now."

"Girls' can by the gym, checking her makeup. She thinks everybody can see the scars."

"Everybody can. She shouldn't be putting makeup over wounds that fresh." The man sighs. Smoke and frozen breath hang between them. "Try not to piss off more people than you need to. We have to work here too."


ANY GRADE WORTH failing is worth failing well, but it's hard. He has to work at it. The local population (minus Jason's family, who've lived here four generations and never married the neighbours) has an average IQ of about 80. There are tests to prove it, lying around in the principal's office where anyone could find them. Nearly everybody graduates, just the same.

Jason makes a point of passing the classes he really doesn't want to take again. They were bound to throw him a passing grade sooner or later, and this makes it easy. Industrial arts earns him a 62%. Career education gets him an 81%.

Career education strongly recommends joining the army. They watched a recruitment video and everything. Jason got ten bonus marks just for showing up.

JASON FAILS GRADE 11. No one's impressed with him, but his dad studies him for a long time, then hands him over to his mom for further study, and they conclude separately that there's nothing fundamentally wrong with him, beyond the obvious. He's not illiterate. He's ranked second out of seven participants in the ongoing all-family Scrabble tournament. (His mom's back on the leader board for some reason. She wonders when she came back. Why she never comes in the house.) He scored 260 in his last game on the strength of his knowledge of words that use Q but not U. He leaves his dad notes that are properly spelled and punctuated. When his mom leaves him alone at her place in the city, he reads whatever books she's left around. The fact of his scoring 36% in English is just a tiny hole in the universe that they're learning to work around.

His parents are *disappointed*. Other children have been known to fail grades, but *other* children have parents who are cousins. *Other* children have fetal alcohol syndrome.

*Other* children have brain damage from being dropped on their heads or excessive drinking or unreported car accidents. And they did have him inspected, in the car wreck's aftermath, just to make sure he was fine.

Other children weren't going to university anyway. Jason's reminded of this when his nasty-looking academic transcript arrives in the mail, provincially certified and official.

Brenda comes looking for him, right down into his basement where nobody comes without Jason's permission. "You couldn't show some *easier* symptom of being a troubled child?" she asks. "I'd happily support your right to listen to Satanic music. You could draw all over the walls of your room, maybe? Give yourself an ugly tattoo?"

Jason shrugs. He's been watching TV in the dark. He took the set downstairs more than a year ago, and his dad didn't even notice for ages.

Brenda drops a plastic drugstore bag onto his bed. She says, "Just reassure your parents. Your mom, too."

"With makeup."

"They need to be able to see what's wrong with you. This will help."

The makeup doesn't work for everything, but it gets his dad's attention. Jason wanders through the kitchen with his eyes all kohl-edged, and his dad's head snaps around and he stares. His mom watches him in the rear-view when she drives him to her place for the odd weekend. And then she starts warming up gelatin in a pot on her stove, just in case he wants to spike his hair.

Steven and Jason's dad expect him to redeem himself somehow, though, so Jason's commandeered into a summer of checking and fixing fences. He's surprised to find his range of skin allergies no longer carry much weight. If he doesn't want to ride horseback to check the fences, he's welcome to walk. So he goes out, under protest. Spiked hair under his cowboy hat and black nail polish under his gloves. They have miles of pasture beyond the home sections, and there's three strands of wire along most of it. One post every fifteen feet. Jason's punishment is specifically to check the staples and the wire tension, and fix what needs fixing. Keep the horse he's been issued clear of the wire, because horses can't distinguish between loose wire and snakes, and any idiot knows that if you let them get too close together, the horse will turn inside out and head for the hills and never come back.

Sometimes metalheads helping out their own parents drive by and salute him. Maybe they're his new friends. He's not sure where his old friends went.

Probably, he should have gone to some of his hockey games. But he had other things to do. Jenn wasn't going to watch herself.

Jenn, who passed grade 10 (who made *honour roll*, and not by the skin of her teeth — definitely not by the skin of her face) doesn't have to fix fences. Her parents got her a new fucking horse, after her mom and Jason's mom adopted Djinn as their own personal horse-baby. She takes off with Donna for days at a time. She comes back different. Brighter and sharper. Less scared of the universe.

She's not scared of him, either, he notices. She's watching him, but not in a jumpy way. More like she knows what to do if he turns out to be trouble.

The days he doesn't have to work in the sun until his brain melts and Jenn's temporarily detached herself from her girlfriend, Jason drives Jenn into Saskatoon and they hit the second-hand stores. He collects shredded jeans and black T-shirts and thrift-store jewelry that he doesn't actually have the balls to wear, yet. But if these are going to be his new people, he has to go among them in their native garb. The guys he meets browsing the racks of cast-offs are either deeply grunge or something a bit more ambiguous.

He might never attract the tough, drunk girls he still likes the look of, but slippery boys slide up behind him and kiss his neck while he's looking at chain-link necklaces with skulls hanging on them.

That thing he likes, it never used to show before. He wonders if he should change his colours back, before people start recognizing him on the street. If people can actually see him . . .

Then, what?

He'd have too much sex? Not an option. He doesn't think it is. He's seventeen and he's never been fucked out. He doesn't *get* too tired for sex. And his sex life broke apart when Jenn came off her horse. She won't do for him, so he has to find options. The constant jerking off in the grass while he's exposed to the sun and wind is going to end him, but it'll be a death of histamine reactions or skin cancer, not sexual exhaustion.

Jason's never going to be sexy enough to stop traffic, and Jenn doesn't want to look at him, but he has his moments. He scrapes together enough money for a single ticket to a Pantera concert, because one of the metalheads stops his pickup and invites him. He needs friends so *much*.

*Don't leave me alone here.*

But he isn't any sexier when he vents half a year of trauma and sexual frustration by shoving a stringy-haired guy twice his size when that guy gets in his way. The guy answers Jason with a single, clean punch that fells him like a dead moose. A black eye crawls to his surface, and it brings its friend, massive facial bruising, with it. The whole world slides a bit whenever the band hits a new metallic chord.

He thinks he might throw up.

Blond guy he's never seen before sinks mole-claw fingers into his shirt and drags him back out of range.

Jason says, "I'm not . . ."

"Not gay. And getting your face smashed in proves it. Do you need help?" Faces kissing-close so they can hear each other under the concert's scream. There isn't enough space in the sound register for Jason to hear sarcasm.

"Just need to get back to my seat."

He can't quite walk, but there's this pretty, soft boy holding him up. And it's probably significant that at two in the morning, they're still hanging out. Sitting on the tailgate north of Saskatoon, where the concert ended and the silence broke his ear drums. Except for the weird sex undercurrents, they're disturbingly farm-boy-wholesome. It's the wrong time of night for aurora, so the lights Jason keeps seeing are probably a result of his concussion.

"You're a mess."

"I know. I don't think I can drive home."

If people recognized Jason in his right skin, *this* would happen. He'd wind up concussed, needing a trip to the emergency room, and possibly attached to a new boyfriend.

It's not the same as having friends, but it's something. Seth drives them to St Paul's, where they mercifully don't recognize Jason at all, and calls Jason's mom while they're checking him for skull fractures. He writes his phone number on Jason's arm, before he takes off.

Eventually, a Chinese doctor with bad skin walks in with Jason's mom. "Concussion," he says.

"Something hit me," he says.

"Of course something hit you. Person?" The doctor throws a glance at his mother.

"His name is already mud," she says. "It doesn't matter if he was fighting."

"Do not let him sleep." He says other words too, that Jason can't process. He feels like throwing up.

His mom buys him coffee at an Esso restaurant. It's barely hot, but still strong enough to burn his eyes. For some reason, it makes him think about elevation. Most of the time, he feels like he's deep inside the earth, digging along, but really, they're thirty-five hundred feet above sea level. The air here's cold and thin.

"Don't nod off, baby."

"I'm gonna throw up again."

"Open a window."

The road bumps. Some tiny animal just perished in an awful moment of rubber and hydrocarbons. He's glad she stopped drinking. It's easier to roll over the animals, sometimes, than try to avoid them every time they jump.

His mom says, "I should probably tell you that if you ever pick up a gun again I'm going to kill you myself."

He stares at her.

"Just so you know."

*Splat*. Insects die all over the windshield. The day's getting hotter, and all the bugs are flaring out of the grass to get their hot-blooded sex-moment of feed-fuck-die over with.

*Spludge*. Ground-dwelling rodent bursts under the truck in a moment of perfect physics. His mom doesn't even slow down.

Jason throws up into a fast food bag that was lying on the floor. She hands him the rest of her coffee to rinse his mouth. Spit out the window into the flying swarms of insects.

# « CHAPTER 3 »

THE HIGH SCHOOL LIBRARY isn't the only one in Bear Hills. There's a branch of the Wheatland Regional Library on 1st Street, and in that library, there's a section devoted to Girl's Own books from the 1940s and 50s. Cloth-bound, usually red, with a black outline of either a horse or a girl or a girl and a horse etched on the cover. Rearing horses. The girls have puffy blouses and shoulder-length wavy hair, lifting slightly in the library wind.

It's those damn fillies again. They're everywhere. That particular shade of sun-drenched blonde hair spontaneously generates short fiction for young adults while no one's looking.

*Horse Stories for Girls*
*The American Girl Book of Horse Stories*
*Canadian Horse Stories for Girls*
*A Horse of Her Own*
*A Horse in Her Heart*
*Stories for Girls Who Love Horses*

Most of them feature the tale of a girl who took a terrible fall from her pony and then has to overcome her fear and ride again. Now and then, a loved one (parent, schoolmate, secret lesbian lover) perishes in the initial accident, and she has to overcome that too. Trembling on new-foal knees under her breeches (or jeans, depending on who's doing the writing), she approaches her chestnut nightmare and rediscovers the joy of galloping through the meadow while her hair whips in the wind.

They aren't morality tales by any stretch of the imagination. After she read her way through that section, though, Jenn went on to read Larry McMurtry's westerns, in which the horse you love will eventually murder you. Those are cautionary tales. She should have kept them in mind.

*See your pretty pony? You've got it nicely groomed. Shiny feet, big soft eyes, silky mane. Someday, randomly, it's going to have a fit, rear up and flip over backwards, and crush you between the saddle horn and the ground. You won't survive that.*

*With this in mind, place your bet somewhere between "Gotta get back on the horse" and "Discretion is the better part of valour."*

Real cowgirls don't believe in discretion, of course. It's how they cull the human herd — sending everyone out to play with livestock and seeing who comes back alive. Jenn's skin stands out in school, jagged in the crowd of soft, freckled faces, but she's not the only girl walking wounded. Other girls stagger around on crutches or in neck braces. Mostly from car accidents — a little drunk, Saturday night, when they decided to see what was going on at the pit — but the odd one's been earned on horseback. Those girls walk differently. They look smug.

They look like boys who've won fights. She keeps reminding herself.


SHE ISN'T GOING to be able to ride Djinn again. It's the better part of valour. But she feels terrible, like she left something small and vulnerable in a dark place without feeding it. It's the sort of thing she had nightmares about, before. Apocalyptic animal accidents.

Djinn's safe. She has a different protector now. It doesn't really help.

When they sent Jenn's mother home from the hospital to sleep, she found Djinn standing bloody next to the barn. She hadn't gone to bed first. It's her farmer instinct, in spite of her law practice, to check on the animals first. So instead of sleeping or eating or bathing, she caught Jenn's horse and cleaned her up. There were witch-knots in her mane and buckshot in her neck. Not deep, but messy. This faintly psychotic horse-aura permeated the barn. Horses are skittish anyway, and scared of shadows. Djinn was convinced all her equine nightmares were real.

It wasn't easy to get the blood off her. Jenn's mother hauled five-gallon buckets of steaming bathwater from the house and washed the horse that way. With a sponge, in the cold. Wrapped her in towels and old quilts like a baby and sang to her. Jenn's father stayed at the hospital until Jenn's mother came back, and then he went home and took over. Neither of them got much sleep. The nurses thought they must be bathing with the livestock. About the third day, they found Garry and made him take over, but he's ambivalent about animals. He didn't engage as much as Jenn's mother thought was necessary.

He didn't feel *responsible*.

Her mother phoned Sarah.

It's going to be years before Garry recovers from that. Sarah drove all night to get to the farm, and bypassed him completely. No warning. He came to the barn to check on the horse, which wasn't going to die, and there was his wife (his ex-wife), singing to the thing and feeding it dried fruit from the organic co-op. Just like they'd never had to untangle conflicting restraining orders and criminal charges and years of recrimination.

She said (separately according to Sarah, and according to Garry), "I read that the Arabs used to feed their horses dates, so I thought she'd like them."

"Jason isn't here."

"I know. You aren't either. Just me."

He watched her from the house. His parents' house. She wasn't allowed to come in.

SARAH DECIDED THAT Jenn needed a present. Jenn wonders, even as an adult, whether Sarah worked it out. She didn't say anything, but she's protective of Jason, and if she couldn't find a specific frame that would make a pasture shooting entirely Garry's fault and not Jason's at all, she wouldn't bring it up. But she felt responsible, Jenn thinks. It's the best justification she can think of for the guinea pig Sarah smuggled into the hospital. Twenty-dollar animal in a cardboard box filled with unexpectedly aromatic hay.

"There's some sweetgrass in it. A little bit of sage, too. If you like, I'll bring you more." Standing there in her slightly ethereal way. Witch-woman, Jenn thought unfocussedly. Clutcher of steering wheels. Sea-swimmer. Absent family member.

"Thanks."

There was a little bow in the guinea pig's hair.

It's a little fat creature that lurks in her bedroom. Jenn's mother took it away before the nurses caught them keeping rodents in a semi-private pediatric room, but it was there, in her bedroom, when Jenn came home. Her father made it a little pen and a hutch in the shape of a barn. The roof lifted off so she could peer in at it. It crawls out at unexpected moments and drags limp produce from one end of its cage to the other.

She loves it. She loves it so much she thinks she might have to start a zoo, just to fill the space in her chest that opens up whenever she looks at the guinea pig too long.


SEX IS NOT the beginning of anything. It completely fails to rupture time in the way she was promised.

At almost-seventeen, Jenn's in the third year of her brain intermittently screaming SEX while she's trying to cope with the other problems in her universe. Some people, it probably hits them sooner, but thirteen was too early for her. It predated anything useful in terms of sex ed, and post-dated the period when she was comfortable asking her parents. She hunted a lot of books up, in the school and Wheatland libraries. And she isn't stupid. She knows they're not accurate. But sometimes it's all the information she has. Jason's pornographic sampling didn't help, either.

It's the wrong details. Even the best stuff, the vampire books and the dark romances featuring dead things, are about the wrong bodies. The wrong kinds. She's left with the impression that sex-ecstasy comes from penetration, or maybe his orgasm. Semen flowing into the girl's body like hot light.

If that's not part of the equation, she's not sure how this is going to work at all.

In grade seven, their human development class watched a film from the 1970s, complete with movie projector: *Bodies for Girls / Bodies for Boys*. It sounded like a suggestion — *you get these bodies, we'll take those ones, and we can all meet up again when we've screwed our brains out.* Jenn remembers wanting a time-out option, one that would let her ignore the question for another year or two, until various levels of incest and violence had wiped out that segment of her class she least wanted to deal with.

In Bear Hills, everybody is *somebody's* cousin. Just, Jason's her only one, and every year she's less certain she wants to touch him. The odd time, at pit parties, she's tried it, but there was something fundamentally wrong about it that might not have had anything to do with the fact that they're related. Other people noticed, though. She found a note pushed through the slats in her locker that said, *Your kids aren't going to have any eyes.*

If marrying your cousin could make you go blind, there'd be even more accidents on their roads.

Nobody said she had to *marry* him.

Other films they were showed that year (and the next year, and the next year, in between sermons on the importance of self-esteem and charts of out-of-date street names for drugs) were meant to dispel myths about sex. They weren't myths Jenn had heard before. Blindness, hairy palms. What did the monkeys have to do with it? *What* would fall off if you didn't leave it alone?

She's fairly clear on what you can get pregnant from. You can't, no matter how many times someone asks, get pregnant from oral sex. Even if your friend's cousin totally did get pregnant that way. Really.

· In biology, one of the last classes she was in before she was shot in the face, they were treated to a fairly graphic video, circa 1989, about the physical stresses of pregnancy and childbirth. The bits about potential tearing were their very own horror story. The bits about doctors making cuts to keep the vagina from tearing were worse. Aimee, who had hysterics at that point in the afternoon, was four months pregnant. One of those ones who'd been very, very interested in sex back in grade seven. She'd just started to show. Hadn't exactly announced it to the teachers yet.

Jenn remembers the bio teacher crouching next to the supply room door, talking to Aimee about epidurals and C-sections. *Don't panic. Please.*

The video kept running. It showed a new baby: red, bloody, tiny, howling. Possibly with no eyes. Or three. It could have been locally produced.


SEX IS THE beginning of the moment that she looks at herself in the bathroom mirror, naked, and nothing hurts. Sunburn digs down into the cells of her shoulders, there's too-soft flesh on her belly, and her skin is livid where they sewed her back together, but that's all suddenly livable. She's not damaged beyond repair. She feels good. No joint pain, no lung damage, no thinning bones, no torn cartilage, no stripped nerves, no failing organs, no cells about to reproduce out of control. Both of her eyes are fine. She can use her hands. The dermatologist at the university hospital had some concealer suggestions, when she finally nerved herself up to ask.

No one in the house except her and Donna. Her parents calmed the fuck down at some point, and they're gone up north for a while, camping. Tori's taken off with one of her friends. She complains that Jenn ignores her.

She does. She can't deal with herself and her sister too.

Donna's there to keep Jenn company. She's good for her. Calming. She has her dad's touch with people.

Sex smell crawls all over Jenn's brain. Curled up behind Donna on the bed, watching movies on the TV they carried upstairs. Their favourites: *Reality Bites* and *Dangerous Liaisons*. Warm air, still cooler than the air indoors, pours through the window screen. The strange weather shifts that'll mark their adult lives haven't really started yet. It's just August, night, not quite hot out. They're both barefoot; they have jeans on, but no shirts. Both of those, and their bras, are on the floor. Donna's toes keep nudging up the leg of Jenn's jeans and stroking her.

The walls have this faint shimmer where the TV light's reflected off silver horse statues on her trophy shelf.

She can't remember which movie they're watching.

Kisses Donna's shoulder. Her left hand is wrapped around Donna's body, rubbing under her breast.

She picked Donna up from town, earlier, at a time agreed on by their parents. Pulled off the highway partway home, and leaned over and licked Donna's belly. There were crush-marks at her waist, from her clothes. Dark skin underneath marking a permanent bruise from a whole life of waistbands just that much too tight. Jenn peeled the denim back and tongued her navel until Donna wiggled and pushed her off. Kept pushing until Jenn was leaned back against the driver's side door, and then licked *her* for a while. Chest to waist. It was a surprise how much she could feel in the unexpectedly unscarred space under her right breast.

Jenn's been able to smell her since then. Warm sticky-wet and distinctly female. She knows what it is. Not her skin and not her sweat, because Jenn's smelled both of those before. She's licked her all over. Sucked on her breasts and left bruises on them. Donna's hair is clammy from being hot all day.

It takes more nerve than Jenn expects to slide her jeans off. Donna has floral panties, wet in the middle.

The sound she makes when Jenn licks her startles them. Whining moan so you'd think it hurt. A leg hooks over Jenn's shoulder so she'll know how much she likes it.

*Stay* **there**.

All over her *face*.

Jenn licks her. Pushes her tongue up into Donna, and she knows it isn't what Donna wants, but she can't not do it. And Donna doesn't hate it. She whimpers when Jenn pushes a bit. Rubs herself against Jenn's face.

They took sex ed for four years and no one ever told them how to do this.

Everything Jenn knows about bodies other than her own, she learned from the distorted world of Jason's porn collection. It isn't quite right, and it doesn't entirely match either her body or Donna's, or what she thinks either of them might like. But figuring out the details is what girls have sex for. Proving she's smarter than she looks. But how smart is she? Jenn's brain kicked into *sex now* mode sometime while Donna was licking her belly this afternoon, and since then she's been intellectually blank, like maybe the intelligent-critical-verbal part of her hurtled out the window in a giant cloud of road dust and hysterical joy.

She needs to lick her right . . . *there*.

*Fuck* . . .

And just keep doing that until Donna twists against her face and the muscles holding flesh and bone together spasm and she makes this noise like a dog tangling with something big and wild off in the distance, tearing breathy metal . . .

Donna shrieks . . .

Jenn knows she didn't hurt her. It's just that Donna sounds nothing like porn, or like Jenn's studied quiet, and she wasn't expecting the noise. Doesn't quite trust herself even now that she's reduced Donna to soft *yes yesyesyes* and fingers in Jenn's hair, and Jenn isn't shaking at all.

Donna rolls her down after that, and does this quick thing with her fingers, fast like a soft machine. The voice in the back of Jenn's head is their grade nine sex ed teacher, the one who said, *If you think girls are going to really enjoy it the first time, you're going to be sorely disappointed.*

Except, she does like it. It's nothing like what was described to her, and she's inarticulately relieved. Whenever she pictured having sex, there were always tears and apologies, or this frozen mortification that she wouldn't be able to escape. Not hot-sweaty skin to skin with herself growling *fuck me* and sucking on Donna's neck and wrapping legs around her hips and telling her exactly what she's going to do next time she holds her down.

Like every time they chased each other, they were just waiting for this.

Later, Jenn's less surprised to be playing blind-man's-bluff at two in the morning, pursuing Donna through the house with all the lights off. There are no yard lights, either, because she turned them off earlier — walked out barefoot with her jeans pulled on over sticky skin and one arm over her breasts and palmed the switch. No internal lights except the LED clocks on the stove and the microwave. Flicker of Donna in the kitchen when she blocks the aqua-pale computer numbers with her shoulder.

*Gotcha . . .*

Naked in Jenn's mother's architecturally perfect kitchen. This house her parents built out of polished wood and light and gorgeous glass tile, that most of her life she's been afraid of smudging. Bare-assed on the almost-cool kitchen floor, it's funny.

She's never going to mention that they did this. Just in case Donna's father has multi-dimensional hearing. Just in case Jenn's mother needs to take the kitchen apart and disinfect it tile by tile.

Jenn leans over and licks Donna's nipple. Her knees are warmer than Donna's waist, and they're both wet. In the morning she'll check for tell-tale smears. She can smell-feel Donna, almost moving.

And then Donna slaps Jenn's ass. "I'm it," she says. "Run."


JENN'S FATHER WANTED to be a rodeo cowboy, once. He talks about it, sometimes, when the mood takes him. From the time Jenn was little, he's taken her to roping events. Offered to teach her, just like he hadn't witnessed her history of animal accidents. Her mother said, *Utterly no. No.* And it's not like Jenn wanted to. But she wants to be as comfortable in public as the girls who rodeo, and better than them, too. Not so marginal. Circuit rodeo is comprised of five sports: saddle bronc, bareback bronc, bull riding, steer wrestling, and calf roping. Barrel racing is peripheral, and it's strictly for girls. Little-Jenn, following her dad, used to have plans for the bronc-riding competitions.

*You just have to be nice to them. Talk soft. You'll be the first girl — the first person — to ride a bronc to a standstill.*

Later, she understood that wasn't the point. They pick rodeo stock for its ferocity, and they strap them up so they'll always move. Your bronc stops, you lose.

You *lose.* Still boggles her.

Getting back on, though, is the point of rodeo, and it's what her father wants for her.

She can't picture herself bull riding, and even her teenage self isn't big enough to wrestle a steer down. They're inherently guy-sports. Real men (or even boys who wouldn't claim to be "men," yet) don't race horses when there are cattle to be thumped into submission.

It isn't to say that men don't race at all. They race against women at pickup gymkhanas, as long as they're taking place in remote areas, and as long as the men in question aren't visibly queer. If you're going to race girls, it has to be the best game in town.

Nobody ever found the last guy who entered a barrel race at a pro rodeo. Somebody's wearing his teeth in a hatband.

*This here's ma trophy from th'ambiguously gay cowboy. Goes with ma "bulldoggers do it in the dirt" T-shirt. Not that ah'd wear a T-shirt to a rodeo. Ah got standards.*

The inflection isn't local. Rodeo engenders it. You take up any cowboy / horse sport and the accent slides in. You can live all your life in the middle of Canada and still say *y'all* and *yous* when you're in rodeo company. The language comes in over the secret radio. Little receivers in your brain activate after the third good solid crack of head against fence.

A smart guy once described it as the accent that makes *ice* sound like *ass*. Texan by way of the media-fed south you pick up from country radio. Edges of *Deliverance*, just to keep it interesting.

Jason stopped coming to roping days with his dad and Jenn's about the time he figured that out. He thought it was *funny*.

He thinks all kinds of things are funny. Even now, he leaves offerings of porn in her bedroom, with selected pages hilighted. Jenn's first reaction is usually a wish that the girls would cut their nails short before they hurt each other. She's a nail biter now, herself. Learned it from Amber. Doesn't even bother painting her nails purple to hide the damage.

She's going to *get* him, one of these times. Catch him out and tie him up, drive him over here some night to the post-roping booze-up, and throw his psycho little ass to the blue-eyed inbreds. He'll come home in the morning all grinning and spit out his front teeth and say *that wathn't tho bad.*

They won't be even, then, but they'll be closer.

Donna's father comes to roping weekends, too. He conducts the "interfaith" prayer meetings that trigger Sunday mornings with a kind of enthusiasm Jenn can only attribute to his being in deep, serious denial about the state of his family. Or else he knows. He's trying — officially, the Church of the Family in Christ is trying, but he *is* the church, so — to excise the limited safe-sex education segments from the Bear Hills Comprehensive curriculum. It's encouraging the children to *fornicate*. If the schools keep encouraging them, the youth of the community will descend into a life of carnal filth.

He doesn't look at Jenn when he says this, or Donna. She thinks sometimes that he couldn't imagine what they do. It's not in his universe. As long as they're not fucking boys, he'll always love them and never notice, and the trouble he makes will only wrap around everybody else.

Girls who come to roping days might go to church, but they don't wear their God clothes. Irony and cowboy culture don't mix; you don't pour yourself into jeans tight enough to show the pattern on your panties and then top it off with a CHASTITY NOW T-shirt. You might see the occasional I ONLY RIDE WITH JESUS. But it's sincerely meant, and if it sounds dirty, it's Jenn's fault, not hers.

Lapsed families skirt the edges of the prayer meetings. Their bumper stickers say, *Jesus was my co-pilot but we crashed in the mountains and I had to eat him.* The stickers aren't on their actual trucks, because those have to go into town occasionally, and the God people will smash your tail lights. They plaster them on their tack boxes instead. Maybe on their hockey bags. A couple of the guys who rope used to play hockey with Jason.

He's apostate from his own kind of religion. It's another reason for him to stay home.

Jenn started coming to these roping meets when she was maybe three. Little girl with cowboy boots stuffed into the legs of her jeans, because real cowboys wear their leather on the inside, and a big straw hat. She'd watch her dad go tearing across an arena after a terrified calf. Catch it by the head, jerk it off its feet. Horse dragged it down while he jumped and ran and threw it and tied up the calf in maybe twenty seconds.

Jenn's mother said she couldn't do that. She'd wind up finger-less the first time she dallied a rope and caught her hand in it. The way Jenn does. Her dad's still disappointed. If Jenn had learned, they'd be able to team rope together. Her dad needs a son instead of two introverted daughters. He needs a kid who believes that fingers that you lose grow back like lizard's tails.

He should try Tori, Jenn thinks. She's a braver, stranger kid than their dad gives her credit for. If he could stand to walk into Tori's room full of Barbie dolls, he might find what he wants.

THE FRAGMENTS SHE remembers later of the last two years of her publicly funded education involve curling up with Donna in cul-de-sac corners of the school over their lunch hours. Their books spread all over the floor and Donna's head settles in Jenn's lap. Basketball games crash on the other side of the cinderblock wall. Jason lurks around the edges of her consciousness and watches her. He studies enough not to fail grades again, and he's always at her shoulder, or two seats behind her. Jenn braces herself for the day he throws a book at her head and finishes her off, but it doesn't come, and while she doesn't relax, she stops expecting gunfire whenever he turns toward her.

Not entirely, but if he kept the gun from November, she's never been able to find it. If Sarah took it away, Jason'll never get his hands on the thing again.

Mrs. Walker, their math teacher, loses it six months into their grade-eleven year. She sits down in the pudding they (a collective *they* that comprises the entire classroom in teenage hive-mind, but no individuals at all) carefully smeared over her ergonomic desk chair, paying careful attention to the colour match between custard and upholstery. She gets up wailing, runs out of the room, and never comes back. They all sit there, very quiet and well behaved, while her voice snakes through the building, articulating all the reasons why the children are going to hell and she's isn't going with them anymore, or ever again.

Mr Morrison comes from across the hall and teaches them to draw human figures for the rest of the afternoon. Jenn isn't clear whether he's furious with them or incredibly impressed with their collective ingenuity. She's lost her urge to sidle up to him and confess, *it wasn't me.*

The new math teacher never looks anyone in the eye, twitches when he talks, and every test he gives back is folded into origami. Morrison adores him. During lunch hours, the two of them go out to Morrison's 1982 Volvo station wagon and get high. The afternoon classes are amazing.

*Fucking* numbers *man. You wouldn't* believe.

And there are whole months when nothing interesting happens at all. Jenn crashes at Donna's house after school and wakes up in the middle of the night with an afghan thrown over her and Donna under the covers, pressed back against her through the layers of blanket. It's cold in the manse. Jenn brings extra pajamas so she can crawl under the covers with Donna and not fear being caught by Donna's father in the morning.

Donna's parents don't say anything much. They hug Jenn and feed her like she's one of their crowd of kids. The extra daughter they forgot they had. The little ones stare at her, though. And when she brings Donna home with her, nights, Tori sits across the dining table from them in the morning, with this expression like murder. She wears pink single-knit nighties and kitty socks to bed, but it doesn't soften the effect.

Jenn and Donna wear University of Saskatchewan T-shirts and sweats, and after a while they just exchange clothes when they need to. What fits Donna is oversized on Jenn, but not that much. Only Tori really notices the difference.

She's judgy. It's a reason not to go home.

Jenn rides the school bus home eventually, because she needs clean underwear and time with the horses, and her mom rolls her up against the wall and hugs her hard. Whispers, *Where the heck do you keep disappearing to?* She knows it isn't a real question. Only, she doesn't phone home every night anymore, and her mom isn't ever going to stop worrying about her. She looks so *tragic*.

Jenn gets the point. She comes home in the mornings, when she can, to shower and eat breakfast with her parents. They perk up and replace the cold cereal she's eaten most of her life with glorious, artery-clogging plates of wonderful. Eggs and bacon, when they're in a hurry to leave for work. Pancakes and sausages and maple syrup when they're not Hashbrowns. Whipping cream in her coffee.

She can think of a way to tell them she's all right. She wishes they'd stop worrying about her, when they think she can't see them.


JASON'S BRANCH OF the family never had pet horses until Jason's mom buys Djinn from Jennifer. She does it formally, with negotiations on price and hours of storytelling over coffee and the requisite envelope of hundred-dollar bills. Jenn keeps the hundreds in her jewelry box. Takes them out and counts them when she's alone.

Jenn's parents have a rule that you only take cash for horses. She heard, on TV, that all American hundred-dollar bills have some cocaine on them. She thinks Canadian hundreds must all be marked with nicotine and horse dander. Some chewing tobacco. When she goes with her dad to horse auctions, she meets old guys with no front teeth who carry maybe two thousand dollars in their jackets at all times, all in brown folded bills.

Djinn doesn't leave. Sarah says she isn't going back to Garry's house, and she apparently means it. She drives out to visit her horse and plays with her, rides her and grooms her, has lunch with Jenn's dad, and goes home. She doesn't even usually wait to say hi to Jason.

They don't go back into the pasture. Djinn stays in the yard, where Sarah can watch her. Sometimes they ride along beside the road. Jenn sees them — skinny, serious woman on the jumpy little horse. Flat-out running on summer fallow in the half-dark. Jenn comes to the barn and finds Sarah with her face pressed to Djinn's like the two of them are in love.

She does move the horse, eventually. An artist friend of hers has a family homestead a few miles away, where she can ride and pasture Djinn without intersecting with anyone else. Gordon Watson comes over with a borrowed trailer and moves horse, tack, and woman in one trip.

SHE STANDS IN the mud at a gymkhana in Rosthern, holding her dad's horse, Max, and her new Cricket. In her dreams with horses, Jenn will always be this age — seventeen. The horses will talk to her, but never about anything serious or important. Every other girl around them is in full buckle-bunny gear. Tight jeans and massive belt buckles. And then Donna comes back from the can, wearing her favourite huge striped T-shirt and late-grunge baggy jeans over roper boots, like somebody's urban cousin out to play for the weekend. She looks clueless, and it's a good trick. Lulls the local riders into a false sense of security. Donna is good at this. Jenn's almost good. Cricket's really good. Smart snappy little mid-brown horse who can change leads like breathing and bites anything that gets too close. Even Max. He has big chunks missing from his hips and withers, and they have to be trailered with Cricket snub-tied to the gate to keep her from mauling him.

Nobody stands near them after the first time. The red ribbon in Cricket's tail isn't ornamental.

*Stay back . . . I kick . . .*

They switch horses, weekend by weekend. Donna's father likes this new incarnation of his girl. She's outward-focussed, maybe a little leaner. She has a suntan. She looks like a fat valley girl, and nothing like the pretty dyke who puts Jenn's makeup on for her every morning.

They went with a lot of eyeliner. It gives exactly the right impression.

Their parents — Jenn's and Donna's both — gave them an envelope full of entrance-fee money, when the school year ended, and keys to the truck. Play outside. Be okay. Little edge of *keep getting back on the horse.* Keep busy. Don't join a cult, don't try drugs, don't die.

Be good.

They're very, very good. Jenn and Donna have gas money and a quest to hit every rural fair on the gymkhana circuit. They look like nothing, like nobody's ever put them on a horse before. And then they clean up, make their entry back, and money for burgers. They spit at people who come to close to them, when Cricket's not around to work defense.

Jenn loves Cricket. First horse she's ever seen that growls while she watches other horses run. It's not like loving an animal that might break.

Gymkhanas aren't horse shows. You come in your working gear, the stuff without silver edges and no recent maintenance work beyond a little waterproofing. Spend one day and ten dollars in a serious attempt to end your life through some minor feat of agility. Dance afterwards. Drink, fight, fuck, sleep it off in the truck-cap camper. Go home. Do it again next weekend, seventy kilometres away.

Just occasionally, Jenn spots Donna's mother watching them

102 « WHITETAIL SHOOTING GALLERY

from the bleachers. One or two little kids with her, eating sno-
cones, but never focussing on the girls on horseback.

She leaves them notes, taped to the trailer door. Mostly, they're
updates on what's for supper on Monday. Sometimes, they're Pun-
jabi etymologies of equestrian words, so detailed she's obviously
been copying them out of the ancient Oxford English Dictionary
at the Wheatland library. She leaves them money, sometimes.
Doesn't say hello.

She takes pictures, though. This picture Donna's mom sends
Jenn's mom that Jenn comes home to find plastered to the fridge.
Donna's nose is busted, and Jenn has a black eye. They crashed,
trying to run a Gretna Green race. The organizers were so worried about liability they bought both girls dinner and a case of
beer if they'd sign away their right to sue. There's blood on their
teeth, and they're holding a box with rosettes and key-chain
prizes spilling out of it. They did pose for that, for a local paper.
Donna's mom must have been behind the pro photographer, just
out of their line of sight.

She's watching them. Jenn isn't sure how to take it.

The picture's mounted on cardboard. On the grey-brown edge,
she wrote in black marker, *I lost an eye pole bending in Meadow Lake
and all I got was this lousy ribbon.*

She hangs out with a lot of really old cowboys in the course of the
tour. Men over a certain age — say, over seventy — are attracted to
buckskin horses. Black mane, black legs, glossy gold body. Max, on
loan from her dad, is like a diagram from *The Color of Horses.* There's
a book, something people used to read in school, about a buckskin
pony, and the sight of a real one makes old men weak in the knees.
Jenn'll come back to the trailer, sucking on a Freezee and minding her
own business and find little old men hugging her dad's horse.

Guys like that buy her and Donna beers without being sleazy
about it. They don't even want to ride the horse. They just want
to touch him. Jenn lets them.

Thinks about Donna's belly in the truck's half-dark and doesn't listen to their stories.

The two of them scrub down in cold water — all they can get from public hydrants — on Saturday nights, and it doesn't strip away the horse smell. They both reek like sweat and animals and greasy food that leaves salt grains under their nails.

And it's still amazing. She gets to sleep with Donna every night that they're on the road. Licks her way down from mouth to knees. Pulls her fingers through Donna's endless hair-tangles while Donna licks her back. Pretty, clever mouth on her cunt, and Donna gets way too much of a kick out of hearing her beg.

They get caught, twice. Neither time within an hour's drive of home, but word gets around. Donna starts a defensive rumour about Jason, and by the time it gets back to them, the stories have merged, and half the school believes Jenn's fucking Jason. It's an easier story for people to believe. The family trees in town don't all branch the way they should, and cousin-grade incest is legitimate fodder for comedy. The next cycle, they've forgotten Donna completely, and people think it was Jason out in the field with her, all summer. At the back-to-school pep rally, Dustin Pattison stands up at the podium with this shit-eating grin and says, *Congrats to Jason and Jenny Hiebert, reserve North-Saskatchewan gymkhana champs. Please accept this box of condoms with our best regards.*

Dustin gets detention, a week of lunch hours washing the hallway baseboards with a toothbrush. Donna laughs at Jenn and stays at least ten feet away from her at all times. No one suggests Jason should give the condoms back.

Jenn doesn't talk to him. She doesn't touch him. He doesn't stop watching her, and she doesn't stop hearing, second-hand, the new version of the jokes about shooting Jenny Hiebert in the face.

She goes back to the library, with Donna, and stops her ears. Reads and doesn't listen. And in November, two years after she saw Jason stand across from her holding a shotgun, she spots him at one of the library tables, making a semi-serious effort to create an illustrated report about Iceland. Mr. Morrison comes up behind him, like the guy police, and says, "Swear to me you're using something."

Jason snaps his head back. Stares up at him. "What?"

"Latex, boy. Condoms. Wrapping up your meat."

Jenn waits for Jason to laugh, or puke. Instead, he says, "I am."

"Promise me." Like Morrison isn't joking or even patronizing. He sounds like he stays up nights worrying about this.

He doesn't say anything to Jenn. She wonders if he knew she was there. He doesn't seem to see Donna, most of the time, but few teachers do. Donna's father is a sink-hole of administrative trouble if he decides you're dangerous. More every year. They don't need Donna's love life coming down on their heads.

Other people might be watching closer. The teachers know everyone's locker combination, so Jenn isn't totally surprised when she starts finding care packages in with her books. Just, she can't figure out what they *are*. The rubber gloves are simple, but the baggie of green latex squares is entirely beyond her. Then her Algebra II mid-term comes back folded into a cricket, and when she unfolds it, a second paper falls out. Just this little slip of a pamphlet.

*Amy's Dental Dam*

The graphics belong to the '70s film-strips that dominated sex-ed, but she doesn't remember these particular details. There's even a little section on how to pad your fingernails with cotton balls inside the rubber gloves, for safety.


ON THEIR ENGLISH B final exam, it says,

"If thou dost marry, I'll give thee a plague for thy dowry: be thou as chaste as ice, as pure as snow, thou shalt not escape calumny."

*Identify and give the significance and context. Write a short essay relating this quotation to your own life.*

That was Morrison. For the rest of her life, Jenn's not sure which one of them the question was aimed at, or if he just wanted to remind all of them how careful they have to be.


THEY GRADUATE FROM high school. It takes all day. Pictures start shortly after dawn. There are family gatherings and group portraits. Dinner. Ceremonies. A slide show involving each graduate's baby pictures. Their grad party is Jenn and Donna and Jason and forty-six classmates stripped out of their black-tie formal outfits and poured back into jeans and shirt layers. And all their friends. The district's grads are staggered so that no two fall on the same night. Everybody comes.

It's a barn dance on acid. (Not joking. There's blotter acid in plastic wrap stowed in a beer fridge, next to the horse dewormer and the actual beer, in the machine shop.) Four-hundred-odd people run loose through the Wiebes' barn and house, kissing and drinking and sobbing, fucking and watching their parent-chaperones commit adultery. Jenn and Donna's girls form their adolescent pack for the last time and jump the barbed wire around the yard to go howl at the moon.

Hockey boys streak past, high on aurora and covered in blood and dirt by morning.

The bonfire flares like a moment of satanic terrorist arson whenever someone's drink hits it.

Caligulan orgies have nothing on a rural Saskatchewan grad party. Every year, someone finishes the night ten miles away, naked and disoriented to the point of psychosis, clothes left on the quarter-mile fences.

You wear old clothes, in case it's you.

# « CHAPTER 4 »

THREE YEARS AGO, Gordon Watson left Vancouver and moved into his family's homestead house, three miles away from Jason's family. He said he was sick of teaching. That Vancouver was getting too expensive, that it wasn't an organic place for him to work. Jason listened to his mom on the phone to someone and concluded that Gordon's mom had finally died, and he'd inherited the house and nothing else. He wouldn't have taken it, but he needed a place to dry out. Less than one bar per square mile in the Bear Hills. Some of Gordon's more exotic chosen chemicals aren't available at all. Jason's dad visited him sometimes. Brought him food and non-alcoholic fluids and massive bottles of vitamins.

They could hear him screaming, sometimes, from the road.

He got better.

Even now, though, Gordon isn't integrated with the Bear Hills population. He shops for groceries in Saskatoon or Battleford, and lives entirely within his own yard. His regional existence is limited to his first initial, last name on the latest incarnation of the rural municipality map. Gordon lives on forty acres with barbed wire strung around them. He doesn't do anything with the land except drag the occasional dead tree home for firewood. His place is almost entirely bush. It makes a barrier around him. And for long stretches of time, he leaves, and plants grow up in his driveway, or snow builds up in it, and the barbed wire gate catches junk and stops looking movable, and people forget he exists.

He's Jason's very own neighbourhood monster. A Selfish Giant without anything interesting in his garden. Or...maybe just a troll. Scruffy, ugly guy who hunches around at the edge of social awareness and snarls when passersby get too close.

Jason gets to be the very big goat who makes it all the way across the bridge. He walks into the yard, kicks leaves off the doorstep, and chews on ugly old meat with the monster he carried to the hospital and home again.

Jason's responsible for Gordon now, and he doesn't quite understand how that happened.

Some of the things he's heard about Gordon are true. His family had another place, a ranch in the southwest of the province, and it was parcelled up and sold to pay for Gordon's bohemian life. It was gorgeous down there, but Gordon only wanted to be away. There's nothing cowboy in him, and he wanted out so badly that his mom retreated to her family's homestead, and then died out here. Gordon's sister took the land around the house and sold it. She said he could keep the house.

Gordon spent years in Vancouver, and now he won't set foot there. He spends months at a time in Ontario and the U.S., doing installation art, or in northern B.C. and Alaska, among the freaks. Different kind of freaks than the ones in the Gulf Islands colony. Organic drugs and neo-pagan ceremonies and people with no furniture and no carnivorous tendencies at all. They take him in when he goes off the rails, as long as he's happy to exist on legumes and the spirits of the air. So eventually he comes back down because he misses red meat. He tells Jason about hitch-hiking from remote communes into industrial towns for one really good hamburger.

At this stage of his life, Gordon's way farther out than the established lefties that Brenda does legal work for. Left of unions and grain co-ops. His is a kind of purist existence that wasn't ever meant for the masses. You get far enough to either end of the political spectrum, maybe, and you stop being able to deal with other people.

He has deviant ideas, but Jason's dad would rather Jason ran towards Gordon than off to the right, towards everyone else in the community. Jason's just a little too attached to the local culture for his parents' comfort. They must think they're in real danger of losing him. That he's internalizing rural conservatism, and one of these days he'll start thinking that the KKK is a really neat idea.

It isn't going to happen. He grew up believing in the cruelty of right-wing politics the way other kids believe in the vindictiveness of God. It's not something you can just slide out from under. Ideologically, this leaves him some room to maneuver. He has enough political leeway to chase Gordon all over the province.

The places they go (oh, the places they go!) aren't entirely unfamiliar. When he lived with his cousins, Jason's aunt Brenda and uncle Steven would take him along to meet with people. (Meet with The People, straight out of Marx. Except, Brenda told him, very seriously, Marx only wrote for an industrial society; he'd have had no idea what to make of Saskatchewan.) They thought he might feel safer in adult company than left with a babysitter. They drove two hours up north to the lake towns, and then Brenda and Steve would sit down for coffee and policy papers with ancient farmers and Jason was turned loose to do war with the pigs sleeping in the yard. He vaguely remembers being up by Turtle Lake, perched on fish-drying racks overlooking the water, contemplating the weirdness of his family while unpleasantly hungry porcine bodies patrolled below him.

Jason learned to drive because his dad was showing signs of going the same way, and Jason had no intention of being a political hanger-on for the rest of his life. He doesn't like being "in tow." And now he's in tow again, because Gordon can't drive safely until his eyes heal, and every now and then he needs a lift somewhere.

All the fucking time.

Jason doesn't hate it, not really. Two weird guys (because he's learning to internalize his own weirdness) rolling down the grid roads of Saskatchewan in darkest winter in a red '82 Corolla, spewing rust and a certain amount of pot smoke behind them. It gives him a place to be where he can't always be watching Jennifer.

The Corolla's a drafty machine. Ice holds all the gravel on the roads in place, and there's high snow between the wheel ruts. Little bits of car get left behind on the snowdrifts. Gordon's flying and Jason rides the second-hand high, and they eat a lot of strange things as a result. Gordon's friends cook with the same experimental determination that Jason's mom uses in her sculptures.

*Behold the Bean Explosion!*

*Curry Your Brains Out!*

*Against the Tyranny of Brown Rice!* (It's made with brown rice. The title's ironic. It began as performance art.)

Gordon operates in rock-star mode behind his sunglasses. The winter's dim to the point that yard lights on sensors never turn off, and it's dark in the houses they visit, but the red-eye of the constantly stoned is secondary to the level of ocular damage from which Gordon's currently recovering. He looks exactly like a guy who took the rear half of a shotgun blast to the face. So he covers it up. Clamps a hand on Jason's shoulder and just follows him around, or gives directions. The artist has no eyes. Instead, he has a not-very-pretty boy chauffeur that he introduces to the provincial freak population.


FORTY-THREE KILOMETRES east of Saskatoon down the straightest road in the world, Jason asks, "What were you doing there?"

"I heard gunfire."

"What were you doing in our *pasture*?"

"I go for walks. Sometimes with your dad. Sometimes without him."

"You had a gun."

Gordon says, "My dad came home from World War II when I was four. He used to go out and hunt Germans in the pasture. I got the habit from him." Jason watches him in the rear-view mirror. If he stares hard enough, he'll strip away Gordon's skin and get at the truth underneath. "I'd never fired the gun before. I just carried it to remind me of him."

"You fired it then."

"And it exploded in my hands."

"You said you heard gunfire."

"Yes. I was . . . strung out. So I fired back. It wasn't a good idea. I never cleaned that gun. It shouldn't have surprised me that it exploded. You don't remember this?"

"I only heard one shot. But I think I was deaf."


LATER, JASON SAYS, "Jennifer."

"I didn't see what happened, Jason. I just heard the shot."

"Jennifer."

"I'm sorry for your cousin. But my gun exploded in my hands. I didn't shoot her. I didn't hit anything but myself. I don't hunt little girls for sport."

"Jennifer."

"You should have been more careful. That's all I'm saying. It wasn't me that shot her."


JASON THINKS, SOMETIMES, it *could* have been somebody else, shooting Jennifer. It could have been Gordon. Could have been anybody. There are hunting accidents every year. Just because his family's pastures are posted against hunting doesn't mean that every asshole actually pays attention. Not everything is easy to solve, who did what and who shot who.

And, comparatively, only about once every five years does a genuine psycho emerge somewhere on the prairies. It's someone who lives for two decades in a trailer that never gets cleaned, and then comes out one night and shoots the neighbours, one by one, like they're mice in a silo.

And then the RCMP come, establish road blocks. They talk back and forth to the psycho over the phone, or by loudspeaker and screaming, for six hours or a couple of days. Then the psycho shoots himself. It's cut and dried like that.

Mass funerals follow. The odd traumatized survivor staggers over to a CBC cameraman.

*We coulda seen that coming, really. Guy's been crazy for years.*

Very clearly a terrible person. Not like anyone Jason knows at all.


GORDON SAYS, WHILE they're on the road, "I'm not good with guns. My father wanted me to be able to hunt, to take care of myself, but I couldn't do that to an animal."

"But you *shot*."

"I eat meat, too. But only if I don't have to watch it die."

"I'm just trying to understand," Jason says.

Gordon sighs. "Do you know what a startle reflex is? I . . . I have a fairly extreme one. I don't know why I was carrying the gun. I'd never shot it. I never cleaned it. I hadn't fired a gun in forty years. But there was gunfire, and I . . . I answered it. I thought someone was shooting at *me*."

"You remember that?"

"I don't remember everything. But I remember a lot." Blurred, bloodshot eyes look at Jason over the tops of cheap sunglasses.

Road goes by them. Snow. House. There's a yellowish coyote in the flat snowy distance.

Gordon continues, "I've been a dedicated pacifist since 1965. Last winter I spent a month naked, praying for peace for Yugoslavia. The things happening there are inhuman. I can hardly imagine them." Coyote in the field jumps on the snow crust, breaks through to catch mice underneath. Jason slows so they can watch. "I've been a near-vegetarian for six years. I can count my lapses on my fingers. This is eating at you, Jason. She forgave you. Let it go."


JASON THINKS HIS parents might worry less about him if they thought he accepted their politics. Funny, that he still thinks of them as a unit when they haven't stood in a room together since he was seven years old. Where he's concerned, they're a unified front. Both of them talk politics with him incessantly; they've been doing it, in various ways correlating to what he could understand, all his life. Only three evenings of his life have been devoted to frank discussions of drugs, sex, and alcohol. He was about ten when his mother informed him that they'd both tried a certain number of mind-altering substances. That he should avoid opiates and cocaine derivatives. That cigarettes would kill him. That alcohol was *déclassé* when consumed in large quantities. She'd quit drinking. She didn't mention the bottles in the bathroom while she lectured him.

His sex talk was embarrassing and conducted with just his dad. The word *respect* came up a lot. The night ended with a gift of two condoms and the least comfortable hug of his whole life.

He wonders what his dad knows. The talk was pointedly gender-neutral. Cautious, like his dad was waiting for Jason to tell him something. Like they couldn't proceed until that thing was said, and really, Jason was being a bit difficult.

*Please, o best beloved, confess a desire to move to Borneo and do it with monkeys. I need a sign that you're not a deviant. I need to know you're mine.*

The guys he played hockey with never had to deal with this shit. Their family traumas were completely different.

Instead of staring at his dad until the guy flinches, Jason gets off the school bus at Gordon's place, afternoons. Folds himself down on the couch, and Gordon challenges him to defend his family's politics. And they argue.

He's holding the line. His parents have no idea.

When Jason was in grade five, just about the time his dad came back, there was a federal election, and he got in a fairly extended fight with a grade six advocate of the Progressive Conservative party. They started balanced on the geodesic-dome monkey bars (silvery, steel, garnished with tongue-skin sacrificed to them every winter). Jason doesn't remember doing it, but Jennifer claims he jumped the other kid. Knocked them both flying, Batman style, into the sand, and proceeded to beat the snot out of him.

Later, when they were both ice packed and more or less duct taped to chairs in the vice principal's office, the fattish guy in charge of elementary school discipline asked them what the hell it was all about.

"Politics."

Blink. Cross-eyes.

"P.C!"

"N.D.P.!"

Blood spit back and forth between two guys whose balls hadn't dropped yet. They wouldn't be able to vote for the best part of seven years, still. Their grasp of socioeconomic policy was tenuous at best. Jason does remember the vice principal looking like he thought calling their parents might only result in a much larger brawl in his office.

This is the sort of thing it would reassure his dad to know. The vice principal might have been right about the brawl, though, if they'd called his mom instead. His mom's a grassroots girl. She has pointy elbows and short, jagged nails she's not afraid to use.

The arguments Jason has with Gordon are nothing like that, though. Gordon's got no interest in party platforms. He wants to debate individual freedom versus collective responsibility. They go over it for hours, while Gordon drinks and Jason sometimes does too, cutting the vodka or whisky with generic cola so he'll still be on his feet when he gets home.

It's not *déclassé* at all. Drinking is essential to the political process.

Jason walks home, after, because he can't think of a way to phone for a ride. Running shoes and jeans, ski jacket and gloves, and no hat. He comes in with mild frostbite and his earholes aching like they've been fucked raw.

In the fridge he finds leftover hamburger and rice, wolfs it down, and tries to continue the argument with his dad, who was drinking his decaf and reading *The Western Producer* like an innocent man.

Wakes up hungover on a Wednesday. There's water and painkillers next to his bed. His dad's handwriting marks the notebook page taped to his bedroom mirror.

**FREEDOM MEANS RESPONSIBILITY.**
**THAT IS WHY MOST MEN FEAR IT.**

— G.B. SHAW

*Don't come home drunk again, if you still love me. Also, you <u>do</u> have to go to school today.*

Jason has the feeling the Shaw quote is something he's supposed to remember and internalize. Or else it's the answer to the arguments he tried to put together last night that he's currently too messed up to remember.

He should whisper it to himself in meditation. If he did that.

His dad does it. Comes in from working during the afternoon, strips down to his underpants and sits cross-legged in the living room, breathing deeply and reflecting on the universe. Quietly scruffy farmer guy with this esoteric inner life. He doesn't talk to Gordon much anymore, but he should. They'd understand each other.

These are important details.

Jason's parents met in Seattle in 1974. Both Canadian, both backpacking down the Pacific coast with the kind of desperation that lands people in cults. There are pictures of them both in loose clothes with messy, shaggy hair, looking like the hippy diagram people in *The Joy of Sex*.

Someday, in the midst of a really ugly argument, Jason's going to tell his mom it's that mental image that made him gay.

They got married in North Vancouver, barefoot in Cates Park. Made it legal at City Hall. Came back to Saskatchewan and discovered they'd travelled fifteen years back in cultural time. In Saskatoon, things were appropriately groovy. In the country, they only knew it was the '70s because the farmers hated Trudeau so very, very much. So it's not surprising that they left for a while. The west coast was their natural habitat. The fact that they came back suggests that Saskatchewan might be completely inescapable. Jason's landscape will haunt him all his life, like family.

Clearly, what Jason needs to improve himself and redeem his more horrific redneck tendencies is to be exposed to as many lefty artist freaks as possible. His dad and Gordon might even have communed on the subject, though neither of them will admit it. Probably, though, Gordon just likes having a chauffeur. He can make Jason listen to him all afternoon.

It's not all bad; they eat at amazing Vietnamese restaurants. Originally, they were probably Chinese restaurants. Small towns in Saskatchewan are theoretically supposed to have Chinese restaurants, and one slightly alarmed-looking Chinese family running each of them, but most of the Chinese families raised their kids Canadian in the '50s, and the kids became doctors and accountants and moved to more civilized places, and the restaurants were bought up by Vietnamese boat people about the time that Jason was born. It's not anything like the expected cultural mix, but like most places, the Vietnamese diner serves the only commercially prepared food for an hour in any direction. And if you grew up on sweet-and-sour pork and wonton soup, it's not such a big jump to hot-and-sour soup and spring rolls and blindingly spicy noodles.

It's better, both in the way that it's more authentic (for whatever value of authentic) and that it's actually closer to being recognizable food. It means when the local kids grow up and leave, they'll be able to look at sushi without going into convulsions. It'll help when they run away to Vancouver to become heroin-addicted homeless people.

In the restaurants, chain-smoking guys with early-stage skin cancer on their faces stare at hot turkey sandwiches bordered with a few flaccid lettuce sheets and finger-sized rice paper rolls stuffed with canned shrimp.

Two hours from home, in some town he couldn't pick out on a map, Jason flips through sketchbooks in some artist's studio and finds naked pictures of the teenaged Vietnamese waiter who handed him the orange pop that came with lunch.

They always visit artists. Some of them are drug dealers, too, but everyone Gordon introduces him to is engaged in the process of creating impractical and improbable objects. Twitchy women paint canvases of mostly fruit in too-vivid colours. Sometimes they add furniture to the fruit for depth. Gordon bitches about them in the car, how they're stuck in the precious practices of the university's third-rate art school, and if they want to be artists so bad, they could at least *try* to do better. There are older women who make pottery. Guys who sculpt. Wild-eyed transgender performance artists who rehearse in Saskatchewan and exhibit in the Pacific Northwest. You can rent an entire abandoned prairie town for the price of a Vancouver studio.

And there are colonies here, too: whole towns that have been swallowed by artists' collectives, wherein massive, wood-fired kilns are dug into the earth and the town hall's been converted into a shop for kinetic sculpture.

Ceramic fish on chains keep flying at his *head*.

Other places, the artists just infest one or two buildings. Like this gutted, raw-painted church. There are three other churches in this particular town; two have actual congregations. They're spectacular buildings, put up fifty or eighty years ago, when Saskatchewan had almost as many people as Ontario and you had to come to church either on horseback or by Model T. They did-n't stay popular. The architecture's warm-water American coastal, designed to keep worshippers cool instead of warm. People froze to death here, looking for God. They died staring into the light: sky and snow reflect through the old, old glass. Wood stove in the centre to keep them warm, but all the heat rises into the rafters without touching human skin.

The church is occupied by a husband and wife team. Really *occupied*, because Jason doesn't think they bought the place so much as just moved in. Ran in wires for lights from the power pole outside. They bed down under electric blankets and cook on a hot plate in the corner. The whole place is tangled with their work but they barely have any furniture.

*We were in Asia for years. We're too used to living with this to go back to clutter.*

*Anyway, furniture's bourgeois.*

It takes him a minute to place the term. Jason's heard *bourgeois* before, but only in social studies units on European history, and the one time he read through his uncle's copy of *The Communist Manifesto*. He'd like to introduce them to his uncle Steven and see if they'd use the word to his face.

And really, the resident artists do have furniture, just not for living, only for work. They sit on cushions on the floor, cups beside their feet. Their tools rest up above their heads on plywood trestles scavenged from the basement. On the other side of that church-supper barrier, the space is crowded with sculptures. Long, barely human arms reach at Jason. He sees ceramic, rope, carved wood. Porcelain. Sketches of the boy they're modelling twist into the sculptural mass.

It's the world's largest, most beautiful piece of child pornography.

They have photos of him taped to white-painted sheets of plywood, too. Black and white. They look wet. All angles in the same post: arms out, suggesting motion. Other boards, along the back wall where the altar used to be, show photo sets they aren't working on right now.

Outside, there are other figures, protected from the wind by tarps. No roof over them. There's a three-sided polypropylene shelter, though, like the sculptures are wintering horses. Snow all over their backs.

"Won't they crack?" he asks.

"It's part of the process." She's maybe fifty years old. One eye tooth rimmed in gold catches Jason's eye when she smiles at him. "The series is about immigrants and the damage they take." Eye-snag. "He gets cold too."

It's a throwaway remark until the boy comes in. He's Jason's age, but only two-thirds his mass. There's a moment of blank, dark-eyed terror while the boy takes in Jason's shoulders, hands, the hockey jacket he pulled on to keep warm because the tea and the wood stove weren't quite enough. His look is a reminder that Jason's natural expression is unpleasant.

Jason makes a point of standing down. Hands spread. Nod. "Hey."

"Hey." The guy shakes his hand, briefly. Hand-slap somebody taught him that he spent a lot of time getting just right.

"Jason."

"Peter." Jason looks at him. Tries to explain why the name doesn't fit. "It's my English name. 'S easier for people."

Little consonant hesitations, but Peter's got a friend somewhere in this miserable cold town who's put serious effort in, coaching him to be normal. Walk like a real boy. Talk Canadian. It only fails because normal people, born in Saskatchewan and raised in wood-heated houses, don't shiver that convulsively. It's cold in here — Jason's fingers hurt, it's so cold — but Peter looks like he's cold all the time. The thickness of his movements suggests he's wearing several more clothing layers than the one Jason can see. He's so fucking thin. His shoes are too big. Layers and layers of socks. Even with his ski gloves off, Peter's still sporting black mini-gloves with the fingertips cut out. His fingernails show frozen white.

Over in the work space, there's exactly one chair. Peter throws his winter gear on the floor, then drops the rest of his clothes. He's down to one layer when he folds himself into the mess of an armchair, burrows into the quilts they give him and tilts his face up into view. Two sets of hands slide over his exposed skin, taking in his shape.

In warmer weather, it's pretty clear, they did that to his whole body.

He's so skinny. He looks like a kid.

Jason knows Gordon's looking at him. Almost-healed eyes.

Just. No.

Jason's nothing like pretty. Peter's got bone lines in his face that Jason isn't ever going to have. A century or so of mixing peasant stock left Jason with the face of a blunt object hurtling through space. Why show him this?

He could, probably, catch a bus to Saskatoon. Most of these tiny places get one coach passing through a day. The church is on the town's edge. It's only a five-minute walk to the restaurant. He can hunker there, ignore Peter's family and wait for the Sask. Transport Company bus.

If he's missed it, if the bus comes in the morning . . .

He can phone home if no bus comes by ten or so at night. Reverse the charges. *Hi, I'm stranded in the middle of bad-touch nowhere, and can you come get me, please?* He tries to decide which of his parents is more likely to believe he isn't drunk.

Gordon clamps his wrist when Jason goes to move. He says, "Breathe out."

Jason stares.

"Listen to me. Breathe out." Squeeze. "I don't have any designs on you." Gordon's a little guy, but he's got strong hands. The bones in Jason's wrist are grinding. "You're not comfortable."

"No."

"Then we'll leave. You only had to ask."

No one cares when they go. No one notices. Jason's not interesting in this room full of stripped-down freezing boy.

In the road's snow-dark, Gordon tells him, "I wasn't lying to you. My sex life is complicated, but I've never had a taste for children."

Jason flickers.

"I know. You're not a child. Except you're seventeen and I'm fifty, so I say you are." He turns on the radio.

They're too far out from Saskatoon for FM signals. CBC radio AM at this hour is news discussion — deep, luminous accents colouring patches of the world. Arts programming later. Jazz at ten.

Breathe in. Breathe out. Watch the road.


GORDON'S MORE INTERESTING than a publicly funded education, but school's still the centre of Jason's universe. He has to keep one eye on Jennifer. And, unless he feels like leaving home and living on the streets of Saskatoon until he freezes to death, he has to go to school. Six and a half hours a day, five days a week, plus bussing, plus homework. He doesn't really know anyone under forty — except Seth, except Peter — who doesn't go to school with him. And it's not like any of them can escape. Bear Hills has as many kids in the Comprehensive schools as it has residents in the town; they're going to notice alienated youth running amok. Only strange, neglected, town-dwelling children cut school, because only they can get away with it.

If no one takes care of you, if you live in the town, you can stay in bed. Or, if you have desperate, twitchy parents, you wait 'til they leave, and then go back to bed. Sleep or read comics.

There are only three TV channels out here, and one of them is in French. In the daylight hours, you can watch *All My Children* or *Coronation Street* and pretend to be your own grandma.

Jason hasn't watched soaps since his grandfather died and his grandmother moved to Victoria. She said she wanted to live a couple of years of her life without snow. When she died, there wasn't a funeral. His aunt just flew out, collected the urn, and they interred her in the family zone of the cemetery, the next spring. Until then, she lived on a shelf in Brenda's office at work.

Wasn't even her mother, but she was willing to keep the urn. She probably still has it, empty now, on a shelf. If anyone else in the family dies, she'll re-use it.

She has her office in the town. If Jason goes walkabout, she's going to see him.

So school. It structures his days. Three morning classes, two in the afternoon. No recess since he left elementary school, but they have ten-minute intervals between classes — smoke breaks for students and teachers. Bell rings, everyone grabs his or her parka and dashes outside. Steps past the chain-link fence that marks the school grounds' edge and lights up.

Smoking on school grounds is not, of course, allowed. Technically, there's a resolution on the school division's books that students aren't supposed to see their teachers smoke. But maybe a third of the students smoke, and all the teachers do, and the trees here are scrawny, abused sticks. There's nowhere to hide.

Between morning and afternoon stretches the lunch hour. Time to go home, if you live in town. Maybe time to appear, if you cut morning classes. For ninety percent of them, though, it's just a hiatus. They're trapped. The school's *in loco parentis* from 8:30 to 4:00, and the children must have a trained eye kept upon them.

Stay the fuck inside.

In winter, it's not that hard. Only crazy people and smokers go outside, unless one of your friends has a place in town you can hang out. Jennifer used to take off with that towering Ginger-thing, but she's stopped going. So now, really, she's never out of his sight.

If you stay at school, you have certain options: 1) join a club (pep rally, newspaper, cooking, peer counselling, calculus); 2) lurk in a classroom until the supervising teacher flees for a cigarette, then pile the desks into pyramids; 3) lurk in non-classroom spaces and molest the object of your affections; 4) lurk in off-limits areas and molest the unwilling; 5) take up intramural sports. Four hundred kids and a few extra all up in each other's faces. The school newspaper is composed of half a page of sports scores and two pages of gossip columns. Who's making it with whom. Who smoked parsley because someone told them it was pot. Who may or may not have, while drunk, done something obscene with a farmer sausage.

The school newspaper is run by small, malicious freaks. They don't bother to make anything up; they just print every rumour reported as truth and then blink wide-eyed innocence at the person who hunts them down and threatens carnal murder. Movies present school newspapers as bastions of investigative journalism. Movies are written by people who never went to high school. Jason's never seen a TV high school half as savage as his. Within the brick walls they're shut up in, you can say anything you want about someone. The only authority-sanctioned response is to ignore such slander. Possibly, if the tale is hideous enough and easily traceable to one teller, that person might be taken by the scruff of the neck and forced to apologize. But that's it, and they don't have any way to check that the story ends there. More likely, it turns into legend, gets repeated for years.

Jason's determinedly ignoring the bathroom etching that informs the world how *Jason H. sucks dicks.* Something very particular about that final *s.* Jason sucks *many* dicks — not just, supposing it's possible, his own. His alternative to ignoring the wall writing is to dig up the shotgun from its burial place, bring a couple of bombs, a hunting knife, and something toxic made out of farm chemicals to school and really have at it.

He isn't going to do that. He might think about it, though.

He does manage to intercept the first layer of stories about Donna and Jennifer, though. They show up in a note to the newspaper, written as a blind item. Something about Jenn's tendency to lie with her head in Donna's lap during lunch time. He spots it on the computer-lab floor when the news staff leaves.

He burns the note with a lighter out in the snow. Then he finds the assistant editor and explains to her, quietly, exactly what he'll do if she prints that shit. And she might claim it isn't her, that she doesn't have the power, but the story doesn't surface. Maybe someday he'll give her some other story to make up for it.

Around him, people fight each other. A brawl in gym class feeds an open war "downtown" at noon. Battle site in an alley three blocks from the comprehensive school, on the path to the post office. It's outside school authority. Still, anyone reported to be fighting there on two separate occasions is forbidden to leave school grounds for the rest of the term, and at that point the fights have to relocate behind the prefab storage huts and take place in the snow. Major battles have a lead-up, but random guys fight every day. Girls fight less often, but more spectacularly. Glittering, athletic girls fight skanked-out, neglected children, who fight the odd, still-closeted lesbians with their hair spikes and boys' clothes that are obvious to everyone but them. Guys crack ribs and fingers. Girls take off skin strips and leave deep bruises. One of those chicks takes you on, and you'll be infertile for years and septic everywhere she scratched you.

Jason used to love watching those girls, when his attention had room for more females than Jennifer. He really liked the silver-white bleached ones with their emery-honed little claws. His mom said once, when she was washing Jason off after Jennifer'd clocked him when they were both tiny, that if Jason developed a thing for scary girls, it was going to be Jennifer's fault.

She had no idea.

HE NEEDS SOMETHING to do that doesn't involve watching Jennifer. Other people are watching him. The newspaper freaks are getting their own back on a scale he didn't expect. He doesn't know if stories about her fucking her cousin are better or worse than stories about her fucking Donna. He absorbs the first round, but after that he's out of the way. There's a limit to how much trouble he can stomach.

He doesn't want her to look at him anymore, either.

Years of hockey taught him how not to fight. Contact play taught him to hit a guy hard enough to fracture vertebrae, and he can always hear his dad's voice at the back of his head, asking him not to do it. Two or three guys were killed on ice, province-wide, in the last ten years. Every time, there were threats to suspend contact play entirely. They didn't. But the Junior Hockey Association organized trips to hospitals so the guys could get blood-and-guts acquainted with the results of a bad hit.

Med students loved seeing them. *This is a cadaver, kids. Feel free to immerse your hands in cold viscera.*

*You can throw up in that sink over there.*

A couple of guys wound up crouched with their heads down between their knees. Their tour guides always looked like they wanted to stick someone in a morgue drawer, just for an hour or so, to really make the point.

They could be taught. Their division developed a reputation for disturbingly clean play. A lot more guys turned eighteen with their dental work intact.

Hockey played in the school gym is lower velocity, so you can hit with your whole body and be reasonably sure that the body you hit won't die. You play in т-shirt and fleece university shorts and a decent, non-marking pair of runners. Plastic puck instead of rubber, but the puck was never a problem the way a hundred and fifty pounds of pissed-off teenage boy hitting your clavicle is a problem.

Landing on your fingertips and watching them bend the wrong way is a problem. The odd really fierce girl's shoulder hitting you in the gut is a problem. Jason's good with that last one. He's the only guy on the court who's not distracted by breasts in motion.

You sign a release to play. Your parents, too. The biology teacher has a standing request for a copy of the students' x-rays. He marks every new break they incur on the plastic skeleton by his desk.

They're good games. They always draw an audience. They even acquire a teacher who can't be convinced not to play.

Two or three people probably notice when Jason trips Mr. Klein. Twenty or so people see Klein crack a fist into the side of Jason's face.

Grey-dizzy.

When Jason pulls himself together, he's ten feet away and staggering. Four guys stand between him and Klein like a wall. Student referee with her hands out looks like she swallowed her tongue.

*I'm good*, Jason says.

Nobody believes him. Hands march him sweaty-cold to the principal's office, and turn his face to the light.

*How many fingers?*
*Two*
*What's the date?*
*No clue. Friday? Thursday?*
*Who's prime minister?*
Jason blinks.
*I know you're political enough to know that. Come on.*
*Chretien.*
*Good man. Go and change, and we'll get you a cold pack.*

Klein's outside, crouched like an angry student, and he looks at Jason like he wants to skin him. And Klein's not his teacher anymore, hasn't been for four years, but.

Jason has an all-new problem. He has a thirty-something frat- boy grade eight teacher who's *pissed* with him on an entirely personal level. Nothing to do with Jason's academic implosion. He's angry at Jason's tripping him, but mostly at being hauled into the principal's office like a kid.

They're not going to fire him. Doesn't mean he's not mad.

Nobody asked that fucker to join the noon hour games. He plays like losing might kill him. And they're all aware that he hates teaching, thank you — hates the sheer volume of insolence, snark, obscenity, contempt, disrespect thrown at him in the course of a day. Hates the way bored students try to get under his skin. But it's so easy. He's the biggest stupid kid on the playground, just with a few grey hairs and a B.Ed. He'd be way better off as a prison guard. That way he could beat the shit out of anyone who answered him back. Or he could join the army and be one of those guys on the TV news who picks up and tortures random kids in third world countries.

Those guys were from Saskatchewan, he remembers that.

Anyway. They don't need the newspaper freaks to circulate this story. *Everyone* knows that Jason and Klein have a problem.

People expect it to work itself out passive-aggressively, though. Jason will refuse to answer questions, and Klein will undercut his grades, and Jason will almost/not quite fail grade twelve, and that'll be it. They forget that Jason's too old to be this guy's classroom victim. He's just some punk kid who achieved what all students (even the sweet ones, the distracted ones, the unconscious ones, even maybe Jennifer and Donna) fantasize about. He took out a *teacher*.

Morrison hides Jason in the library for a couple of days. Jason stopped going after their weird condom talk, but the big guy holds him by the collar so he can't get away. Morrison offers him subversive texts, and duct tape, if he tries to move.

*So now you know, boy.*

*What?*

*The better part of valour's getting punched in the face.*

*That makes no sense.*

*But you know you won the fight. Why not back down, now?*

Jason shrugs.

Even Morrison can't watch him forever. He has a whole tribe of little freaks to govern, and Jason just has to wait until he's distracted and walk away. Morrison's nice, and maybe almost as smart as the average teenager, but he's operating on the theory that Klein's an adult, and he's wrong about that. He acts like he hasn't met the guy. Unless Jason belly-crawls to Klein and expresses how very, very sorry he is, they're still going to have to fight this out.

He waits for it.

Until hockey season ends and it's May and the weather's gorgeous. It's the beginning of the limited time Jason actually enjoys living in Saskatchewan. Caragana windbreaks flower yellow. Elm and willow spread, and the lilacs start, and Bear Hills' massive, secret population of very old people emerge from their little houses and start gardening. The place looks like some kind of small-town TV fantasy.

It's time for animal babies, and for all of nature to commence its mad fucking!

It's very pretty. So, he's told, are some of the girls. School offi-
cials are nervous. They've all made it this far — almost all the way
to graduation — and they have no business getting anyone pregnant now. The usual stay-indoors rule is suspended. The hockey
boys and assorted other boys are told in no uncertain terms to go
outside and play, far away from the female population.

When Jason's class — the one that graduated ahead of him,
last year — was almost finished elementary school, and they were
all huge and hulking over the kindergarten kids, they invented *It*.
*It* was the game that was not tag, because it was too huge, too
complicated, too *adult* to be tag. They recruited Jenn's class to
play so there'd be more of them. Jenn didn't play, but for six
weeks, almost two entire grades, boy and girls, randomly hunted
each other.

It probably gave Jenn ideas. She was always happier playing in
private.

What they do now is a version of a tag game, but this time no
one is *it*. Everyone hunts together.

Every guy with the energy and inclination to keep up takes off.
They go all around the town, like the ants marching, but faster.

Three days of it. 11:55 AM to 1:10 PM.

Run.

He runs through thick leaves and this alley full of the buffalo
bean flowers he used to pick for his mom until he realized they
were always covered in ants. Staggers to a halt. He's trying to
breathe. There are ten feet between him and the most vindictive
teacher he's ever been cursed to meet. All the other assholes have
dodged around them and taken another route back.

He's never seen a teacher come this far into the town proper. Most
of them live in Saskatoon or Battleford and commute out to Bear Hills
in the early morning. They settle in the staff rooms and only come
out to smoke or deal with the small, evil children they've been hired
to educate. Most of them would rather be dead than live here.

Jason had no idea you could teach and still have time to scout good fight locations.

Golf shirt and black polyester slacks. Running shoes. Klein grins, and Jason realizes the guy has bridge work. He took it out, just for this.

This moment when Jason looks into thirty-six-year-old eyes and understands that Klein actually has no memory of being his age. Thinks he does. Doesn't.

He takes a shoulder to the chest when Klein first hits him. Full body collision. There's a foot- and hand-scrabble while they go for purchase, and then hard fists all over. Body blows come over and over again. Klein beats his chest, shoulders, kidneys. Thighs now and then. Keeps all the bruises under Jason's clothes.

Except, now and then if you listen, you can hear Jason's cartilage go crunch. There's a softer sound when he hits Klein in the face again. He had to make it count.

Blood going down his throat isn't a new sensation, but then Jason realizes it's going to smear his clothes. *Shit*. Warm slide of it on the black and red of his T-shirt, and the ice-blue of his jeans, on his white runners when he spits blood.

He hooks a leg and brings the guy down. Kicks him maybe twice.

Then Jason stands over him and bleeds on him a bit. He says, "Jesus. I used to be in your *class*."

When he turns, using a bare arm to staunch his nose, he sees the remains of Jennifer's girl-pack watching him — not Jenn or Donna, but Amber the nail-biter, and Ginger. They look interested.

They follow him all the way back to school. He goes into the boys' washroom, and they lurk at the door, like they've decided he's food and they might get hungry.

Any minute now.

JASON GOES BACK to the alley later and studies his blood in the dirt. There's something that could be a tooth, crushed into the gravel, but all his teeth are still in place. He wonders if Klein lost another one while they were going at it. He uses his toe to scrape the mess into a pile. Builds up a wall of granite chunks picked out carefully from the loose stones, pink layer around the first grey one. He spits on top. Marks it with a leaf. Tiny shrine.

All his life he's built things like this without being able to explain them. After the accident, when he was new in their house, he invaded Jenn and Tori's room, then built tiny Barbie shrines in the pasture. Stick-shelter, leaves on the bottom, severed Barbie head with its mutilated hair up on a pile of soft organic matter. Shoes and purses around her. He hung the body from the shrine's frame with orange plastic twine.

Tori knew, he's sure. She didn't say much, but she set little detection traps around the door of her room, so she'd be able to tell if anyone went in without her permission. And once or twice he saw her playing with dolls that had been carefully stuck back together. Like movie-monsters with huge tits and orange skin.

He's not the only one who does this. Guys at school hoard chewed gum in wrappers until they have enough to build a new student. Store it all in the one unused desk in the back row of the algebra room, sculpt forms out of an entire grade's used gum. All that work just so the janitor putting desks into storage the first week of July finds that chewed-up, curled-up extra person sandwiched by wood laminate and cheap metal.

Discovers when he rips off the desktop that it's a perfect, aspartame-sweetened bog-man.

Guys who've farmed all their lives pick a sheltered spot for their dead machines. Let them all sleep together, turning from International Harvester red and John Deere green to rust colour.

Their wheels go flat and their tires house mice. They're waiting for the great matrilineal combine herds to visit the boneyard and fondle the radiators of their ancestors.

Maybe all farmers have fantasies of elephants.


AFTER THE GRAD parties have died, Jason feels weirdly empty. He wasn't quite ready for it to all be over. It gives him a reason to go back to Gordon's. He can show up on some random July night at 1:00 AM, smelling like hay and diesel, and Gordon will be awake. He'll have collected people. It's the summer Gordon starts giving very serious parties. Metal lawn chairs stay ranged around the fire pit, and people sit in them. They smoke up and eat beans out of cans heated in the fire. It's better company than Gordon showed him at the artists' colonies; these are his street-people friends from his intermittent junkie periods. They heard there was a good thing going on and started hitchhiking across Roger's Pass and out into the prairies just to check it out.

Jason can fold himself right in among them. It's how he meets the guy who claims to be Coyote.

Night in summer, he meets a scruffy Indian guy squatting by the fire with all this hemp jewelry around his neck and ribbons braided into his hair. Nice moccasins, not made of the electric-bright leather and rabbit fur most people have. He's also high. High as a kite.

High as the fucking *moon*.

For a while, Jason really believes the guy is Coyote, or some other animating spirit of the world, because the first thing he says? "What we need, man, is elephants. No, seriously. Not the fucking sad tiny circus elephants. W'need S'katchw'n elephants."

"Been dead kind of a long time," someone tells him, serious. "Last ice age."

"You have no imagination," Coyote says. "Where do animals come from?"

*Mud.*

*Fish.*

*Other animals.*

*Evo-*lution.

*Jesus.*

*Noah's ark?*

*God made 'em.*

"No," says Coyote. "See." Standing up, he looks deeply, frighteningly sane. "The world. Is on the back of a turtle."

"And the turtles go all the way down!"

"No. No, *fuck* you and your *Brief History of Time* reading like you know what it all means. Little crippled physicist's hooked in to the universe. You listen to me. Animals come. Because you *sing* to them. Anybody can make an animal if they know how. Not mad scientist shit, either. A real animal."

Fire spark. Jason wonders what they're burning. It doesn't — quite — smell like tires. Brush wood underneath, but there's definitely something inorganic being destroyed up top.

On the other side of the fire, "You're so full of it."

Coyote's still on his feet. He walks around the fire steadily, trying really hard to look sober. The woodsmoke follows him.

He says, "I. Am. Coyote. I am Nanabush. People know not to call my name Weesakeechak in winter. Do not make me fuck your shit up."

Gordon says, "Coyote must think he's a black man in the ghettos of L.A. Sit down. I'll build your damn elephant."

Coyote looks... something. Mollified. He drops down, mutters to himself for a few minutes, then goes away to see if there are any hot dogs.

And later Jason comes back from a piss in the trees to find Coyote chewing on a handful of mystery meat and cheap sugared bun. Big kick of chutney relish on his breath when he talks.

"I know something you don't know."

"Okay."

"You, little man, are queer. Bent. A fucking fairy. Gayer than a purple hat."

Blink.

"No, see," says Jason, "I knew that."

"Oh." Coyote chews. "Wish I had ketchup." Pause. "Too bad you're white. You're smarter than the average farm boy, aren't you?"

"They keep telling me."

Grin. Coyote has no front teeth. "Good. You keep Gordon company for me. I want my elephant."

# « CHAPTER 5 »

JASON NEEDS SOMETHING to do if he isn't planning to go to university. His mom watches him when he visits her, but she's seen his transcript and she doesn't have the money to pay his tuition herself, so she doesn't bring it up. His dad puts him to work farming. But even in summer, there's a limit to how much time he can spend on grass and livestock. Eventually, he gets tickets to a field party south of Battleford.

It's a good one. There are a couple of local metal bands, but most of it's electronic music. He hasn't heard this stuff before, but it works for him. In the huge, open night, it eats up the world and rattles down to the magma at the bottom of the earth's crust.

He comes back with a boyfriend. It's a new thing that he's trying.


FENTON LOOKS LIKE he wants to comment on the sheer volume of old leather Gordon's collected, but Fenton is a tiny punk with a taste for redneck metal bands. He has no room to judge. They were bored, and Gordon's place is close. It's somewhere to go hang out.

This isn't love, just Fenton has his moments. He's small and strange and interested in Jason's anatomy. Only, it's like Fenton's from another planet. He's lived all his life in Saskatoon. The only time he saw Bear Hills before Jason brought him out, he was riding a Greyhound home from a music festival in Edmonton, and got out to stretch his legs. He's never lived in the country. He thinks this is the edge of the world.

It should be funny: Saskatoon's not exactly urban. It's a tiny city surrounded by empty country and flavoured with rednecks. It's still insular, though. You grow up in one of the city's suburban tracts and you might never notice there's a world outside. Beyond the limits of Saskatoon, there's a blank space that stretches six hours to Edmonton or eight to Calgary. The trip smells like air conditioning and snow, and diesel from the road.

When they're in town, Fenton leans against the truck like he's stumped into an S&M version of *High Noon*. He graduated more than a year ago, but he just came out this spring, and — so Gordon tells Jason — you're sixteen until you come out. So functionally, he's a baby. Fenton wears knee-length baggy cut-off jeans and *TOOL* t-shirts. He dyes his hair with Kool-Aid. He's so femme you could start a riot at a hockey game just by turning him loose. If Jason were ever, *ever* planning to come out, he wouldn't do it like that, but he can see the appeal of scaring the shit out of people.

He thinks maybe Fenton hasn't been in a lot of fights, yet.

And Fenton's happy enough just to come hang out, afternoons. Jason blows off whatever he's doing. Attempting to fix a tractor wheel. Inoculating calves. They go see Gordon.

Fenton is fascinated by the piles of leather. Gordon's visited every auction he could find listed; he brings back old saddlery, harness, farrier's tools. Sales where people came for the antiques and usable farm equipment, Gordon buys out the contents of the barn for ten dollars. Takes it all home in the back of his Corolla and reduces his garbage-bagged collection to its leather components. There are saddles half-flayed on his porch, abandoned when he got tired peeling the leather away.

*'S my fucking elephant skin.*

Appropriate joke to follow about fucking elephants, and the damage it does to one's bedsprings.

Coyote got into Gordon's head. It's sort of interesting to watch.

Jason hasn't tried to explain Coyote to Fenton. Not that Fenton wouldn't believe, exactly, but he might take it a bit too intensely, like it's an article of faith instead of some weird shit that happened. He'd build a little, entirely serious shrine and burn incense and just... no.

So they sit between the saddles on Gordon's porch and watch him stitch up the first elephant bits. Then Jason watches, and Fenton lies in the shade and reads the copy of *The Naked and the Dead* that Gordon threw at him to shut him up. Later, Fenton watches, and Jason curls up on the floral velour couch that's landed on Gordon's porch, possibly straight from space, and sleeps.

He wakes up and sees Gordon under the willow shade, cutting leather off saddle trees. Some of the antique ones are gorgeous, when decades of accumulated dirt and animal sweat and oil are stripped away. Hand-tooled ornamentation under the water damage, with vaguely Spanish designs stamped and stitched into everything. It's old school — the idea that a good western saddle should be decorated everywhere you can sink a needle or a knife ran wild over those seats. Leather conchas fall off like coins when Gordon cuts through the thongs holding them to the saddle frame.

Jason shifts and goes back to sleep. He wakes up in the early evening with his head against Fenton's knee and his bare feet sunburned. *The Naked and the Dead*, lying open on the porch, smells like alcohol.

Fenton doesn't look drunk. Gordon, though, is drinking like he might have to swim at some point tonight and he needs to be a fish before that time comes.

OTHER DAYS, FENTON comes out and Jason's wired, and they go out on bikes. Fenton bitches that he's never been a jock, but he can almost keep up. Anyway, the ringing in Jason's ears thins out the sound of whining.

His ears have rung for two and a half years. It's the echo of that enormous gunshot sound that he only half remembers. He blocks the reverb with music, blasting tapes through his headphones hard enough that he burns out a set of earbuds every two or three months. He has a Walkman. Rechargeable batteries all over his basement den. On the tractor, he wraps himself in sound. On a bike, he doesn't even have to turn the volume up all the way. So he blasts *Back in Black* and surges ahead of Fenton down the grid roads, towards Gordon's place.

Not all the roads are graded. The one up the west side of Gordon's place is only dirt. He hopes Fenton'll like it — the trail could have been designed for mountain biking, if you accept that you're mountain biking in Saskatchewan, so the hills are small and the ground's all sand. Tree roots go straight down to the water table. The rock bones of the planet are hundreds of feet down. So it's soft, but the trail is gorgeous and long and rough and riding it burns through his thighs. Fenton can almost keep up; Jason only has to stop and wait for him occasionally. He goes two miles up the road, riding in wheel ruts and over tangled, allergenic plants. Pigweed clogs in his spokes. Russian thistle pokes through shoe nylon enough that Jason doesn't put his feet down if he can help it. There's creeping portulaca here, and buffalo beans full of ants, and spear grass. The ride ends in a sand quarry.

Jason's been coming here for years, since before Gordon lived adjacent. There was a time, living in the island colony, when his whole family biked. He remembers his dad driving him into Saskatoon and helping him pick out this bike from the big two-storey cycle shop on 20th Street, where the hookers are. His first bike (red, banana-seated, predating their coastal excursion) came from there too. It had handlebar streamers. Training wheels that caught on the yard weeds. This bike's silver, mountain-framed, and Jason's put on six inches since he got it. He learned to adjust the height for himself in the farm machine shop. He's taken it apart and put it back together, winters, to remind himself how it feels to ride it.

He should wait for Fenton, stay with him, but Jason's competitive on levels that Fenton hasn't really discovered yet, and if Jason wanted someone he always had to be *nice* to, he'd be dating a girl.

Anyway, he likes being chased. Fenton's not as fast as Jason is, but he's smart enough to find ways around that. Jason just has to piss him off enough to make him play dirty.

Shirtless Fenton on his own bike, perched on the edge of a dune in the quarry, snarls at Jason. Half *slow the fuck down*, half *I'm gonna get you, asshole*. It's really sexy. Fenton doesn't have fight reflexes, though. He's too attached to the white lines of his face and body. He hasn't got any idea what a little rough-housing could do for him.

Jason's halfway up the dune before Fenton understands that Jason isn't just coming up to meet him. He scrambles back, then, instead of launching himself at Jason like he should. He goes down hard when Jason jumps on him. Whimpers when Jason collides with his gut.

The ground gives out while they're wrestling. Sand-slide down to the track with Jason holding Fenton down. Grinning at him, because it's *funny*. The fucking *earth moved*.

He's still waiting for Fenton to get the joke, or at least the reference, when Fenton hits him in the face. Jason hears his nose go crunch, and it isn't sexy at all.

HE'S STILL IN the dirt when Jennifer comes looking for him. He's been single for three or four hours. Boyfriendless. His blood clotted a while ago, but his nose still hurts. Lumps of dried blood are clumped somewhere between his nose and his throat; he won't be able to spit them out for at least another day.

Jenn says, "It's good to know you can take care of yourself."

He flips her the bird. There are little dark blood-spots in the sand around him.

"Your boyfriend kind of stormed into the yard. Took his bike and his car and left. That psycho you hang out with hadn't seen you, so your dad decided to send out a search party. You guys have a fight?"

"Yeah."

"What about?"

"I'm an asshole redneck jock. And he's a whiny fairy with no sense of humour."

Jennifer shifts in the saddle. Her new horse doesn't have Djinn's neurotic appeal. In Cricket's last life, she was something predatory. Fifteen hands of don't-fuck-with-me.

Maybe in its next life that horse will be his boyfriend. They might suit each other.

She says, "Are you riding your bike home, or do you want to ride with me?"

"I'm going to lie here for a while and feel sorry for myself."

"Something might come out of the woods and eat you."

"Your horse might eat me."

"Fine. Next time, send up a flare or something so we know you aren't dead."


JASON GOES HOME, pushing his bike, when the mosquitoes rise. It's early evening, no wind, and if he lies out here all night he won't have any blood left by morning. He had bug spray at one point, but he sweated it off. He needs the extra-strength toxic shit they smear on the cows' backs to keep the bugs off all summer.

Sand in his shoes feels like the blood-grit in his nose. Two miles goes slower when he's on foot, and when he sees the back edge of Gordon's place, he starts thinking about how he can get through Gordon's bush with the bike on his shoulder, because that really would cut twenty minutes off this miserable slog. Or he could actually ride the bike, except that he hurts in ways that won't be eased by straddling a metal frame.

Lights flicker through the trees in front of him, and for a minute he's grateful for the rescue, but the girl who gets out of the car isn't Jenn. It's Donna.

She isn't looking at him, maybe can't even see him in the twilight. Without the car's beams as backlight, it takes him a minute to understand that she's climbing through the fence. The electric current that Gordon runs through the unbarbed strand is minor, but Jason's still surprised that she touched the fence with bare skin. Her hair catches momentarily, and then she's through. Dark hair's left on the barb; bare shoulders covered with bug bites twist a bit while she shakes off the pull.

Walks away from him into the bush, toward Gordon's house.

Jason finds paper napkins in the glove compartment of her car and a half-empty water bottle under the seat. The water's warm and stale, and the napkins are fast-food relics with soiled edges, but together they're enough to wipe the worst of the blood off his face. He leaves the bloody paper mess on the car hood for her to find. See what she'll make of it.

FENTON LEAVES SOME of his clothes behind, and since he won't answer the phone when Jason calls, Jason guesses the clothes are his now. Scattered around the basement, in with the condoms that Fenton was really picky about, he finds a pair of army boots. An army-surplus sweater with satin epaulettes. Pentacle on a black shoelace. All those and the pride T-shirts Fenton gave him, when he felt like hinting that Jason should maybe come out. Be that guy. Jason was naked on his knees in Fenton's shitty bachelor apartment when Fenton gave him the first one. Examining the state of his hickeys in a bathroom mirror when he was awarded the second.

*I'm not gay but my boyfriend is . . .*

*Dip me in honey and throw me to the lesbians.*

The second one, no matter who you run with, is hilarious. Most of the guys Jason knows crack up if you just *say* "lesbian." When they were in elementary school, maybe grade four, somebody informed him very seriously that *lesbian* was an army rank. A special one involving sharpshooting. Same person told him that *gaylord* was a baseball player's cousin.

So if sometimes he plays street hockey in Bear Hills in his lesbians T-shirt (black, red text that looks just enough like the *No Fear* shirts everyone else is wearing this summer), that's fine. Guys read his shirt, choke on their laughter, and then he can knock them down.

Normal people wear shirts that say, *He who dies with the most toys STILL DIES*, and, *play hard / win everything / die anyway*. Jason liked those T-shirts, when he first saw them. He had one in his hand, last time he was in the mall, but then he heard Gordon in his head laughing at him. Because it's a fucking T-shirt, made by a multinational company. To make you play basketball in expensive basketball shoes.

And he's not sure that wearing a T-shirt that commercialized nihilism wouldn't cause Coyote to drop by and beat him up.

Anyway. Hockey.

He wasn't prepared for the number of guys who are leaving to go to university. The pick-up street games that get played in the paved area in town between the schools and the Church of the

Family in Christ involve a lot of older guys. Everyone who didn't go on to anything better. Guys like him. And even Jason wouldn't play these games if he didn't have a reason to. But he does: he's watching Donna.

She's usually around. She *lives* here, at least a little while longer. But she ranges out a lot, like maybe her dad's insane followers make her nervous the way they make Jason nervous. The church people are getting stranger. Not build-a-bunker strange, not yet, but going that way. In five or ten years, Jason thinks, they'll abandon Bear Hills and go somewhere farther out, maybe up north or to the B.C. interior. They'll start one of those cult-towns that looks respectable but later spawns TV news documentaries and scary magazine exposés.

Donna will be long gone by then. She's not stupid, and she's not that kind of crazy.

Donna's mother . . . he's not so sure. Her mother comes out, most nights. First just to watch the games, but then she starts nursing. Sits on the church steps with her arms around her knees. She pretends she's not grinning at all of them. She has a big first aid kit at her feet.

While she's holding a cold, wet towel against his bruised face, Jason asks how she knows to do this. She smirks at him (white teeth, little yellow stains at their edges, lines around her eyes). Says that Bible camp teaches you things the heathen would never believe.

Complicit look like *heathen* for some reason doesn't include him.

All the good mothers of the Church of the Family in Christ go out to a lake camp in the fall and run naked in the trees.

Of course they do. It explains everything.

Up close, she's so completely Donna's mother. And yet, she's married to that *guy*. The one who warns against filth and degradation and pedophiles and the Satanism of everyday life. Who took up that weird crusade against the drama club.

Donna's mother braces Jason's head while he spits blood out into her icy-green guest-bathroom sink and considers that he might have permanently broken some of the veins in his face. The first sign that he's an old guy now. Her other hand rests on the small of his back, right on his dirty lesbians T-shirt. Makes slow circles. *Don't throw up, baby. Breathe. Your face will put itself back together in a few days.*

*No it won't. I broke it. That asshole Klein broke it.*

*Nobody actually breaks their face. Breathe.*

He's braced to deal with her husband pushing the bathroom door open, but not for Donna to do it. She has soft pants on, and her T-shirt shows ink writing up her inner arms like math homework gone insane. Like nobody told her she doesn't have to do homework ever again if she doesn't want to. But she's right there, in her *jammies* like he hasn't seen her in years. She takes the wet towel and holds it while her mother goes looking for ice.

It's not that Donna's bigger than he is. She might weigh as much as Jason does, but he knows he's stronger. But she pushes him, hard enough to drop him down onto the closed toilet lid. Leans over him and tilts his head back toward the vanity lights. Absent-minded hands rub the nasal blood off his lip. There's still a clot stuck to her forefinger when she brings her hands up to touch his blackening eyes. Outlines him in thick blood, like eyeliner, and all he can do is stare at her.

THE ELEPHANT PROJECT moves indoors for the winter. It fills whole rooms of Gordon's house. The mud room is stuffed with leather; the back bedroom is full of hemp. Coils of rawhide appear in odd corners. Drilled lumps of glass that are going to be elephant eyes refract on the kitchen table. The elephant's brain is a coil-bound pad of sketches and a battered elephant joke book. Magazine cutouts sandwiched in glass: elephant toenails. Fragments of pictures of a box of Smarties. The elephant's brain says, *Why did the elephant paint his toenails?*

*So he could hide in a box of Smarties.*

*Have you ever seen an elephant in a box of Smarties?*

*No.*

*Works, doesn't it?*

Gordon has sketches for the elephant's frame. It's going to be made of red willow sticks. He can't get those until spring.

In the basement, though, there are other frames. They're smaller in scale, made of woven and twisted tamarack. Not a tree that Jason's seen before, but it grows in the bush up north — slick little conifer that sheds its needles in the fall. They use it to make duck decoys.

Gordon hit the flea markets, and now he owns every tamarack duck in existence. Jason thinks Gordon might have stolen some of them from crazy old men who live in the woods. Somewhere out there are old guys with damaged fingertips and missing skin where Gordon pried their weird folk-art objects from their not-quite-cold dead hands.

Shuffling old guys stagger along the northern highways, looking for their ducks like a slow, slow zombie movie.

The ducks, though. They're not cute. They're just woven baskets that look vaguely like birds. Bits of them are sharp. Or were. Now most of them are just sticks on the floor, because Gordon wanted to see how they were made. It keeps him busy. What with one thing and another, he says, winter's the wrong time to build an elephant. He filled up his whole house and then abandoned the elephant project, and now he's weaving tamarack girls.

They're smaller than the sprawling, ceramic boys that Jason saw from the church-studio window, but they're broader. Less naked. Not that they're *dressed*, but the tamarack medium limits detail. No nipples on the breasts. There are stick-tangles at crotch-level that shield them like pubic hair. His eyes, though, always catch on the fat-rolls just above their waists, below their breasts. On their bellies.

No faces. Stick hair.

In the middle of one of the faceless heads are carefully inserted canine teeth. They're real, though Jason isn't sure what animal they were grown in.

Gordon says, "What do you think?"

"I think I'm scared."

"You should be. They're primal Venus figures. Unanswerable to men. Una*ffec*ted by men."

Gordon's proud of himself, like he's discovered the cure for cancer, or proven that not just God can make a tree.

He has more teeth in his sweaty hand.

"You're going to give the other one fangs?" Jason asks.

"Not the way you're thinking." The toothless girl-figure is crouching low enough that Gordon can bend over her like he's going for a little cellulose action. When he points to her spread thighs, Jason's not sure it's not just a random grope. "There."

Jason feels his eyebrows moving together without his help.

"Vagina dentata, boy."

Blink.

"Girl with teeth in her cunt."

Jason screws his eyes shut. He says, "Why?"

"Man's ultimate fear. The woman who seduces and emasculates."

Jason says, "Don't."

"It's part of the whole. An essential part of the installation."

"It's disgusting."

"Feel free not to look, then."

It's what his mom said when he complained about the yoni sculptures, back in the day, but Jason wants Gordon to know that this is fundamentally different. The tamarack girls have all the same flaws as the ducks: they're rough and wooden and utterly lacking in the fine details of a living thing. They still look essentially human. Their feet aren't differentiated into toes, but they have arches. Short, heavy girls with big feet. They look like every woman he knows.

IT'S NOT ALWAYS cunt teeth, but everyone's afraid of something.

For example (and this comes to mind immediately, proof you don't escape high school just by graduating). A teacher gets spotted walking out of Saskatoon's only Novelty and Triple-X store, and his students will tell that story forever. Years from now (not that many years, less than ten), you'll be able to get that shit online. Collect all the filth you want in the privacy of your own home, and nobody will be able to see you.

Until then, you're doomed by a single pair of furry handcuffs.

The issue's not so much magazines. Everyone has porn, and everyone knows how to get it. You expect men to have pornography. There are barns full of it, and basements. There are TV gags about daddy's *Playboy* collection. You don't live in infamy over magazines.

The issue, really, is dildos.

Big, scary, orangish fake rubber-plastic dongs.

They keep manufacturing them, so there must be a market. People out there who want dildos. Who're willing to buy them and use them. Deviants.

The opinion of the Bear Hills collective adolescent culture is that such people buy dildos that are large, intricately veined, strange smelling, and vaguely sticky to the touch. They really want to use dildos on teenage boys. There are teachers who keep such things in locked steel filing cabinets. It's the ultimate disciplinary threat, and handy for use in a variety of degrading pleasures they'll certainly take, once you're naked.

The dildo Donna waves at Jason is nothing like that.

It's pretty. Translucent evening blue, with shimmery starspots hanging in it. About as long as his hand. Smooth. Balanced on its scrotum-suggestive base, it shivers slightly with the room's vibrations.

Right there in the manse powder room, where anyone could walk in.

Jason doesn't care that the door's locked, or that he and Donna are the only ones in the house for as long as her mom is outside watching the hockey game and her dad is leading a prayer meeting somewhere miles away. The dildo's existence commands cameras. Every eye in the world turns toward its pretty blue curve.

She's good. Donna poured everything she knows about Jason's debased little psyche into a half-pound of shiny rubber and waved it in his face, and now she owns him. He shouldn't be surprised. She's been kicking his ass since his balls dropped, and now she has the resources of an entire university at her fingertips. All so she can drive home for the weekend and scare one boy. She can hound him with the dildo. Chase him through town with it. Duct tape it to his car. Leave it next to his name in the rink bathroom. Slide it into his hockey bag, his coat, the back of his jeans. Touch him with it.

Slide into his basement while he sleeps and take pictures of him with the dildo cuddled like a stuffed animal against his chest, blue glitter catching the flash and the holes in his T-shirt all showing. She can get in; he doesn't have any doubts.

Or, he can be her boyfriend. His choice.

There's this second where she looms over him. Big, hulking *girl*. Breasts up by his face. Whatever bra she's wearing, it does its job. Nylon and elastic, extra reinforcement. Those breasts might as well be suspended from her collarbone. And she's full of knowledge, new stuff he doesn't have access to.

He couldn't possibly say no to her. So this must be consent.

It means he has to visit her. Go to the city and hang out with her on the university campus. Go to classes. They don't seem to notice he's not registered. In the big science lectures, there's no way they could tell. After harvest, she expects him every day. He's supposed to show up on her doorstep in west Saskatoon, say *hi* to her nice,

Christian roommates, drive her to class. He has to get up before dawn. In the darkened lecture halls, he sometimes falls asleep.

Donna watches him. Not for the usual reasons, he thinks, but she must get off on it. He watches her in case she decides to devour him without warning. He watches doors in case Jennifer walks in. She doesn't. She's gone into the elsewhere of the city, taking classes that are different than Donna's classes, living in the residence towers and moving in one of those human packs he sees shifting from building to building. Lucky her.

Jason wonders whether he looks just enough like Jennifer to make Donna happy. There's some family resemblance, and his tractor-riding sunburn's reduced his facial skin to a precancerous mess. But Donna takes him around and introduces him to people. Band people. Art people. In the Arts lounge, while they're taking up an entire couch and watching the big-screen TV, she leans over and bites him on the neck. Sucks. Leaves him with a hickey and smeared girl-pink lipstick. Her smell (hair spray, peach deodorant, fruit-soap bath products) gets all over him and won't wash off.


HE DOESN'T WANT to fuck her, but she's interesting.

He likes all freakish girls, and Donna's smarter than most of the ones he's met. He shares space with her because they're supposed to be dating, and she leans against him and fills scribbler-notebooks left over from elementary school with numbers. She's developed a love for linear algebra that he won't try to comprehend. There's ink all over the book and on her hands. It's smeared at the corner of her mouth where the pen exploded while she was chewing it. It makes her look weirdly tribal. BiC-blue war paint. Somewhere under the baby fat layers of her, there's a woman hard enough to cut him.

And he might not be interested in her body, but she's interested in his. Intellectually. Maybe sexually. Maybe she really is still in love with Jennifer, and this is just scientific curiosity. The years of human development classes they were subjected to taught them to identify the human reproductive organs as they appear from the inside, in a sliced-off side view. They weren't told about the touchable bodies of the opposite sex. It's the fault of the curriculum that Jason's brain sketches ovaries and fallopian tubes when the world invites him to think about women's body parts.

He even drew them into a few of his porn magazines.

It's possible that *vas deferens* is all Donna's thinking when she touches him.

It's cold out.

After classes, in his truck cab because they can't do this where her housemates might be watching and he doesn't want to drive home, and it's dark and the windows are fogging. It's a cliché. It's not like they're going to get anyone pregnant here. She's just... holding him down. She traces muscle and hair and bone on him, and he shivers, twitches a bit when she tweaks his nipple.

Jason decides to see how she likes having bare skin in this cold. He hooks fingers into the waist of her jeans and pulls. They don't give. Jeans are supposed to stand up to an inhuman level of abuse, and hers have creased into knife-hard lines. He has to pull the buttons loose before he can peel the denim back. There's a faint pressure scar from years of jeans digging into her belly. Fresher red cross-hatching from the press of her tucked-in shirt.

She isn't prepared for it at all when he pushes her back and rolls up and licks at those marks.

DATING DONNA MEANS studying with her, and if he'd known he could feed off smart girls this easily, he would have tried it years ago. In the biology lab (and why don't they notice him there, where they seem to at least know most people's names?), they dissect animals: fetal pigs, frogs, crayfish, starfish, earthworms. Cut the little bodies open, slide their organs out and draw pictures of them. Hand in a lab report.

Donna's reports are works of art. She diagrams the preserved corpses of small animals in carefully shaded pencil crayon. She does muscle studies to supplement the lists of organs. All she wants of Jason is that he actually cut the thing up.

He's farmed most of his life. He hates farming, but he's basically good at it, and he's held more disgusting things than pig fat before. Norbert the fetal pig was never really alive. His tiny, immature testicles never dropped. Cutting them loose doesn't hurt him at all.

And then, across the lab, he sees Jennifer.

She has actual pig parts in her hand, maybe the only girl in the room who does. She looks at them close. His pretty, scarred-up cousin holds an eyeball at eye level and looks back at it. She has to know he's there, but she doesn't look around, and she doesn't look at Donna, either.

Guy from the next table presents Jason with a severed fetal penis at the end of the lab session. He smirks at Donna while he does it.

It doesn't mean anything in particular that Jason goes with that guy and spends an hour making out with him in the vast university parking field. Both of them smell like formaldehyde and porcine body parts, and they don't exactly remember each other's names.

Donna knows. She doesn't seem to mind very much.

She's *curious*.

It's the kind of curiosity that drives them back out to the farm so she can have the run of his bedroom. She sits on him in the cold underground, leaning towards the space heater's glow. There are blankets all around them. Jason might not even freeze when she takes all his clothes off.

She likes his street hockey bruises. There's spread-out purple blood just under his skin. Yellow-green spots from the blows that rained down on him last week and the week before. Raw pink places show where his blood vessels have just barely ruptured. He's trying to be careful of his nose, so he leads with his chest, and bruises happen.

He's unspeakably grateful that her nails are short. If she could, he's not sure she wouldn't open him up like the small, sad pig and sketch what he looks like underneath his skin.

Always touching him. Lines of his hair. Places that make him twitch.

She says, "Tell me about the guys. The ones you've had sex with."

"It's none of your business."

She sits down harder. Heavy on his hips like she doesn't really care his dick's under her and she might kill it. She's still dressed.

She says, "You wanted to know about me."

"No."

"Yes you did."

"Fine."

"So. You tell me and I'll tell you." Eyebrow quirk.

Psychotic cunt. If she was a boy he'd love her forever. So he tells her.

Everything he loves about sucking cock. Flesh in his mouth. What men taste like. Pulse on the underside. Breathing through his nose so he won't gag. The pre-cum slide on his lips. Semen on his tongue.

"You like the taste."

"No. It's like coffee — it tastes awful but I don't really care. Taste's not the point."

Pause. She slides down onto his leg, then lays her hands on his pelvis and studies the frame. Says, "Can I suck you?"

"What? *No.*"

"Why?"

"Because it's not up to my brain." He sighs. "I'm sorry."

Donna says, "Never mind. Turn over."

On his belly, his cock's protected, at least. Easier for him to relax. She rubs his back. Apology for the knots she tied his body into with that one question, or maybe she's just touching for her own sake. It doesn't matter: it feels good.

The aches whisper that he's only nineteen and he already randomly hurts. He didn't even work hard today. By the time he's old enough to live his own life, away from here, he's going to be too crippled to do half the things he's fantasized.

She strokes over his back, muscle and fat-soft places and spine-bone to his waist. Fingers under his boxers' elastic reach to his tailbone, out over the curve of his ass. She drops a hand down to the leg-hem of his shorts and rubs up under the flannel.

Donna's the only woman in his whole life who'll touch his balls like this.

Curious. She feels the shape of them. Works the sac between her fingers, measuring texture. Tugs on the fine hairs. Then rubs hard like she's mapping out what's underneath.

Mental image of all those mimeographed diagrams of the testes. He shudders.

"You okay?"

"Just thinking."

"Hmm." She eases off. Rubs her finger-pads slow along the seam of his scrotum. And then she shifts her weight, leans in close against his back, and tells him about Gordon.

SHE WANTED GORDON to teach her to draw. This was more than three years ago, when she was still trapped in high school, and the idea of real, applied art classes seemed incredibly remote. In school, they got standard assignments (draw an animal) and random chunks of theory (build a colour wheel; it should really turn) and busywork. And she wanted to draw. Better than she could. For real. And Gordon was right *there*, within shouting distance of Jennifer's place, and he used to teach at Emily-fucking-Carr College.

154 « WHITETAIL SHOOTING GALLERY

His work's in the National Gallery of Canada, and it shows up in touring collections; there are books about him.

"My mom's an artist."

"Your mom's not what I had in mind. No offense."

She was fourteen. She found him meditating in the pasture, when she was out there and Jenn was elsewhere. So she asked him.

*Teach me.*

The fact that she can draw well enough to apply to art school —

*You applied to art school?*

*I'm applying now. Emily Carr. UBC, too. Not the point. Pay attention.*

— is because of his teaching. He guided her hand. Showed her how to look at the world. So in that sense, it worked.

Just. He wanted her to be his muse. She did it for four years. And she didn't realize how sticky it was going to be.


DONNA LEAVES A note taped to the basement wall, next to the light switch at the foot of the stairs:

*you think you're so smart*

*but I've seen you naked*

*and I'll probably see you naked again*

Jason's not sure whether it's directed at him or at Gordon. Her protector or the guy she wants him to take down.

Jason hasn't had a chance to play knight since he stopped running through the woods with Jennifer. Jennifer used to be the wizard, and he was the knight, except for that one time they don't talk about, when he was the princess. Now Jenn is a witch, and it's not the same thing.


DONNA'S A WITCH, and she still sings in church. Every Sunday, two services. She goes home for it. White blouse, black slacks, flat shoes. The mess of her hair is twisted and pinned to the back of her head so her eyes show. With her usual mask of too-dark concealer and black eyeliner stripped away, you can see an almost-real girl.

She flickers when Jason comes in. She's up front, in full voice, staring up at God and not at him at all.

Jason's never been to church before. His parents wouldn't have taken him together, and separately, they were even less likely. The sum of his Christianity is picked up from Bible stories on TV and the group sings of *Jesus Loves Me* in elementary school. They spent two years singing the Lord's Prayer, too, after their teachers gave up just making them recite it.

Donna doesn't sing anything he recognizes. It's nothing a congregation could sing with her.

And then she's finished and he can't just leave. He has to sit through an hour-long lecture on purity and the place of Man, because he's too chickenshit to stand up in front of his girlfriend's father and walk out. The guy has a terrible look on his face, and he stares at Jason. He's going to redeem his daughter's barely-faithful heathen boy-thing or burn out in the attempt.

It's not that Jason doesn't appreciate it. It's nice somebody cares about Jason's eternal existence. Only, religion doesn't work on him. It feels like white noise. Nothing in him cries out for God.

These people believe in Jesus on a level that Jason doesn't even believe in sex.


HE DOESN'T BLAME Donna for ruining Gordon for him. He thinks maybe that was just coming, the future hurtling toward him. Jason hated the tamarack girls for weeks before he figured out what they were. Not just naked girls but *his* girls, naked. Donna and Jennifer and even Tori. And his aunt Brenda. And his mom. All the fierce, bright women that he knows.

The teeth — Gordon put cunt teeth in all of them — just make it worse.

Jason thought about burning them, the dolls. A little gasoline, a couple of matches, a call to the volunteer fire department once he was sure the whole house would go up. Still. He's never seen a fire catch the wind and move cross-country after snowfall, but it's still a risk. He's invested enough in the land not to want to send up sparks. Also, he thinks he might miss the elephant if it died.

So instead he deals with it like an adult, as much as he knows how. He lets himself in, Saturday afternoon, and finds Gordon lacing the elephant's toenails onto rawhide.

Jason says, "Give me the pictures."

"Hmm?"

"Of Donna." He thinks. "And Jenn. And Tori. All of them."

"Jason —"

"All of them."

The naked Vietnamese kid might have been sick and freezing in that church, but at least he knew what they were making out of him. Jason's women never signed up to be the models for this kind of sick shit.

"I can't."

"I'll call the police."

"I *can't*. They're . . . I put the pictures in the dolls. To give them minds."

"Then take their heads off." *Or I'll tell.* He could make a suggestion to Brenda. She's a lawyer. She could eat Gordon for breakfast.

While Gordon's thinking about it, Jason digs through the mess in the mud room and finds a saw.

HE BRINGS THE artwork to Donna. All her math runes and the raw places where her jeans dig show up in the sketches. Gordon convinced her to take her clothes off. Jason's not sure how Gordon did that, but Jason's never done anything an adult told him to, unless he wanted to do it anyway, so he's not an expert on the power of authority. The sketches are bad, but at least Donna knew about them. The photos are worse, and he doesn't think she knows about those, so he doesn't show her.

Donna and Jennifer, topless, in the bush in his family's pasture, running. Donna squatting to piss with her jeans around her knees. Arched against a tree, scratching her naked back. Jenn stripped halfway down after riding, sponging herself off in what must be the barn.

Gordon must have been stalking them for years to get pictures like that.

STANDING IN GORDON'S basement with a severed tamarack head in his hands, Jason says, "You shot her."

"No."

"You're fucking crazy and you *shot* her."

"I've never shot anybody."

"You shot *these*." Waving the photo that was crammed in the head at him.

"That's not the same."

"Are there other ones? Are there negatives?"

"No."

"If I find out you're lying, I'll kill you."

"Jason."

"Are you at least sorry?"

"Jason."

"*What?*"

"Do you even remember what happened?"

He remembers being deaf, and the smell of cordite. Smoke and dry grass. Blood and burned skin and the horse panting. Somebody shot Jennifer, but it doesn't have to be him. Maybe he missed. Maybe he never picked up a gun at all.

He couldn't have shot her. Not really.

"Jason, you were *right there.*"

"You were hunting them for years. *Years.* God, you make every-thing dirty."

"I heard gunfire. My gun blew up when I tried to shoot it."

Jason's tired of this. He throws the tamarack head at Gordon, hard enough to knock him backwards. Goes digging through the remaining girls with the saw and his bare hands. Every girl he rec-ognizes, he stuffs in his jacket. Then he goes back and picks up the rest, too. He has to get them all away from Gordon. Gordon shouldn't be left alone with anything female.

Behind him, Gordon says, "Can you understand this has noth-ing to do with you?"


HE GIVES THE sketches to Donna, but he gives the photos to his aunt Brenda. Sits with her at the kitchen table and tells her every-thing he can remember about Gordon. All the way back to finding him with his face burned off in the pasture. All the way back to seeing him at the Salt Spring Island colony. Everything he's seen and most of what he suspects.

Jennifer isn't home. She visits only occasionally. He's grateful — he couldn't do this if she was here. He can barely do it for her mom.

Brenda takes notes. Listens to him like he supposes she listens to the assholes she defends in court. She doesn't have to like him; she just has to listen, remember, repeat. She wants evidence and clear statements. She wants to know what happened, as if Jason actually knows.


DONNA VISITS HIM on weekends. She carries her sketchbook in her book bag, and some of Gordon's drawings are taped into it. Like she didn't even hate the pictures, she just wanted them back.

There are pictures of Jason in that book, too. Donna stays over, some nights, and he wakes up at two-thirty or three to find her sketching him, as close to naked as he sleeps. He'll never get those drawings back from her.

When he joins a senior rec hockey league, she comes to a few games. He stays over a couple of nights at her place in the city, once she's decided she's sick of her roommates. When the school year's over, she'll never have to deal with them again. And school ends early for university students — in April, not June. So she's going sooner than he expected.

Her parents paid for her first year of university. She doesn't think they'll pay for art school. She talks to people on campus, and shaggy pot-smelling guys who swing by her place and freak out her roommates. Gets a job planting trees in northern Alberta. And then she disappears. Not off the face of the world, but out of Jason's. By the time he moves to Saskatoon, she's gone. Packed everything she owned into a Girl Guides–approved backpack and took off. She sends him postcards, occasionally. Maybe twice a year. So he knows she goes to UBC, where she finds a way to fuse her artwork with that math obsession she's been carrying around. She might even finish a degree. And then she hitchhikes through the Rockies, down the Pacific coast and back again, joins a wymmyn's (with two y's and no phalli) agricultural collective on Vancouver Island.

She's good with computers. When they get a decent internet connection out there, she puts her little company online.

It's impressive. All-vegan porn — still pictures first, then videos. No animals are used, abused, or consumed by anyone in the production of this smut.

She collects tattoos. Those come as picture-postcards, no text attached. He keeps some of them on his fridge, where guys stare at them and ask what exactly Jason's into, anyway.

He just likes thinking about her. That blunt, red-haired witch crouched somewhere in the Pacific.

# « CHAPTER 6 »

JENN SAYS, "I need you to take care of Bentley."

Jason rolls over. He sleeps like a hurt thing, curled in on himself and making little whimpering noises that have less to do with psychic damage than with the state of his sinuses after all those times he broke his nose. She can feel him wake up under her touch. He shivers. It's enough movement to expose the laptop sleeping against his belly, warm like a purring cat, though more likely to ignite his sheets.

There's porn stacked underneath the computer, to keep it off the bedding, but he might not remember that. She could whisper *fire, fire, fire* in his ear and see how long it takes for him to panic.

He's having a relationship with that little machine. It's his girlfriend. He calls it *Rei*. She's not surprised he sleeps with it.

She's a little surprised he named it after a girl, but she's never been clear what all Jason's kinks are. And he's better off with an imaginary girl than a real one.

There were whole years she didn't want any kind of relationship with Jason. There are things she can remember about him, from when they were teenagers, that make her skin crawl. But Sarah asked her to check on him, maybe four years ago, and after that, Jenn was responsible for him. For making sure he's not dead.

He's good at taking care of animals, at least. A lizard scurries out from under his bed and settles on the warm laptop like it's the best hot rock ever invented.

"Hey," he says.

"Take care of my dog, will you? I have to go out of town for a day or so."

"Is there a reason your guy friend can't do it."

She doesn't want to talk about Shane. "You owe me," she says.

He doesn't ask what for. Instead he sits up. "How bad is it?" Like he's really worried. "Is anybody dead?"

"Not yet." Really, she should have phoned him instead. Explained on the drive over and just left Bentley in Jason's living room, but she wasn't that awake herself. And she's not always sure it's safe. Her dog's enormous, but Jason's house is full of crawling things. If he doesn't take the right precautions, she might not see her dog again. "I have to go up to La Ronge because some asshole took a bear home and it tore a chunk out of one of his kids."

"It can't wait until morning?"

"It'll be morning when I get there."

He nods. "Do you want me to make you some coffee?"

"Sure. Thanks."

Jason's kitchen at 3:17 AM is entirely too male a space for her to deal with. He's the same guy he's always been — tall and vaguely jock-looking and still not as heavy as she is. Sometime this winter he dyed his hair, so he now has dark roots and red tips. It wouldn't be unsexy on someone a bit more fey than he is.

His fridge door is the usual horror show of tattooed body parts and random strangers' dicks. She thinks this is why his mother doesn't check on Jason herself. There might be girl parts pictured in the mess, but Jenn's not willing to dig through just to find out.

She reminds herself that dog eyes can't process images. That her dog looks like a bear in the dark, and Jason lives like a bear with furniture, and they're neither of them quite as dangerous as she wants to believe. Too bad.

Curls up on the floor to kiss her dog goodbye.

TRAVELLING BY CAR at night makes her dizzy. It didn't used to. She remembers riding the school bus and not needing to hold onto her head with both hands. Most of the school year, it was dark when she left home in the morning and again by the time she got back. She remembers Christmas lights on the snow. The bus dropped her off at the road, and she walked towards the house in the dark. Then the yard light's motion sensor would pick her up, or pick up Tori's faster movements, and it would flare yellow-brilliant and burn her retinas if she didn't remember to screw her eyes shut.

That memory's mixed up, right now, with vague thoughts about cold-demented deer streaking across the road.

Jason's coffee didn't help. She's sick with the flu and drugged out to the edge of her attention span. The decongestants she took left her sinuses feeling burned out, and her painkillers are a distant memory against the force of the virus working its way through her skull. The only time it doesn't hurt, she's asleep, and she can't settle down in a moving vehicle. Without sleep, her anxiety levels will eventually rise up and drown her.

She leans toward her purse to see whether she's carrying her meds. Zoloft, this cycle. And it does help. It's her raft on the elusive serotonin ocean with the tide always going out.

They make two stops so she can pee. Nothing's open at this hour, so she pretends the snow gives her some cover while she squats in the ditch. No idea whether Shane's watching.

He might be. People have odd little pleasures, and once you've sunk down into biology, it's easy to forget human norms altogether.

Shane isn't even the most demented wildlife agent she knows. She shouldn't have slept with him, but that isn't his fault. He's appealing. He makes a decent work partner, too. In the past year and a half, they've worked humane society detail, collecting small and medium-sized creatures who need rescuing from human hands. Badgers in barns. Raccoons in the garage.

She remembers the wolverine in Black Lake entirely too well. And it wasn't even her arm that needed reconstructive surgery, after.

They shot the wolverine, in the end. It was a stupid, miserable day, but she's still grateful they didn't have to bring it all the way down to Saskatoon in the truck over the winter ice roads. Someone would have decided it belonged on display in the zoo, at least for a while. The flesh and blood of zookeepers and biologists buys a new carnivore installation. Show the children!

And then some asshole would have climbed over the double barrier and the warning signs, and reached through the page wire, and been chewed up by the nasty thing that only wanted to be left alone. The zookeepers would have been sent in to retrieve the body.

Or else it would have worked its way loose, savaged a volunteer, eaten the red pandas on loan from Chicago, and raged through suburban Saskatoon.

*Crazed zoo predator slays 8, consumes bookmobile; zookeepers presumed to be at fault.*

"Are you awake?"

"How cold is it?"

"Display says –22°."

"No, I'm not awake."

SHE ROUSES A LITTLE in Prince Albert. They put gas for the truck on Shane's credit card, because no one was awake to pre-approve expense forms. Jenn buys sugar with the cash stuffed in her pockets. Gummy animals, pixie stix, Willy Wonka-brand confections. *Nerds! Everlasting Gobstoppers! Thank you, Roald Dahl, for bringing the world a story that led to a cracked-out movie that led to the*

*most brain-rattling candy available on the Western Canadian market.*
*Thank you.* She contemplates the energy drinks in the cooler but
doesn't buy one.

There's a rack of CDs positioned for impulse purchase. It's horri-
ble stuff, but maybe at this stage you have to be a cultural throwback
to buy CDs at all. There's a lot of country music in the display, and
some adult contemporary horrors. Half-hidden behind *Sounds of*
*the Highway*, there's a Jon Secada disc.

Fear this: there are people whose entire musical knowledge is
gleaned from convenience stores in rural Saskatchewan.

She says to Shane, "Do we have music?"

"I brought my discman and an adaptor for the tape deck. You can
dig through my CD bag." Shane's eyes flick over the display. Maybe
he's their target market. If someone didn't buy those albums, they'd
have replaced them with sugar and dried meat by now.

When she's sorted through his discs, Jenn decides the gas station
music might be an improvement. It's not that what he has is awful,
exactly, but Shane's musical taste locked up within a couple of years
of his finishing high school. He hasn't bought anything new since
1997, leaving them doomed to roll across asphalt and ice listening
to the Goo Goo Dolls and other sweetly unirritating post-grunge
acoustic rock of the broken-hearted white-boy variety.

She doesn't think he's broken-hearted. Not really.

If they can settle back into being friends, she'll re-educate him
at some point. Dig out her iPod and hook it into his veins. Maybe
try, in her edge-of-the-world white-girl way, to share her unexpected love of hip-hop with him. Explain how much it's possible
to love something that's so explicitly not *for* you.

Shane looks at her and sighs, and Jenn abandons the idea.

"Do we know how big the bear is?" she asks.

"Small."

"Smaller than a Chevy?"

"Smaller than a coyote. Guy thought it'd be a good pet, didn't
seem to get that baby bears have claws too."

"Where did they even get one this small at this time of year?"

"I have no idea. I got called when you did. Go up north, they said. Rescue a bear from human interference. Take Jenn; she's good with bears. You like her. Buy yourself a coffee." Shane grins, but he's hunched in on himself. He didn't want this.

He just wanted to take care of people's cats, but then he had to go and develop a wildlife specialty.

Shane's vet work encompasses large dogs, small house pets, and the university's collection of land-bound exotics. He's good with the muskoxen, who were hand-raised by the biology students and who kiss up for treats. The only genuine wildlife specialists at the university deal with raptors. Some owls. People bring the birds in, injured, and the school either puts them through full rehab or patches them up and brings them to the zoo. The zoo's only a couple of miles away, after all, and it has a cage housing a number of battered owls. Survivors of freak accidents who can turn their heads completely around.

Big yellow eyes, slightly crossed from a nasty knock on the head.

Shane looks a lot like a damaged bird, but that's not his field. The raptor vet is a predatory guy, and probably drove Shane away. He twitches like a man who's been mauled by bird-people. He digs at his own skin sometimes. Scratch scratch scratch along his arm.


DRIVING NORTH FROM Saskatoon is pretty in the summer, haunting in the winter, and nothing in the dark. The prairies close up and the trees push through, and then the dirt falls away and you're surrounded by bare rock. Big juts of granite. Forest fires strip down long sweeps of brush, leaving behind just lodgepoles and black ground. Fireweed springs up in the summer.

It hasn't snowed much this winter, but Jenn still can't see the lakes. At night, there are ditches, and snow, and the road — black asphalt and black ice. Occasional oncoming lights. So she has to imagine it, this empty dip in the world. High plains to the south drop down to sea level in the Arctic. Bush starts halfway up and continues to the boreal treeline. Then a few hundred miles of muskeg and caribou. Saskatchewan itself isn't quite the far north, though; it's only the hollow centre of the country.

No seas here. Lakes all through the north, all frozen over.

The last century's weather patterns speak to profound landscape changes. She read through the outline in university: prairie geography and prairie ecology, and it came up again in native studies. At the turn of the last century, you could expect six weeks at –40°C. It was a weather pattern long enough to twist the resident plant life into desperate, fast-growing forms. The animals were all hung with deep, shaggy coats that used to be incredibly valuable on the open market, but aren't anymore, since the advent of warm synthetic fibres and paint-throwing anti-fur activists. And it doesn't get that cold anymore.

The last decade, they've started calling –25°C cold. Some winters it almost doesn't snow. Then it rains all summer and the crops (because people are still trying to farm; there's no money left in trapping) get weighed down by the water, and rot.

It's an interesting sight from the air. Looks like crop circles. Maybe why her home region has a massive online reputation for alien abduction stories.

None of the current field crops were prepared for radical climate change. There are people at the university and in the bio-research park on the campus's fringe working on the problem. The last generation of farmers has mostly sold out or taken to intense nordic drinking.

Hence the alien abduction stories, if you think about it.

The wildlife doesn't deal well, either, but it's harder to hunt all the animals down and fix them than it is to engineer new cereal crops. So they get twitchy. Wander into the wrong ecosystem or come tramping into cities and settle. You wake up some morning, and there's a moose in your suburban tract of grass and vinyl fencing. Coyotes chew their feet in downtown parks. Geese are strewn through the city all winter because they don't feel the need to go south anymore.

Snowy owls in fields at midwinter show up fluffy white against brown wheat stubble.

ON SOME LEVEL, every farmyard in Saskatchewan looks the same, but then you go north out of farmland into the bush and there's no way to predict what you'll find. There might be a tractor, an old one with a front-end loader or a blade on it for clearing snow. Fuel tanks, probably, and a shed for general storage and snowmobile shelter.

There might be drying racks with the skins of dead things.

Sled dogs bay on the ends of their chains. Big, hungry animals. You can spend your whole life around dogs and still lose skin and bone to a dog team.

There might be carved wooden animals. Junk sculptures. Road-accident shrines.

At least this yard looks like it belongs on this planet. Some dead machines lie at the edge of the cleared area, but nothing looks overtly mutilated. There are dogs, but not deadly ones — just shepherds inside a chain-link kennel. Dog houses and plastic kids' toys in the snow. A big log beside the house is half-carved into a bear.

The inhabitants are obviously into the whole bear thing, but Jenn and Shane aren't prepared for the sheer number of animals.

Three bears isn't impossible. It's almost proverbial, in fact, but it's a lot of bears. The Mountie who drives in ahead of them is disturbingly smug. His partner, guarding the stairs to the house's basement, is less amused. Something's gashed his left pant cuff and boot.

Jenn can't imagine who carved a basement out of ground this rocky. They would have had to break this cave open with dynamite.

They might have. People who live up here work in mining or logging if they aren't just living in the woods because they've always been up here. Truckers up here, too, and guys who hunt for a living. If you live in the rocks long enough, you start being attracted to dynamite. It's probably related to not being able to dig a hole to China as a kid. Most places, you can dig until you get bored. In Jenn's yard, when she was a kid, you could go down two hundred feet and still be in sand. Here, there's barely an inch of dirt over the granite. They have to haul in dirt just to build up the roads, and even then, every time a grader comes through, the rock shards rip through people's tires for days.

Makes it hard for anyone to escape.

So. There are three bears. Two of them are nearly a year old. Huge, rangy cubs, cheerful and playful and wide awake in spite of the winter. Someone built them a kind of plywood den in the basement bathroom. Lined it with old newspaper and sawdust. Jenn is used to animals, but in the zoo they clean up after them. This smells like bear musk and shit.

The third bear's in a tiny pet-bed.

Baby.

Smaller, even, than that. It's naked. Ugly. Bears only spend a couple of months in gestation. They're born frailer and tinier than any human, even one desperately premature. Naked and starving. They crawl into their sleeping mother's belly-flesh and suck on her for months. By the time she wakes up, they're old enough to walk.

The house is infested with bears, and this one's going to die.

"Where's their mother?" she asks.

"No one will tell us."

"This cub's barely two months old."

"Okay."

"Who *took* it?"

"We don't know."

"Make them tell you."

"It took four hours to get the guy to tell us he even *had* bears."

The Mounties won't come downstairs. She doesn't really blame them. She won't be touching those cubs without leather armour, and maybe kevlar.

Zookeepers aren't usually issued bulletproof vests, but Jenn asked for one at the La Ronge station. She suspected some kind of dedicated crazy, and she has long-standing and well-documented issues with guns. And it wasn't such an outrageous request. The RCMP all wear kevlar now since the bush dwellers started using Mounties for target practice. The detachment offered Jenn a vest sized for a woman, but women field officers are probably slimmer than she is. Less endowed, anyway. So she's wearing a man's XL vest, open at the side.

The infant has nails like knives. Bears are born with no strength, but they come out armed to move a sleeping mother bear. As soon as she's got it, there's a bone-scrape of claws along her armour.

She almost can't believe the cub can move. It's so thin. It smells like the milk they must have been feeding it, but not enough. Cow's milk, probably, and likely the powdered kind. Anything perishable that gets hauled this far north is expensive. She can't picture people spending five dollars a litre to feed a pet. They might have used condensed milk. It's still not enough.

"What were they feeding this guy?"

"Um. Baby formula, I think."

"Fuck." It's not a tenth of what a bear needs. A human mother could mainline McDonald's and still not produce enough fat to keep a bear alive.

Claws scrape across her kevlar, insistently. It's kneading her. *Lie down and spread your fur and **feed me**. I know there are nipples under there. You smell female.*

This mental image of herself nursing a bear — they have care-

fully curved incisors; she might not even lose a tit in the process —
would probably scar the Mounties watching her for life.

"Do me a favour," Jenn says. "Find me some liver and a blender.
Maybe some lard."

Shane says, "How're we going to move three bears?"

"Very carefully."

"That's helpful."

"I'll carry this one, if you think it's safe."

"I think you might not have any clothes left by the time we get
home." Pause. "I can't wait."

She grins at him. Shows him her fangs.


SOMEONE HAULED THE bear keeper back to the house and tied
him to a chair. He looks like a refugee from a gangster movie, if
gangsters dressed redneck. Dark marks on his jeans look like
blood — little baby handprints, and isn't that disturbing? — and
there's more on his shirt. Shredded cuffs. A little bruised, too. Not
quite like someone hit him, but maybe like they gave him a good
shove into the wall.

In La Ronge, guarded by exhausted, chain-smoking social
workers, he has kids. Lots of them. If you measure reproduction
in terms of most large predators, four is a lot. Maybe only three
and a half, given that there's a largish chunk of one missing, now.
Little person in a twin-engine plane, headed for emergency care
in Saskatoon.

Shane says, "Where'd you get them?"

"I told you guys down a' the p'lice station."

"I'm not with the police. I'm here for the bears."

"Fucker."

"*Hey.*" Mountie at his shoulder doesn't quite slap him upside
the head. Might like to, but he's holding it in.

"Gonna kill my bears."

Shane sighs. "We're not going to kill the bears. You did that."

"What were you *feeding* it?" Jenn asks. She's angry, down below the early-morning cold freezing her heart.

"Milk."

"It almost starved to death! You didn't have any fucking idea of what you were doing!"

"Language," whispers Shane.

"I took good care of 'em. Little ones were born too soon. One died. This one held on. Not my fault."

"Where did you *get* them?"

"My brother gave 'em to me."

"Where did he get them?"

"Hole in the ground."

"What'd he do with the mother?"

"Didn't say."

"Can we just throw *him* into a hole?" Shane asks one of the uniforms.

"We'd be investigated."

Jenn says, "How old are the cubs?"

"I've had 'em a month."

It means the surviving infant's at least five weeks old. It doesn't weigh enough.

They're going to yell at this guy for hours. He'll be charged with child endangerment and a slew of wildlife offenses. They'll probably drop one set of charges or the other, but only after a year or so in court, when the guy's so broke he'll never do this again. An institutional object lesson. And he'll probably never get his kids back.

Jenn walks away from them, back to the kitchen. Digs through the box they brought her and starts her baby-milkshake. Condensed milk, cold animal fat, liver. Throw it into the blender and liquify. "Baby bottle?"

The guy in the living room yells, "In th' dishwasher."

"Thanks."

He's using rubber livestock nipples. They have huge holes, big enough to drown a baby. She adds infant-sized rubber aureolas to her mental shopping list. Someone, someday, is going to pay for the fact that her brain can't separate work, in all its deeply maternal glory, from kinky sex shopping.

"What were you *thinking?*"

"Thought someone should take care of them. I got my kids. Two of 'em are my grandkids. I take care of people. You think I meant for this to happen?"

The bear keeper twitches toward the baby. Jenn turns her body half-away, automatically, and the bear scratches sleepily against her belly. She says, "Repeat after me."

He glares.

"*I will leave the bears alone.*"

"I'll leave bears alone."

"*I will not raise bears in my basement anymore.*"

"I won't raise no bears in my basement."

"*I will take up a sane hobby, like birdwatching.*"

He says, "How come you get to keep the bears?"

"I won't keep them in my house."

JENN SLEEPS MOST of the way down on a wash of flu medication, holding the bear underneath her jacket, feeding it whenever it rasps against the kevlar. The big cubs rattle around the back in their cages. Meat-and-milk smell hangs thick in the truck cab.

Shane says, "That's disgusting, you know?"

"Spoken like you've never eaten more or less the same thing."

"I cook it first."

"Barbarian."

"Seriously —"

"Seriously, you think this is disgusting? I used to have a roommate from Nunavut. What's Nunavut now. She only liked her meat frozen. Said the texture was better."

"Did you try it?"

"No. It was pretty gross just to watch. But it was still eating animal parts. Accept it or go vegan."

THEY STOP IN Prince Albert again for baby supplies. More things are open in daylight, and they can sort themselves out in the frozen parking lot. Straighten their clothes, check for blood, find the necessary plastic money. There's a blanket behind the seat, smelling like old animal feed, but fairly clean. Jenn wraps it around the cub and walks through the great sliding plexiglass doors of Wal-Mart.

They engage in the entirely normal practice of shopping. Sex-paired adults with a baby, down out of the north, they stroll into the source of all things and are greeted by an older woman in a blue vest who gently directs them through the vaults to infant supplies. There, they gather up plastic packets of flannel receiving blankets, rubber bottle nipples, and plastic disposable liners. Jenn studies the array of soft, bright plastic teething rings and wonders how long any given one would last in a bear's mouth.

She has to resist the urge to shop that Wal-Mart induces in her. It doesn't really matter where she is, since the stores are all the same, and they all have the same approximate range of everything. Bedding and yard supplies and hardware and a surprising selection of plus-size women's clothing. She thinks about socks — whether she needs them, whether that matters. Makeup. Movies.

They wander everywhere, acquiring towels and diet cola and Febreeze and extra work gloves. Chocolate and low-fat pretzels. Breakfast sandwiches from the ubiquitous McDonald's by the door. Cheap, vicious black coffee.

Every time someone old enough to be her great-aunt leans in,

Jenn has this urge to let the baby bite them. Blood all over the greasy lino floor. Screams lost in the vast overhead space of air vents and flickering fluorescent light.

This is what she imagines she'd be like as a mother: vaguely bloodthirsty. Maybe inclined to arm her children. Turn them loose with small knives and box cutters and see what happens.

They stand out in the cold, drinking their coffee, while Shane smokes. This place is still new enough that there's nothing much beyond the parking lot but snowed-under farmland and brush. Whited-over dirt piles where the concrete ends. Around them, other couples are smoking and holding infants. They fit right in.

Older guy in expensive sunglasses steps carefully across the iced-over crosswalk to the door. Turns to look at Jenn and says, "New baby?" in a tone that suggests she's going to hell very soon, though she can't tell if it's for reasons of second-hand smoke or fornication.

She eases back the blanket and shows him the tiny bear's skull.

Gone like a ghost who'd never grace Wal-Mart with his presence.

She stands listening to the bear's soft whimpers until Shane finishes his cigarette.

THE ZOO IS OPEN all winter, but it's usually empty of visitors. Some kind of repudiation of Schrodinger's cat: the animals still exist even when nobody can see them. Possibly Schrodinger wouldn't have had doubts if he'd used a bigger cat. A lynx, maybe, or a cougar.

On the other hand, Heisenberg was entirely right that you can only know the animals' position or their velocity, not both. They're funny that way.

Only a few crazed grandparents of persistent toddlers show up in any given week. Small kids stare at the suddenly everywhere animals. They learn what nobody outside the zoo hedge knows: in winter, the zoo is *better*. Small, fragile animals come into the barns where they can be peered at close up, and burrowing owls race through a Habitrail™ suspended from the ceiling. The big, northern predators stay in their pens, but they come out in the snow and romp. The wolves, Frank and Desmond, chase each other through the snow and roll around in it. The lynx have taken to climbing their dead tree and pouncing at shadows.

Dance of the swift fox with a dead mouse in the frozen twilight.

This is how zookeepers are made. Little eyes peer at the animals and think, *Me too.*

All this fun while no one else is looking.

You'd never think it was happening here. The zoo's just a fenced corner of the old Forestry Farm Park, locked into the suburban swell of east Saskatoon. A horde of vinyl-sided townhouses surround it. All the same yellow-pink colour, like a shade of nauseated panic rendered into latex paint. The stucco boundaries of any given community are higher and thicker than the ones around the zoo. It makes Jenn wonder what's in those developments that might try to get out.

Children, probably. Families with two point eight children each. A little higher than average, to make up for how Jenn isn't going to have any.

In the pre-evening dark, Jenn can spot a few of the carnivores pacing. Raw meat for them. And it has to be warm. In the wild, lynx die because their jaws are too delicate to eat the frozen meat biologists leave out for them. It's a snowshoe hare a day or cold kitty death for them, and Jenn's crop of half-grown kittens can't even be trusted to hunt if she turns a hutch of rabbits loose in their cage.

The wolves like their meat warm. But what they'd really like is to get loose. Eat a few stunned, vacuous pets from suburbia and then run for the hills. They've been dreaming about it all their lives, and now they're eleven years old and a bit creaky, and still waiting for the day someone forgets to latch the door.

The coyotes don't look as sure they want out. They're rangier, smaller than the wolves. Yellow scraggly dog-animals, they look like they might just figure their cage locks out themselves some cold afternoon. Maybe they already have. Maybe they sneak out at night and chase the pronghorns 'round the paddocks. Stir up trouble for the few monkeys. Nibble on a moose leg. Back in their cages before morning, and no one's the wiser except the lynx family, and the lynx won't tell because they're just grateful they don't have to hunt snowshoe hares every goddamn day.

Coyotes *laugh* at Jenn and her baby bear. *Way to be child-free, zoo lady. Look what it gotcha.*

She tells them that smart coyotes don't get caught and stuck in the zoo. The river valley's full of them. You see them running along streets near the edges of town, just before morning.

*They're not so smart. You **feed** us. And **they** never caught a peacock.*

The bear moans against her chest. There are no volunteers available to come in on short notice. The office yields an animal-adapted Snugli that holds one bear surprisingly well. How can she leave it alone? It's a tiny, deaf creature that's always starving, waiting for her to rip off her bra and let it nurse.

*Mummy mummy mummy mummymummymummy*

The bigger bear cubs went in with the foxes. They're happy now, romping in the thin snow and chewing on small rabbit carcasses, fresh from the petting zoo/rabbit generation system. It's a good life for them. Fantastic, even.

The little one's coming home with her.

It's not what she told the ripped-up bear keeper, but he was an idiot. Four children and three bears and no safety gear. If he knew anything at all about bears, it was only what he read on the Internet. Those sites don't come with appropriate safety warnings.

*Increase fat content. Watch for claws. Growl to the bear, sometimes, to tell it you love it. Not suitable for small children.*

In your home, you may have children or predators, but not both. Jenn can't imagine why most people pick children.

Shane drives her home in the afternoon, bear in her arms. He carries boxes of supplies in while she holds the baby, then sits beside Jenn on the couch in front of the TV and falls asleep. Growls into her ear in bear tones. Warm male body, close up. He smells way too good.

"Wake up," she says.

"Mmm?"

"You have to go away now." *Before I throw you down and fuck your brains out again. I can't be doing this; I'm too sick, and you keep crying.*

He goes.

Jenn and bear alone. Bentley-dog's still burrowed in at Jason's. The phone is off. There's microwavable food of some sort in the freezer, for the next time she feels prepared to eat. Right now, everything smells like bear formula, just that far off appetizing that she might never eat again.

Or, well. Not for a while.

She needs a shower.

The incubator lives in her second bedroom, left over from her nursing the lynx kittens some random idiot gave them right before Christmas. Just another sign the animals are restless; there shouldn't be new babies in December. Not even human ones, but humans are stupid enough to fuck in March with no latex between them, and apparently nothing can convince them to stop.

They should steal all the warm-baby shells from neo-natal intensive care at the hospital and give them to the animals. People have too great an advantage. She'd rather give the animals a leg up.

MESSAGES ON HER PHONE.

*Jennifer, it's Jason. I'm kidnapping your dog to go see my dad. If you're by my house, feed my lizards, okay?*

*Hello, baby. It's Mom. It's about 10 o'clock on Friday, and you're not home, which I know means you're out having a life, but it also means I have no one to talk to, and I'm in this hotel room all by myself. If you're nursing something bitey, phone me up and tell me about it.*

*Hello. This is the Saskatoon Public Library. A member of your household whose name is spelled J-E-N-N-I-F-E-R has library materials that are overdue. Fines are accumulating daily. Please return the items to your nearest branch. Goodbye, and thank you for using the services of the Saskatoon Public Library.*

*You have one old archived message.*

She needs to erase it, but she can't figure out how to do it without playing the message through again. For months she'd hung up without dealing with it.

*Breathe deeply. Press 4 to continue.*

*Are you screening your calls? Don't avoid me. I promise not to ask you to marry me again.* Shane. July 17, 2004. He sounds like he might be about to cry.

She breaks up with people early just so she doesn't have to answer calls like that one. She stopped taking Shane's calls after he asked her the first time, and even last night he had to use the office phone to make her pick up.

*Press 7 to erase or 9 to return to archive.*

FOOD COMES OUT of the fridge only a little worn and dubious. Most of what she has is cold meat, because she craves protein all the time, now. It might be a leftover habit from her time on the Atkins diet, but it's also possible she just always wanted meat. At one point in her life she still snacked on cookies, but that time is prehistoric. There are no written records or survivors.

Doesn't matter. Her body likes this. It whispers, *Vegetarianism is for pussies.*

Liver goes in the blender. Cold liver milkshake goes in the microwave. Bottle liners spill all over the counter. She took care of the Shane problem precisely so her kitchen wouldn't look like this.

The bear wails. Little deaf/blind animal with no mommy. It should set off all her hormones, but mostly the sound burns through her virus-clogged head and reminds her that she won't sleep for real until at least Monday.

Maybe she can give it to her mom. She seems to remember girls in high school did that when they got pregnant.

Wail.

"Eat, why don't you?"

*Mmmph.*

There.

In six months, this baby will walk on its own. All involuntary parents should be so lucky.


IT WAS A POSSIBILITY, but only once. Shane was a warm body, and adorable, and Jenn got too enthusiastic and the condom slipped. It was like cold, sticky water thrown all over her. Jenn got out of bed, showered, washed down her thighs, pulled on her jacket, and hiked the fourteen blocks to the nearest all-night pharmacy. Fifty dollars for two pills and two shots of dramamine to help her keep them down. Take them twelve hours apart. Almost guaranteed to knock the life right out of her.

Shane caught up with her on the walk back. He waited until she got in the car and drove her back to his house, then home when she wouldn't get out of the car and come in. He had her panties in his pocket. At her place, he sat on the steps with her and drank canned diet coke and didn't watch her down the first Plan B dose.

Quiet for ten minutes, and then he asked, "Would it be so bad?"

She didn't answer him, so it's possible that to this day he thinks the answer was *no. No, it wouldn't be so bad.*

*Tell you what. You grow it inside of you. Go off all your meds. Undergo nine months of organ displacement and brain chemical dysphoria. Feed it off your body for another year and a half. Never sleep. Nurture-feed-clothe-wash-keep it. When it's big enough to read full novels and wrestle large animals, I'll take it back.*

If she could have traded bodies with him, then maybe. Maybe it wouldn't have been so bad. Shane isn't muscled, isn't tall, isn't anything other than a basically sweet guy who's just a little bit scared of Jenn, but she likes his body. She could live in it, maybe happier than she lives in her own. No breasts to get in the way of animals. No aching uterine muscle-rips every twenty-seven days. Shane wouldn't have to worry about it. He could just carry child after child, wrapping himself around the soft-growing life inside him, and nest.

It's probably what he always wanted.

SHE'S CURLED UP in bed with her arms full of dog when her land line rings, and fuck it, really, she's in for the night. She gave the zoo its baby bear and took her dog and went home, and she needs some fucking *rest*. She's still *sick*. Anything mauling small children can wait until morning. At the rate people keep reproducing, there'll still be kids in the city at dawn. The grieving parents can pick a new baby from an array of twelve contestants, or they can choose a puppy instead.

Bentley groans quietly against Jenn's hair.

Her cell phone buzzes. It's under her pillow, set to ring high-and-vibe, muffled by two layers of polyester fibrefill but flailing for her attention. Bentley's instantly awake, dragging Jenn upright as he moves, snarling at invisible predators. Big, mad dog like a bear standing over her.

"Shh, baby," she tells her dog. "It's okay." Flips open the phone. *"What?"*

Her mother says, "Are you okay?"

"It's nighttime and I'm sick and I'm sleeping with the dog." Bentley makes soft talking noises as he resettles. Paws drape across Jenn's legs to hold her down. "Is someone dead?"

"No, no. We're all fine. Just ... I got a call about half an hour ago. Gordon Watson walked away from Royal U. Hospital. And we don't *think* he'd have any reason to come looking for you, but ..."

"What?" Watson, last Jenn heard, was in the Psych Centre, prowling behind barbed wire with the rest of the dangerous crazies. He spent five years in the Prince Albert penitentiary before they certified him and sent him down.

"He had ... I don't know, flu, I guess. Something where he couldn't keep fluids down, so they ran him over to the hospital for an I.V., and they didn't restrain him because they thought he was too sick to get up. And then at some point when the man guarding him was asleep, he got up and left."

Her mother sounds calm. She would. Her mother's worked a basic law practice in central Saskatchewan all Jenn's life, and she's seen enough to get past the usual social muttering of *savages savages savages, all these people are crazy, they should be taken out and shot.* She has this sympathy for weirdos.

She wouldn't take Gordon's case, though, and she'd known him for years.


THIS IS WHAT HAPPENED.

Jenn's mother had records — pictures and a couple of affidavits that she filed with the RCMP. They weren't enough to prove anything in particular, though, and the Mounties had more complicated problems than Gordon. So they moved. A year and a half after Jenn left home for university, her parents sold their horses, cashed out of the family farm, shifted her mother's law practice, and moved with Tori into Saskatoon. They resettled in the wilds of the city's east side, just like they'd never had aesthetic aspirations beyond a vaguely postmodern mcmansion with a pregnant garage in front. Tori took to urban education like a nymph to water, and Jenn never saw her lurk in a corner again.

She wonders, sometimes, what it did to her mom to give up the farmhouse. It was the work of an architect friend of hers, and Jenn thought her mother would die there.

Her parents aren't quite lurking behind fortifications, but their house is buried in a maze of cul-de-sacs, miles from the nearest bus stop, if you count every corner-twist you have to make to get there. They used to come check on Jenn every few days at her apartment in the university hinterlands, to make sure she was still alive.

Gordon stayed where he was, in the Bear Hills bush behind his electric fence. There he successfully created an art installation, first shown in a small gallery in North Vancouver, that was so offensive it attracted protestors. Not even the usual morals people. Dreadlocked kids and chicks with drums and a couple of human rights groups came. A radical wymmyn's collective broke in, the second week, and ripped the sculptures apart, left guts exposed: pictures of little girls, all naked. Shreds of the already-dismembered bodies all over the floor.

*That* was enough for an arrest warrant. Jenn's body was too big and ambivalent to qualify as child pornography, and Donna's was even less childish, but little, little girls were good subjects for charges.

Gordon shot at the Mounties who came to collect him. They hadn't even known he had a gun.

Gordon was making an elephant, this massive thing that filled

his yard, and he was chemically altered to a regionally appropri-
ate/borderline psychotic level. He announced through a vintage
bullhorn that Weesakeechak was whispering in his ear. Climbed
up on his porch roof with a half-destroyed rifle and fired randomly
at the cars.

No dead bodies resulted, but they dragged him out in a righteous
fury and added a couple of attempted murder charges that stuck to
him after months of debate over the validity of art and the nature of
child pornography. Three curators and two university art critics
came in to explain that Gordon's deconstruction of the female body
and his approach to gender and cultural perceptions were an elab-
oration of pre-Christian wood-nymph imagery. Five months of
police excavation of Gordon's yard produced no bones of little girls,
and they never matched the photos to anyone who was missing.

And there was this huge, hanging issue that Gordon is *queer*.
He's the least likely guy to prey on girl-children.

They needed less complicated charges.

Gordon's bullet ripped out the tendons of a girl-Mountie's left
shoulder, just below the edge of her flak jacket. During the trial,
they showed a lot of pictures of the damage and emphasized that
she had been a pretty girl, before Gordon shot at her. That worked.
Gordon's been in jail for six years, chewing on his fingers and howling at the moon.


DONNA SENT JENN photos of the gallery raid. She lived in Vancouver by then. Feral, marathon-fit wymmyn in west coast rags
and feathers took the already beheaded tamarack girls apart with
knives. Donna was there. She's very clear about her involvement
in the protests. She writes Gordon long, complicated e-mails, and
ccs them to Jenn and Jason. Some of the pictures she attaches are
downright pornographic.

# « CHAPTER 7 »

JENNIFER BLAMES HIM for all sorts of things, but mostly the things that aren't his fault. For instance. She holds him responsible for the people who invade her zoo. Just because the walls aren't high enough to keep people out. Jason's seen more impregnable suburbs, barricaded behind noise walls and floodlit for beauty or security or to scare the Indians away. It's not one of those things he's supposed to say out loud — not if he likes working for the government, not if he likes keeping peace in his own neighbourhood — but the way people built this city, you'd think the Indians were *right there*, waiting to take over, circling on wild horses like that essential shot from every TV-broadcast western.

When the moment's right, they'll storm the panic-pink mansions and claim this development in the name of Big Bear. Reparations for lost property to follow.

Karmic real-estate transfer.

In the zoo, Indians aren't a problem. They come in sometimes and tour, two or three moms and a grandmother and a pack of little kids. Serious looking couples with their toddlers in strollers look around like they expect to be kicked out. School-trip groups come in from the city's southwest, kids being introduced to coyotes and moose by middle-aged white Catholic school teachers. Kids stare at coyotes. Coyotes stare back. Owls ruffle their soft feathers and make pinched faces at the creatures on the other side of the wire.

It's a nice space. Better than the world outside. He can see why Jennifer likes it.

The problem is, two or three years ago when Jenn was still enthralled with her new zoo job, she invited the family on an after-sunset tour. Just because they could. She included Jason in the general e-mail invite. She must have been feeling generous, because she even wrote, *Bring your friend-thing, if you want.*

Jason was experiencing a period of bad taste in men; he admits this. One of his series of flickering, whip-thin junkie boyfriends came along, and *he* liked the tour more than he should have. Kept running out ahead of them and leaping out from behind trees. He leapt onto Jason's back and demanded to be carried. He loved the monkeys just way too much.

And then he dumped Jason's ass and wandered off into his own delusional, chemically-induced version of the city, where he apparently told all his goddamn tweaker friends how *it's all happening at the zoo!*

*I do believe it. I do believe it's true.*

*Woo!*

So, weeks and months after Jason's last sight of that particular pretty boy, other party-boys on speed came in over the zoo fences at night. They must have looked amazing — androgynous bodies under black hair with electric-bright tips, in hoodies and skinny jeans and beautiful sneakers. They raced each other around the snow-cleared paths like their lungs weren't burning and they weren't freezing cold in their too-thin clothes in the subarctic night. And they fucked *everywhere.* They left used condoms and wrappers to be eaten by curious mountain sheep. Thongs were found hanging in the raptor cages. No one, as far as he knows, actually tried to defile the animals, but the zoo staff were worried enough to check.

It's not his fault the zoo had to hire guards.

Jennifer phones him because she holds him *personally* responsible for the gay tweakers invading her animal-space. Tells him he has to come down. In the background, he hears a too-high voice demanding *penguins! The absence of penguins is breaking my heart! This is a totally inadequate zoo: the penguins would love it here. Why aren't there penguins **right now**?!* And then Jason has to come, because he knows the voice. He brought that one into the zoo, the first night.

He can't remember the asshole's name.

He gets there before the police do. The cops are off breaking up house parties and dumping random Indians off-road so they can either freeze to death or walk back to the city with no shoes on. Zoo-invaders don't rank among the disturbers of the night, since the only people they scare aren't human.

Jenn says, "Take him."

"Fuck, Jennifer, he isn't *mine*. He's just a guy I used to know."

"I don't care. You brought him here. Get him out." There's an edge of *or else* in her voice. Weeks later, he's still waiting for her to finish articulating the threat. But he put the word out, the best he could, to stay out of the fucking zoo.

He might have written on a bathroom wall that animal sex gives you Hep-C. It was all he could think of.


IN DAYLIGHT, HE makes an attempt to look like an adult. He needs to eat, and if he doesn't want to go back to farming, he has to shift for himself. Self-abuse and Grindr-trolling aren't paying jobs, so he works for the provincial government, troubleshooting computers. Mostly, he solves simple software problems for unhappy civil servants who tell him fairly good jokes. He has them trained to attempt the *turn it off, count to ten, turn it on again* process before they call him, so the problems that land in his lap are real ones. Not thrilling ones, but they let him spend his days digging through other people's work computers, reorganizing abstract data and getting one or two good looks into people's almost-private minds.

He wonders if some of them understand that adult content sites are riddled with spyware. They have people's whole lives on file — finances, education, child custody — and the hard drives are so corrupted he thinks he should touch them with rubber gloves. It's comforting to know that everybody likes porn, but really. Boundaries.

The computers belong to the government. This particular government's been feeling fairly self-righteous lately, and it has no sense of humour at all. When Jason bills for his time, he doesn't mention that a staggering number of their psychically tortured office slaves (he's seen the places those people work, and he's surprised they don't all go on shooting sprees) store intrusively intimate photos of the human body on their hard drives. The administration would fire their asses without giving a moment's respect for the range of interests involved. Some of them took real research.

Girl-on-girl. Man-on girl. Man-on-girl-on-other-man. Shoe worship. Bondage. Cling-wrap bondage. Erotic tales of Roy Orbison in cling wrap. Genital close-ups. Costume fetish. Spanking. Military men. Star Trek characters. Big breasts. Small breasts. Girls in the shower, panting softly to themselves as they lather up their hair. Stuffed animals. Fur suits.

Other things, too, that make him think of biohazards and wince, but if it's all consenting adults and they're not, say, torturing bunnies, he's not going to do anything but take notes.

It begs the question, though: *if there isn't a website devoted to it, is it even really a fetish?*

Once, all he found were pictures of men kissing each other, mostly not even naked. The computer's problem, when he eventually found it, wasn't related to the user's online interests. He likes the woman attached to that hard drive. On his next trip through her office, he "accidentally" left behind a CD-R full of slightly better quality photos of the same kind of thing. Though he doesn't share her taste in men, it's the sort of interest that should be encouraged. She likes guys, apparently, who look like him — post-athletic, a bit geeky. It's his work skin, not what he thinks of as his real self, but still. It's reassuring.

The system grinds along. He reassembles lost connections. In mid-afternoon, while he's eating a crappy sandwich he brought from home, he sends blind-addressed e-mails to people, suggesting links catering to their fetishes. This is almost always worth it. When he comes back to his office from field work, there's chocolate waiting for him, and a whole tuna-noodle casserole. It's pretty good.

DAYS WHEN JASON doesn't have to rescue the welfare state from a bloody, computer-driven death, he sits in the office basement and reads his e-mail. The questions from people attempting to become competent enough not to harass him on a daily basis get answered first. Then the interoffice stuff. *Please note that technical staff is to be included in the dress code. While we recognize that you do not work with the public, please refrain from wearing any garment marked with obscene text.*

Personal stuff last. If it's sex-related, it goes home, so only his very clean, public self gets e-mail at work. E-cards from his mom and his aunt. Bad jokes from guys he used to play hockey with.

The message from Gordon's been sitting in his inbox for two days. He's not sure if it was written before or after Gordon disappeared. Not sure whether he should send it to Brenda or the police. He deletes and undeletes the e-mail twice before he opens it.

*From: Gord Watson <sculptureman115@hotmail.com>*
*Date: 22 February 2005*
*To: Jason Hiebert <jason.hiebert@gov.sk.ca>*
*Subject: some things i am thinking about .*

*dear jason*

*i am thinking about the sculptures i built when you had that summer off, not when you went away to school (university) but before that. you remember. i think they (sculptures) must be very damaged by the weather. i cant go back and look at them right now and i think my sister would sell me back to the state if i call her to ask. maybe you could go and look? the yard is very safe.*

*my new friend is a strange guy. i met him in p.a. but he is out now. he was in for "mischief". indian fellow, kind of skinny. he built little fires out of t.p. and cigarettes, which were contraband, in prison. he can build fires anywhere really. i said last week to him that he was the devil but he laughed and called me names. he says he is coyote and I think he might be right, though he doesnt look like coyote. i think this government would put coyote in jail. they put me in jail.*

*do you still work for them? i guess you must do, since you have a government address. they read your mail, of course, but they already know what i think, and i will not tell you where i am going. you should have a hotmail or the new gmail. they are both corporate but that is the way of the internet I find.*

*peace for you,*

*gordon*

JASON HAS A computer tower in pieces, trying to figure out what crawled inside it and died, and when he looks up his dad's there. Big, greying, bearded guy leaning against the door frame, the way he used to loom when Jason was a kid and probably in some kind of trouble, waiting for Jason to realize he'd been caught. This time when Jason was five or so, he used a chair to climb right into their giant chest-freezer in the basement, and he sat there on the loaves of frozen bread and bags of peas, eating store-brand chocolate ice cream with his fingers. It had to look disgusting. And after a while he looked up, and his dad was staring down at him, looking somewhere between furious and like he might have to swallow his tongue to keep from laughing.

His dad says, "Can I take you to lunch?"

Jason pauses to shake the decades-old kid-guilt out of his system. Pull himself together. "Why?"

"Because I don't want to eat alone, you ungrateful creature."

"Yeah, okay."

They do this. His dad is the only one of them who still lives on the Bear Hills farm. Every few weeks he gets lonely and comes into Saskatoon and offers to feed Jason in return for company. Every half-year or so, he drives out to B.C. and spends a week sleeping on Jason's mom's couch. Jason wasn't expecting that, and he hasn't yet figured out how to ask what's going on.

He offered to buy Jason lunch, but what actually happens is his dad drives them both back to Jason's house. He's made curry. His dad has keys, but he doesn't exactly have permission to just walk in and start cooking whenever. He has keys in case Jason's murdered by a random pickup someday, and the smell starts to bother the neighbours. This doesn't smell like death, though. It smells amazing.

Venison curry. It washes fire through Jason's sinuses like he's never been cold in his life.

"You took up hunting?" Jason asks.

"I traded for it. I was hauling wood for Todd Czelnik, and he offered me a bunch of meat. S'good. I've been eating it a lot."

The venison is darker-tasting than beef, and vaguely bloody under the spices. It is good. He hardly ever gets to taste this. Between his parents' deer-induced trauma and the family's beef operation, wild meat hardly ever crosses his path. On his own, Jason only really makes hamburgers; everything else he eats comes frozen. But he misses it, eating big chunks of animals. Reminds him of his mom. She wasn't a very good vegetarian colonist. She told him once that if people weren't meant to eat meat, they wouldn't have incisors.

"Your mom sent you some stuff." His dad says it very casually, like they still live together. Like they never stopped talking.

"Is it scary?"

"Well, some of it's animal bones."

"Really?"

"No. Most of it's vitamins. She makes me take those too. Something about bachelors not eating right." He pauses to stuff his mouth with tomato and bell peppers. "Her freezer's full of microwave dinners . . . she sent you these guys, too."

Jason blinks. His dad has a ferret in his lap. Like, an actual pet weasel. It looks domestic — it's wearing a little harness. It looks up at Jason very seriously, then returns to licking curry gravy out of his dad's palm.

There's another weasel on the floor.

He says, "You've got to be joking."

"She said it was time you learned to take care of something besides yourself."

"I have lizards."

"I told her. She says they don't count."

His dad cleans up the kitchen. It's crusted with tomato juice and the dark-yellow spice stains that curry leaves, and Jason wouldn't bother, himself. He'd leave it to set, and go back to microwaving. He only has a stove because it came with the house. The ferrets follow him. Only one is wearing a harness; the other has a little collar on. They wander into the lizard room and study their new housemates. From the warm, reddish dark, Jason says, "Tell her I don't want them."

"I don't want them either. You going to let them die?"

Sigh. "No."

"There. Was that so hard?"

His dad comes to find him in the animal room. Jason thinks he should install a couple of beanbag chairs and use it as a space to get high, if he still got high. It's the sort of thing he misses, not being in contact with Gordon. His dad leans down to pet the weasels, and then the lizards. He fishes in his pocket. Holds out something small and white. "I lied. There are bones too."

It's a snake skull. Jason suspects it's supposed to be symbolic, but his mother's developing a new language for herself, and he doesn't know what this one means, yet.

THE POLICE WERE in Gordon's yard, but not recently. They just came up here to see if he'd gone back home when he disappeared, but there's enough Mountie blood in the dirt that they wouldn't hang around just on the off chance. Jason can picture them pausing to spit on the ground just before they left. Maybe burying some kind of talisman to keep the psychopath away.

It's there — scraps of uniforms bunched up with a zip-tie. They nailed it to the gatepost.

Barbed wire on unanchored posts is strung across the driveway's mouth. When Gordon lived here, the fence was electrified — not a huge current, because that would have attracted attention he didn't want, but enough to rattle your teeth. He said he didn't want loose cattle wandering in and damaging his sculptures.

They talked a lot about the electric fence at Gordon's trial. The Mounties said the fence running through his back pasture was hot enough to start fires. It must have happened after Jason stopped coming around, but he guesses it's not impossible. Gordon's sister said she didn't want to pay for upkeep on the fences, and the Mounties tore out the transformer to use as evidence, so nothing's electric now. Even the house is powered down.

The remaining sculptures are fifteen-foot masses of dead metal and old bone. None of them has ever been shown in an art gallery, because they aren't portable. The support frames are railroad ties sunk two feet into the ground. Creosote whispers its carcinogens into the surrounding water and air.

The dominant colour is rust. Old tractor parts out of context are raw, frightening things. Behold the weapons of some earlier time. Watch your fingers.

The bones are legally got. Gordon was never that interested in most laws, but he was almost fanatical in his devotion to the Archeological Site Preservation Act. He found a bone — buffalo or human, at least — he called it in. The university people came out and dug it up. In return, they gave him a break on the price of a thoroughly studied buffalo bone or two, and the ones that turned out to be cattle bones were his for free.

Jason's never asked where the human bones came from. Some of the bones are definitely human. And you can't buy those.

There might be some sort of exemption for Serious Art where human remains are concerned. If the medical school can chop up the dead to educate twenty-year-old medical students and teenaged hockey players in the secrets of anatomy, there must be a loophole for artists, too.

There are only a couple of human bones left hanging. When the Mounties went over the place, they cut a lot of them down to test. When they decided Gordon hadn't killed anyone featured in his assemblages, they brought the bones back. Threw the box of them down at the base of the sculptures and left them there. When the cardboard dissolves completely, the bones will be part of the piece again, and Gordon's declared, *officially*, on some form registered with a government office, that this is now part of the process. He owns the bones, and there are laws protecting finished pieces of art from casual desecration. The Mounties had to issue a formal apology for the original damage, too, though it was a fairly strange one. They issued it to his face, and Gordon was chained to a bench at the time.

Other sculptures in the yard are made of old glass and hemp twine. There's a frame like a homemade swing set, crossed with deadfall branches. Braided ropes loop around the decaying bark, then the strands come loose, each leading down to a different bottle. Patent medicine flasks from the turn of the last century. Tiny jars for long-extinct soft drinks. There are a few old-style glass telephone insulators hanging, too. Their head-swells make them more human looking than any of the bones.

And it all hangs and strikes itself. Breaks, occasionally. The glass pieces are chipped from impact and coloured from their early chemical lives and decades of sunlight.

Jason likes the piece. It's titled *It Used to Rain Here.*

Gordon was working on this one when Jason found him in the woods. In his first months of damaged-artist responsibility, he picked out a few of the glass chunks. Later, Gordon took hundreds of pictures of the assemblage, from all angles in all lights, and developed them with a bright gelatin gloss. He spent most of the next summer merging the photos into a single, twisted version of his already twisted baby. The photo-collage went on tour. It showed in major civic art galleries in the Pacific Northwest. It showed briefly at the Mendel Gallery in Saskatoon, too. Jason clipped the little newspaper article on the show and saved it. If the iguanas haven't devoured it, the clipping's still somewhere in his house.

If Gordon's sister had any brains, she'd be protecting his work. If Gordon dies, and god knows the guy's crazy enough that he could just take a running leap into a pen full of psychos someday, she gets his estate. There might be money in it.

She doesn't care, though. Says she hates his work. It's only Jason who ever comes out here to check the sculptures for damage.

Jason ran into his mom, once. She was just sitting on the porch, looking at the installations. He waved and went to visit his dad and came back later when he could be alone.

The pieces have complicated lives. Some of them are supposed to weather. Gordon explained it to Jason in terms of west coast totem poles and the nature of wood. Every so often, Jason thinks what he really needs to do on these trips is bring out a digital camera, shoot the whole yard, and let Gordon scrutinize the mess for himself. Except, Gordon can't fix any of it himself, as long as he's in jail, and he'll panic if anything's seriously wrong. Out of jail, he might actually try to come put things right. Jason really, really wants Gordon to stay lost. If he can create some kind of record proving the installations are fine, maybe he'll go up north and live in the bush forever. Join a commune on the edge of Alaska and just learn to live with the absence of meat, if he can get over the border. He should go live far away from anyone he could actually hurt.

Jason brought the ferrets out with him. He thought maybe they could hunt for mice, but they're curled up around each other, right now, asleep in the car.


THE HOUSE IS WRECKED. There's no power hooked up to it anymore, and no heat. Gordon's sister didn't want to come, so the pipes exploded the first winter. Glass broke. Animals moved in. Up close, it smells like an uncleaned zoo pen, rank fox-musk and nearly decomposed shit in the corners.

Jason hasn't run regularly in years, but he only misses it when he leaves the city. Misses his fast, angular, sexy teenaged body, the way it could run for miles. He can't do that anymore. Five minutes running hurts. He ripped his knees apart playing rec hockey and shredded his lungs in smoke-filled bars, back before the smoking ban. He hasn't been able to breathe properly since the summer of three broken noses. Probably he snores, now. He hasn't asked anyone.

He can't even keep his feet like he used to. One patch of shade-ice, and he slips and falls. Rolls through the snow and mud into the chokecherry.

If he could get high-speed Internet to reach out this far, he'd dig himself a cave in Gordon's pasture and live here forever. Summon shaggy, pretty boys to come fuck him when he gets lonely. They could bring him food, he could repay them with art tours. The ferrets might like it here. They could hunt out troves of plant life and protein.

Eventually, he gets up. Cold and dirty and wet. Hikes back to the car and strips off his jacket to get dry. While he's re-dressing out of the tangle of clothes in the back seat, one of the ferrets takes off.

It might come back eventually, but Jason wants to get home before dark. He turns towards the sculptures and catches a flicker of tail. Runs after it.

The sculptures behind the house aren't ones Gordon likes, particularly. They're decomposing fast as spring sets in. Some of the more biological elements — are those dead magpies? — have rotted. Something's been chewing on them.

Ferret.

There comes a time in every man's life when he looks at his unwanted pet and it's hanging from its own teeth trying to consume a sodden *corvidae* husk that's been incorporated into a found-object sculpture via traditionally made hemp rope. At this moment, all a man can do is pull out his cell phone and take a picture.

Laugh his ass off. Maybe catch the ferret when it goes flying.

"Excuse me. What the *fuck?*"

She says, "It's art. *That* isn't part of the vision. Keep your animal off it."

This woman. The first time Jason looks at her, she's amazing, soft-edged, sexy in a way he's been culturally programmed to respond to, even if his dick isn't interested. Biological dissonance makes him rub at his eyes, and maybe there was something in them, because when he looks again there's no girl at all. There's an older Indian guy wearing a dress. Earrings. Hairy legs push down into work socks and army boots. So, not a girl, but still throwing his animals around. The ferret crawls into Jason's coat and curls up.

"How do you know? I mean, that it isn't the vision?"

"I was here when he made it."

"You weren't."

"I was. I'm Coyote. Just because you don't fucking remember . . ."

Jason rubs his eyes again. Rubs ferret-dander into them and feels his allergies react. "Is this look you're working on for my benefit?"

"Do anything for you?"

"Really not."

"Liar." Coyote makes a face, like he was going to pull a full-on drag queen vamp and then gave it up halfway through. "Anyway, no. It's not for you." A piece of the sculpture comes away in his hand, and he studies it. Sniffs. "Anyway. Remind Gordon that decomp includes everything that happens, not just the weather. He has to leave this shit alone."

The ferret caught some feathers before Coyote threw it, and it's chewing on them now, tucked between Jason's armpit and his sleeve.

"And tell your weasel he's *not* part of the process and vandalizing a work of art is a crime in this province. It's one of the only decent laws we've got." Just like Coyote isn't holding a chunk of the sculpture himself. He probably chews on it when no one's around.

Jason thinks he should walk away. Go back to his car and stop reading Gordon's e-mails. He makes it ten yards. Turns around. He says, "Where's the elephant?"

"My elephant. None of your business what I did with it."

Jason doesn't have to deal with this shit. He throws the ferret into the back seat and leaves. When he goes to hook the gate shut, though, there's a sudden hum, and the fence re-electrifies. He stares at it. Stares at the house, where Coyote is drinking tea out of an orange plastic thermos lid. He touches the fence, to be sure, and the current snaps his head back hard, harder than any hockey-hit he's taken in his adult life. No helmet. No mouthguard.

Jason spits and two of his teeth hit the ground. He stares at those, too.

Coyote says, "Give me one of those to add to the sculpture, and you can keep the other one. I won't even come after you."

It sounds perfectly reasonable until Jason's on the highway, driving home and periodically spitting blood out the window. He wishes he could keep his tongue from pushing into the gap.

*From: Gord Watson <sculptureman115@hotmail.com>*
*Date: 13 March 2005*
*To: Jason Hiebert <jason.hiebert@gov.sk.ca>*
*Subject: girls you might remember*

*dear jason*
*i thought you might like to know i am working again. i have a little space and some materials so i have been making little assemblages. its probably good because working gives me a different headspace and now i feel much better.*

*when i was in p.a. some of the women who came to visit their boyfriends gave me pictures of them. they said they dont mind on account of how im queer and wont masturbate to them.*

*coyote thinks this is all very funny. he started being a woman, which i did not expect, and now he has gone somewhere. if he comes to see you please tell him i said hello.*

*peace,*
*gord*

THE FERRETS INFEST his house, and they're always hungry. The websites tell him to feed them ferret chow, if he can find it, and otherwise live/recently dead mice. Just like he has a reliable source of mice. Jennifer does, through the zoo, but her house is infested with bears. He goes by to check on her, after his mom phones and asks him to, and Jenn answers the door wearing a snugli with a baby bear in it. Whatever she's bottle-feeding it smells revolting, but it gets on his hands and when he comes home, the ferrets lick him relentlessly.

She told him, anyway, that the zoo doesn't share its mice. The owls come first, and their mouse supply has to be reliable — an owl can't live on baby chicks alone. He can learn to feed his own pets.

He needs live mice. In the meantime, he's feeding the ferrets cat food, but he can tell it's not the same. They nose the half-empty cans around his kitchen hopefully. They're waiting for the meat to come back to life and fight them a little.

Feeding all these animals is expensive. The iguanas expect fresh, finely chopped produce. He had to research them, too, when they arrived, and to this day he's haunted by the spectre of the iguanas developing a lettuce addiction. The online guides were clear about it: feed iguanas lettuce, and they'll refuse to eat anything else, and then they'll starve, because lettuce can't sustain iguanas. There were cautionary pictures. Two years ago, he looked at those, and since then he's spent money he doesn't always have on vegetables he doesn't really eat, himself, like kale and arugula. He's learned to shred softening melons into lizard-sized pieces and serve them in small, carefully cleaned dishes. But the ferrets should be eating raw meat or small animals, and he's not sure how he's going to finance that.

He can guess what his mom had in mind. She's fucking manipulative.

He cages both ferrets in a cardboard box and drives them out to the Bear Hills. His gums have almost healed, but he's developed an aversion to Gordon's place; he drives an extra three miles on the east-west road grid to avoid going past that over-electrified gate.

His dad lives on the farm alone, now. Jason's aunt and uncle packed up after he told them about Gordon, and moved the girls into Saskatoon. He thinks it must have been like cutting off an arm, leaving that house. It was Brenda's project. An architect friend of hers laid out the plans before either Jennifer or Jason was born, and then Brenda and Steve built the house over the next decade. Even when Jason was little, it wasn't entirely finished. They were picky. No *good enough*. Everything was perfect: polished wood and ceramic tile and exactly positioned windows. The girls' bedrooms were architectural marvels, almost instantly filled up with plastic little-girl crap and disposable toys. Animals and stuffed animals and those Barbies Jason used to have such a thing for.

He got over it, but only once he was old enough to buy his own toys.

Jason's not clear why his dad didn't move into that house. It's still there, with the pipes drained and minimal power running, and his dad goes over sometimes to check it for damage, but he apparently chooses to live in Jason's grandparents' house, where he's lived most of his life. When he has to hire guys to help with harvest, they stay in a trailer next to the barns.

His grandparents' house — he still thinks of it as their house, fifteen years after their deaths, after nine years of living in it himself — isn't locked, but you have to know how to get in. His grandma took to sealing the front door to prevent drafts, years before Jason was born. Aluminum foil and duct tape. One year, she got really into it and added a layer of yellowish insulation, and then never bothered to unseal it again. His whole life, Jason's come in by the back door. It's all he's needed. From there, he can access the mud room and the basement and the kitchen. He and his dad never used the dining room much, anyway. They gradually piled stuff they didn't want in there, out of the way.

Since Jason moved out, his dad has emptied the dining room of its garbage bags of unwanted stuff, but he hasn't refurnished much.

Instead, the room's full of gigantic plants. Hibiscus Grace looms over the windows. She's older than Jason, this huge flowering tree that his grandma nurtured and his dad decided to keep. Almost ceiling height. Next to her, the ficus Jason's mom bought at Safeway in 1982 has produced a forest.

It smells good in there. Wet.

He turns the ferrets loose in the indoor woods and goes hunting. Down to the basement. Since Jason left, his dad's stripped the black curtains off the windows, and torn down the drywall partition. It doesn't look like anything but a basement. Old second fridge full of carrots and potatoes. Old bikes, including Jason's. A few things that might be abandoned art projects.

The chest freezer's half full. It might be the one Jason climbed into as a kid; he's not sure. Appliances die, and his dad buys second-hand "new" ones at Rose's Auction in Saskatoon, or from newspaper ads. He likes the classifieds. Buys all kinds of things.

Behind him, Jason's dad says, "I don't feed you enough?"

"I need meat."

"For you?"

"For the animals."

"Let me see what I've got. Stay out of my ice cream." His dad pushes him gently. Makes Jason stand to the side while he rummages through the freezer bags of yellow beans and paper-wrapped meat. "I think I've got some freezer-burned beef they could have. I was going to stew it."

"Do you have mice?"

"In the freezer?"

"No. In the barns, maybe, or the house?"

His dad pulls a crackling plastic bag of wrapped meat from the freezer's depths. Hands it to Jason like it's glass bricks. "You don't want to eat that yourself."

"Think it'll be okay to give it to them raw?"

"Your mom said to feed them cat food."

Jason shrugs. Upstairs, he fills the sink with hot water and drops what might once have been a steak in to thaw. The ferrets race into the kitchen to investigate, then vanish again into the dining room.

"Have you seen my strawberries?"

"What?"

Strawberries. Two tiny bedrooms are filled with tables and sun lamps, and to call what his dad's created a nursery doesn't really do it justice. The plants aren't just started, they're making fruit. Little green berries under dark green leaves.

"I didn't know you could grow those indoors."

"It's just an experiment."

"It's pretty cool."

"I'm thinking I'll build a greenhouse."

"Yeah?"

"Out there." Nodding to the space between the house and the combine bone-yard.

Jason picks an unripe strawberry. Holds it as he walks outside. It's still winter, here — low-depth snow and layers of snow mould, and the world smells frozen. But his dad's growing things, indoors. He'd make a decent gardener, if he could do it full time. His dad's garden is a weedy thing, set up by Jason's grandma and half an acre across, but it needs hands every day. This last year, his dad didn't even get the vines cleared before snowfall.

His dad's sixty-one. He's farming out here by himself.

The other house is dark, and weirdly hollow. Jason doesn't think he's ever seen an empty house just *sit* like that before. His own house, when he moved in, had crap left over from the last tenants lying in most rooms, and he had to throw it all away before he could spread out his own stuff. By the time the other crap was out, his crap was in. The most intense view of emptiness he got was the empty second bedroom, and he filled that with lizards.

Behind Brenda's house, there's broken glass hanging from the poplar trees on long strings. One small assemblage that looks nothing like Gordon's work. It might be Jason's mom's, but her creations look like girl-parts that've shed their human bodies and wandered off on their own. This is more like a scarecrow made of machine parts and beer bottles — bigger than human and gangling, and for some reason wearing a *Pantera* T-shirt. At its feet, there are two of Jason's old Barbie-shrines, sheltered by leaves. He has to stare at it a while before he understands.

It's a *metalhead.*

He goes back to his grandparents' place. Finds his dad and says, "That's terrible. Is it yours?"

"Do I criticize your art?"

"I don't make art."

"Barbie heads, Jason. Those have to be yours. Neither of the girls would have included all those little shoes and purses."

The meat in the sink is soggy inside its plastic wrap, and the water's laced with old, greyish blood. While it doesn't smell *off,* exactly, Jason wouldn't eat it himself, given the choice. He lays the slab on a board and starts carving away slivers. "You don't know what I do," he says. It comes out sulky, like he's not thirty-two years old, with his own shitty job and a place to live that houses only him and a few small, ravenous animals.

His grandma's plates are in one of the high cupboards. He has to get up on a chair to retrieve them. While he's up, he asks, "Why don't you throw this shit away?"

"I might need it to fight off monsters."

"Plates."

"My house, Jason. You want me to come bitch about your place?"

It's nice china. Pink rose pattern around the edges, maybe a trace of gold leaf. Jason likes how it looks with raw meat all over it, placed carefully on the floor for the benefit of ungrateful weasels.

He sits and watches them eat. Takes the china away after and handwashes it, then sits on the floor in the plant-infested dining room and reads the comics he stashed in the house, under the stairs, before he moved out. Watches it get dark.

"Are you hungry?" his dad asks, from the kitchen.

"A bit."

And then, later, "Are you going home?"

"Not sure."

The lizards have food. They'll be fine for a day or two. Jason thinks he might want to stay here, in the half-dark, where no one can find him. Where he can suck on the gap in his teeth and not think.


HE WAKES UP in the dark. He fell asleep on the linoleum floor, and his dad threw a blanket over him, but it hurts. His bones are all out of alignment. When he stretches, the ferrets shuffle away from him, just out of arm's reach. Sit there and watch.

He can't live like this. He needs his laptop. Wonders if there's any way to get Internet access out here that's faster than dial-up.

Living in Saskatoon made him forget about the depths of the dark. When he steps out of the house, for a second he thinks he's diving under water. The world has no edges, and the sky is huge. Full of stars. Moonless.

Remember to breathe.

He waits for his eyes to adjust. It isn't terribly cold; with the blanket wrapped around him, he can cope without a jacket. And really, he should be able to navigate anyway. He used to have muscle-memory of the whole farm, enough that he could go out at night any time he couldn't sleep and just walk. Go through the pasture. Climb up in the treehouse and consider living there. Swing until he lost track of the ground.

Jennifer showed him how to do that, in the period after she decided she couldn't live in Tori's room and came to take her own back. She made him sleep on the bottom bunk, and it meant that when she woke up in the night, he could hear her moving. She went away, not to the bathroom, and didn't come back. He had to go looking for her. Found her out behind the house, on the swings her dad built, moving high and quiet, back and forth. She did that for years. When she was still freshly scarred-up, he watched her swing from just far enough away that she wouldn't be able to see him and scream.

Brenda's house is locked. Two doors, both cedar and glass. One of them, he thinks, is bolted from the inside. Permanently unused and only present because of the abstract rule that a house should have two doors. The other one is just locked. He moves along the edge of the long verandah, rubbing his fingers under the edge. He finds splinters and cobwebs. Dirt. The key, hanging on a nail.

It's a totally empty house.

Not warm, but there's heat on somewhere, enough to keep the place from freezing. And they can't have taken everything. Jason leaves piles of shit behind every time he moves, just because it's easier. This is pretty thorough: the appliances are gone, even. No fridge. No stove. Downstairs, no washer or dryer. He goes back to the kitchen, opens the dishwasher, and gets a face full of dank, vague mildew-smell.

There's nothing in the cupboards but mouse shit and mouse nests.

Mice.

It's an idea. He opens everything. The house is full of mice. They're in the walls; he can hear them. The cupboards rattle when he throws them open. Closets shake.

You can't keep a house empty. Something's always going to get in.

The ferrets in his grandparents' house are asleep in Jason's parka. He stuffs one under each arm and carries them back across the yard. Turns them loose.

Fur flies all night.

JASON DREAMS ABOUT the ocean. The island colony, so he must only be six or seven years old. He's walking along the beach, and when he looks close there are thousands of crabs all marching in unison in the shallows, going southeast in one movement. Tiny forms, blue and red and sea-floor gold-brown, all marching to the side. He thinks about diving in. Curls in on himself.

There are animals all around him. They could learn to swim, too.

They shuffle with his sleep, though, and the ocean spreads out into red-tipped grass, and he's standing with all of the animals on the bank of a creek, somewhere he thinks must be thirty miles south of home, looking at crayfish, thinking about how they look like crabs. The animals wander away and infest the abandoned claim-house next to the trees. Tell him, *We're going to live here, now. You too. Get your stuff.*

Ferrets in his sleep. Iguanas in the corner. Mice everywhere.

And Donna. The memory of her straddling his hips on his teenage bed is driven by the force of her weight. She was always heavy. She's almost as heavy now. Staring down at him, like he's an interesting spider, and he couldn't get away from her if he wanted.

If she moves just right, he'll fuck her next time she asks him to.

Jennifer says, "I like the part where I could kill you, right here, like this."

He scrambles back to wakefulness frustratingly slowly. Like he's heavy. He is heavy; she's holding him down.

It isn't Donna straddling him. It's Jennifer.

She says, "I wouldn't even have to strangle you or anything. There's a vein right here," touching his neck, "that if I push on it for long enough, you'll probably throw a clot. It might take you a couple of minutes to die, but I'd have time to explain everything. Like a super-villain. Evil genius."

He thinks, *Donna's the evil genius*, and, *Where is she?*

Jennifer's a big girl, and she's sitting on him. Not as close to his dick as sleeping-Jason thought she was. The mattress under him shifts uneasily — that's the source of the ocean, he thinks. Any air mattress is a little like being afloat.

"What?"

"This isn't your house. You don't have any right to be here."

"Visiting my dad."

"You *moved in*. Your crap's everywhere. You brought animals. This isn't your house." Pissy voice. She's whining like a kid, the girl who didn't want to share her bedroom.

"Nobody was here."

It's true. Even the mice fled, mostly, once the ferrets marked their territory. He'd just come here, now and then, to be alone for a while. No Internet access, no stress. No one from work can find him here, if he keeps his phone turned off. It's as close as he can get to a pasture cave. So he brought a sleeping bag, and an air mattress he found for twenty dollars at the Canadian Tire on the city's west edge. This little space heater, then the hot rock for the lizards.

They didn't really like riding in the car, but they settled into the empty house like they've always lived here, and the scratches on his arms aren't bleeding anymore.

He's been thinking about maybe taking up farming. He must be; he left his laptop at home.

Jennifer's sitting on him, and her weight's forward, on her hands, against his neck. She isn't pushing, but she could.

"I think about killing you," she says. "Sometimes because I'm genuinely pissed. Sometimes just for symmetry, you know? Because you keep fucking *watching* me. Why can't you leave me alone?"

"I talk to you, like twice a year."

"You shot me."

He wasn't, until this moment, entirely sure she knew that. He

remembers her looking at him, and the gun in his hands, but neither of those things signifies. Not really. Not after he found
Gordon all burned in the grass behind him, with his own gun. It
could have been Gordon. He's almost sure.

"I—"

"I would have done a better job." She presses a little on the
base of his throat. It feels like he's swallowed something too
large, but he can still breathe. "I'd wait until your dad went to
town. I'd make sure you were hard to find, after. I'd make sure
you were actually dead."

"I didn't shoot you."

"I was looking right at you when you did it."

"Gordon."

"The Gordon thing is weird. And I think my mom believes you.
Not sure about your mom, though." Pause. "But I remember your
gun. What did you do with it?"

"I buried it. Somewhere in the pasture. It was a while ago. Not
sure I exactly remember where." It's more than he means to tell
her, but he's still groggy. The part of him that doesn't believe she
really might kill him wants to go back to sleep.

She raises her fingers, away from the base of his neck to the
curve under his jaw. Holds her hands there. Squeezes, just a little.

"Stop it."

"Fuck you. You shot me, and you followed me around and you
fucked my best friend, and you're living in my *house* like some
kind of insane squatter and I really don't understand what I did to
deserve to be *related* to you."

Jason says, "I didn't mean to shoot you."

She snorts.

"Not exactly. I mean, not after."

She looks like she might actually kill him. Not even angry: she
looks like she's decided, and she has the rest of the day planned. If
she leaves him in the basement, locks the house and takes the ani-

mals away, and his car, she could claim he went home or something. That she hasn't seen him in months. She doesn't even like him; they don't hang out. He has shady friends, maybe someone should go talk to them.

If he dies of a tiny clot hitting his brain, and then the mice chew on him for a year, Jason's not even sure they'll be able to tell what killed him.

Just for a second, she squeezes. He hears a tiny noise that might be him, begging. Then she lets go.

"This isn't your house," she says. "I can't stop you living out here, but if you come in here again, I will actually set the law on you. And if that doesn't work, I will set your mom on you. Get the fuck out. Take your lizards."

She clambers up awkwardly. The air mattress isn't stable, so the fact that she knees him in the balls might be just an accident. She goes to the door and picks up what he realizes is one of those baby carriers. It's braced on some kind of frame to stay upright. He doesn't realize until she puts it on that the frame is body armor. The thing in the sling cries baby-soft.

Her expression isn't maternal, exactly. She just always looked at animals that way. Only Jason's dad looks like that at him.

Before she goes out, she steps back to the bed. Her hiking boots up close smell like animal shit and dirty snow; the smell when she lays the sole against his face is vivid. He can feel it pulsing through his sinuses and the visceral, bloody parts of his face. The gap in his teeth hurts.

Jennifer kicks once, carefully. Jason hears his nose break even before he feels it.


HE'S THINKING ABOUT it every day, now. He's surprised, suddenly, how much he hates his job. Something indefinable shifted. He still catalogues everyone's pornography, but it's less charming than he remembers, and the dust-dry blowback from the computer fans makes his smashed nose ache. The tape holding his face together gets dry and falls off. People stare at his black eyes that never quite go away.

He's an indoor kid who's sick of being indoors. He has to go outside.

They've almost reached the equinox, but there's time between actual darkness and when he needs to sleep. So initially, he goes walking, breathing through his mouth. The doctor who saw Jason at the emergency room was younger than him, and he said something about being too old to go around picking fights. Irritated Jason just enough that when the guy was talking about long-term reconstruction, afterwards, Jason didn't want to listen. His face might actually be ruined. He has the name of a plastic surgeon written in ballpoint on somebody's card in his wallet. There's a vague promise the government will pay to put his face back together, but that's at least a year away. His cartilage and bone have to settle.

There's more bone in his face than there used to be.

By the end of March, he can peel off the tape. The bruises have softened to yellow, and he can flex his jaw without agony shooting through the rim of his skull. He can almost breathe. So he starts running.

Jason lives in a shitty neighbourhood. The houses in Saskatoon were cheap for years, until suddenly they weren't, and the house he could afford — the mortgage he could afford for the house his job will let him pay off in thirty years — is in Mount Royal, where the kids all look at him like it might be fun to take him apart. Nothing to do with his essential faggot identity — just an adult who looks at them wrong. He needs protective colouration.

Running helps. The kids who watch him like animals all smoke, and there's a reasonable chance they won't be able to catch him.

The long stretch of park running north-south lets him cover the western half of the city in an hour of running. It's alternating grass and pavement, with schools cut through it, and blocks where the houses take over, but there's a lingering sense of open country that he likes. Teenagers climb up on the picnic tables and talk all night. He remembers that, too. What it felt like to crawl into somebody's head that intensely.

The last person he really talked to like that might have been Donna. It's a terrifying thought.

He sends her pictures of his bruises. Just simple jpeg files by e-mail. No comments. She sends him back photos of her, topless, and revealing what he gradually understands is a cesarian scar.

She had a kid at some point, and he didn't notice.

He follows her productions. Her online work was more like digital reflections of all his subconscious sexual fears than titillation, but it wasn't boring. A few years ago, there was some kind of legal dust-up, and her company moved production south to the U.S. He doesn't think Donna went with them. When he pictures her, it's still in the ringing glass world of the Pacific.

Running has its advantages. His knees ache and his lungs ache, but his body's lost the tech-guy pudge he was building. It's more interesting these days to hurt all up the back of his legs than to run on the flatline of work and home and Internet trolling for guys who'll fuck and leave. The ferrets like the smell of his running clothes enough that they sleep in them.

He feeds them freezer-burned meat his dad brings in. Thinks about how big the world is beyond the city's edge.


THE PARK'S SOUTHERN reach takes him past St. Paul's Hospital. It's one of the few parts of the city that hasn't fundamentally changed. The hospital itself has a new parkade and murals reflecting indigenous knowledge, but the hookers are still there, and the schoolyard. He keeps waiting for the guys playing street hockey to show up.

One body. Two. Five. Ten. Spread out in the playing fields and knock each other down.

Nobody comes. When he counts, he realizes those guys must be almost fifty now. It doesn't make sense. They're getting old even faster than he is.

ON THE PHONE, his dad says, "Do you want my skates?"

"What?"

"Yours are still here, too."

"They don't fit anymore. Give them away."

"Mine might fit you. The old ones, I mean, from when I was a kid. I think I have bigger feet than you?"

Jason pauses. "The really old ones?"

"Yes. Those."

It's the kind of leading offer that makes him stare at the ferrets occupying his couch and wonder what, exactly, his parents are trying to steer his life into. He can only remember skating with his dad two or three times in his life. His dad's skates only lived in the house because it was *his* parents' house, and they'd always been there. The way Jason goes back sometimes and there are things he stuffed into closets as a teenager and they're still there, underneath the mess of his dad's current existence.

"I'll come out sometime and try them on. See if they fit."

THE SKATES ARE too big, but not that much. Jason borrows a pair of his dad's thick socks, layers them over his own socks, and suddenly there's a real skate around him. They're made of leather so old it's turning brown under the black polish, and their blades are like vintage car parts. They have these curves that don't quite match any modern conception of how physics and the human body intersect.

His dad feeds him a strawberry.

"I need to try these out."

He takes them into Bear Hills. He can't remember, now, how long there's ice in the rink, or whether eight-thirty on a Thursday night is a time when there'd be open ice for aging players who want to try out something ancient and familial in the way of footwear. The town's oddly static. He doesn't come in, much, even when he visits his dad. There's a tiny computer store that he can't imagine surviving in Saskatoon, and a hair salon that might be closed but's still occupied with women he vaguely recognizes as having once been his own age. He buys a Coke at the Co-op. Stands in the snow outside for a minute with his eyes closed and tries to convince himself that the ambient noise isn't fundamentally different here than at the 7-Eleven six blocks from his house.

The rink's hosting an old-timers hockey game. The old-timers are mercifully older than Jason — enough older that he doesn't have to identify with them, yet. They charge him a dollar and a quarter to come in and walk around. The locker rooms are off-limits, but nobody stops him wandering back. *Visitors* has new-old paint on the bathroom stall. Where somebody's carved notations involving Satanism and local sexual practices, he can see there are multiple layers between where he's standing and the colour layer detailing his cock-sucking tendencies. He's almost disappointed.

You leave and they forget who you are.

He wonders who, exactly, his parents would like him to marry. Whether it has to be a chick, or whether they'd be happy with some reasonably nice boy who'd adopt a couple of semi-disabled kids with Jason and co-parent them. Or they might still be satisfied to have grandchildren that are animals. Lizards and ferrets, and maybe a dog someday.

Jennifer's still nursing her goddamn bear. He sees her with it, sometimes, haunting his runs through the city like she might catch him and eat him.

He wants to skate.

Wanders out to watch the game. The stands aren't full, but there are people watching, and kids thundering through the ply-wood-and-concrete tunnels under the bleachers. Their screaming feels intensely familiar, just under his skin. He should get a burger or something. Drink some shitty rink coffee.

The guy working the snack booth looks like somebody's dad. He has the expression Jason remembers from the handful of times his own dad was pressed into service in the rink booth. They keep a roster of parents, whether you sign up or not. Phone you up at home and tell you your shift's in three hours, so get your ass in here. It keeps people from opting out. And it might be some kind of social-engineering plan to ensure that everyone has at least one extra marketable skill. You learn to cook burgers on a grill, run a deep fryer, that sort of thing. If your ranch fails, at least you can work in fast food.

Jason studies him. The guy has grease burns on his forearms. He's heavy the way guys get heavy when they stop looking like the boys they used to be; Jason's only holding that off right now by running half the night. He can't afford to be as old as he is when the number of queer guys in Saskatoon keeps shrinking. Any day now, every queer over twenty-five who isn't married will move to Vancouver, and he'll be all alone.

He says, "I know you, don't I?"

"Asshole."

"What?"

"Boyd, Jason." Pause. "We played hockey together. And."

And.

Oh.

"Sorry."

"You're forgiven. What the hell are you doing out here?"

"I was looking for ice. I want to try out my dad's skates. He's giving them to me."

"Show me."

Jason's not carrying them, but the way Boyd looks from Jason not remembering his name, Jason doesn't get to set conditions. He goes out to his car and brings the skates back. Kid at the door tries to ink-stamp his hand coming and going.

"Nice. Vintage. Those might be worth money."

"I just haven't had any skates that fit for a while," Jason says.

"This game'll go for another hour or two," Boyd says. "But I have keys to the rink at Mayfair. When somebody comes to relieve me, I'll go let you in."

JASON'S ONLY EVER skated at Mayfair a couple of times. He didn't know the rink was still standing. Mayfair hasn't really been a town since before he was born; there are a bunch of houses, mostly unoccupied, and they tore down the grain elevators sometime in the late '90s. Salvaged some of the lumber and set the rest of the structure on fire while there was still enough snow on the ground to keep the grass from catching. But there are traces of almost-town. There are two standing churches, and somebody's living in one of them. And the rink's there, still standing, and still flooded.

They do it by hand, with a hose. Boyd does some of it. Guys Jason's age who want to skate with their kids and don't want to pay Bear Hills prices for the space come out here, swapping the keys among themselves and kicking in a couple of hundred dollars each a year for the light and water. It's almost too warm, now. There's no cooling system in the building, and twice the temperature's hovered around freezing. The ice is heaved under the thin incandescent lights.

Jason's tying his skates, only half-listening, then asks, "You have kids?"

"I have boys. They're nine and six."

"Christ."

"Um."

"And . . . Church of the Family?"

"I like pastor Donald. He got this set up for us. You remember we used to play street hockey in front of the church?"

"Yeah."

"He remembered. He thought we might feel more . . . something. Grateful, I guess, for the state of the world."

"Anyway."

Jason has this vision of Boyd trying to kiss him, and having to express what he thinks about married guys *and* evangelicals, but it doesn't happen. It leaves Jason watching him. Boyd doesn't wear a wedding ring; that could mean something, or not. He could be divorced. He could just be a reproductive disaster area.

He keeps waiting. If he tilts his head just right, he thinks Boyd might break down and forget they're both this old.

The ice is rough, and there's an iron smell in the rink that borders on rotten, but the skates are good. He'll have to get them sharpened, later, but that's not hard. If he lived out here, he could sign on for this place. They'd have their own rink, his hockey-guys and him. And he could get a trailer or something, so he wouldn't have to live with his dad full-time. It's what his mom wants him to do, but it doesn't sound like such a bad idea.

Boyd joins him. He's a better skater than Jason is, at this stage. He skates like a guy who didn't stop for ten or fifteen years, and who knows where the holes in the ice are and how to avoid them. Jason skids away from him, just trying not to collide.

He's forgotten how to skate. He almost can't believe it.

On the Zamboni end, where there's never been a zamboni in this particular rink, the smell is worse. It isn't just iron, Jason realizes. Something's dead in here. Animal behind the boards. He'll have to go in and clean it out, with Boyd, before they can leave.

The camera rigged to the wall catches his eye. There are no

bleachers here; there's no room for them. The sheet metal of the building's only a body-width from the rink boards. Somebody's carefully rigged a camera-ledge at human height. It's not a spy-thing. It's old — analogue, runs on film — but at one point it must have been really expensive. There are lighting rigs, too, higher up.

He goes to ask Boyd if they're making some kind of movie in here, off-hours, and Gordon Watson says, "Jason."

He's just standing at the boards, like a normal person who's not supposed to be in jail. That's his camera; Jason thinks he might even remember it.

He stares.

And really, he wants to ask, *Are you hunting me? Like you hunted Jennifer?*

*What the fuck?*

*Did Boyd show you this place? Am I being set up?*

But Boyd's staring at Gordon, too. There's no reason Boyd should ever have met Gordon before. He might not even know him as the psycho artist who shot at the police ten years ago. And then Boyd says, "Jason. Oh, shit." He points up.

The ceiling of the rink is carefully rigged with cables, each one holding a dead animal. There's a dog that looks like it's been hit by a car. A couple of cats. Something, maybe a fox? There are a lot of deer. They're hanging from the rafters, like the place is a meat locker, only it's too warm, and they're thawing. They're rotting.

It's art. They've all been hit by cars, every single one. He can picture Gordon driving around the back roads of west-central Saskatchewan, picking up roadkill and arranging it to his liking. He could take pictures at every stage, then silver-gelatin print them, blow them up, make it an exhibition.

Jason wonders if Gordon remembers that he broke out of jail. He looks so professional, standing there, like he never lost his mind.

JASON'S CELL PHONE doesn't have a signal. It means he has to explain himself, and Gordon, to Boyd. Explain what he needs. Its urgency. And, eventually, Boyd takes the car and goes to find the police. He leaves Jason stranded in barely there Mayfair, with Gordon Watson and a rotting meat art experiment.

"I'll make you coffee."

Normal, like something anyone might say. And Gordon, he remembers, likes being the host. He's not homeless. He's not living in the church, either, for which Jason is vaguely grateful. He's taken over a converted school bus behind the rink. It's up on blocks, but inside it's insulated, and set up like a cheap winnebago. Gordon lights the campstove on the table and heats water. The bus gradually fills with naptha fumes, and Jason retreats outside.

He isn't really surprised to see the elephant. It's propped up with sawhorses next to the caragana windbreak. It looks normal. Like an elephant made of saddle leather and madness that should absolutely live behind the rink in an abandoned Saskatchewan town.

Gordon's going to make him coffee, in a minute, if Jason doesn't resist. He isn't entirely sure it'll be made of coffee. There might be insects in it, or fragments of the animals that have fallen off their thawing corpses. It's not safe to drink anything here, even the water. So he goes back inside the rink. Without Gordon's specialty floodlights, the ceiling's unclear. He has to find the extension cords and plug each one in separately. Still, when he comes back, it's almost worth it. The animals are all obviously roadkilled, but they've been painted, and their shapes are almost abstract against the corrugated metal roof. Jason stands on the ice in his running shoes and tries to figure out how Gordon rigged the cables up there, to hoist all that weight. How he did it.

The floodlights are hot. He can feel them on his back. If you asked him, though, he wouldn't say they were hot enough to thaw meat. Or, not until the dissolving flesh of a dead buck suddenly gives, and it falls on him.

It's not a full-on blow. Jennifer hurt him worse, but the animal knocks him down, and the ice cracks the back of his head. Jason lies on the ice, surrounded by thawing deer guts. He's still there, in a small pool of melt-water, when Boyd comes back and helps him up. The Mounties study Jason, how he's covered in blood, but they aren't even really all that interested in what happened. They've come here to take someone away, and it isn't him.

Jason finds a plastic grocery bag in his car. He collects the bits of thawing meat off the ice. The animals at home might want to eat it, and he doesn't feel like leaving this mess where it lies.

Annette Lapointe holds a PhD in Contemporary Canadian Literature and teaches English at Grande Prairie Regional College. Her first novel, *Stolen*, was nominated for a Giller Prize and was the Winner of two Saskatchewan Book Awards (First Book Award and Saskatoon Book Award). A Finalist for the Books in Canada First Novel Award, as well as being cited as a *Globe & Mail* Top 5 First Fiction choice, *Stolen* also garnered Ms. Lapointe a Canadian Authors Association Emerging Writer award. Annette has lived in Saskatoon, Quebec City, St John's, South Korea, Winnipeg, and currently resides in Grande Prairie, Alberta.